CAROLINE

a novel

Adrian Spratt

ISBN: 978-1-95386545-8 (Paperback)
ISBN: 978-1-95386546-5 (eBook)

Library of Congress Control Number: 2021921227

Any references to historical events, real people, or real places are used fictitiously. Names,
characters, and places are products of the author's imagination.

Typesetting: Stewart A. Williams | stewartwilliamsdesign.com

Books Fluent
3014 Dauphine Street
New Orleans, LA
70117

DISCLAIMER

Caroline is a work of fiction. No event is based in fact, and any resemblance between any character and any actual person, either living or dead, is purely accidental. Likewise, the New York Defenders Alliance is a fictional entity and has no connection with any actual organization. The New School is a venerable institution in New York, but the classroom scenes are products of the author's imagination. So, too, are the scenes and characters at the Environmental Protection Agency.

PROLOGUE

Outside the West Village restaurant where I'd had dinner with an old friend, I unfolded my white cane, said goodnight and set off for the Sheridan Square subway station. As I approached the next corner, a woman came to my side and asked, "Can I offer assistance?" She assumed I might need help crossing the street. Actually, I was going to turn toward the subway. She said she was going that way and that her offer stood. I took her arm, and we sped along West 4th.

Hints of spring had appeared after a long winter. Even a first-time visitor to New York would have detected the atmosphere of relief and renewal. An image came to me of lit street lamps, neon signs and car headlights staring down the night. Defiance was in the air, the kind that says life doesn't have to be as bleak as winter insists.

"I'm still new to the city," the woman said. She told me she'd come from Kansas to do graduate work at NYU. "What about you?"

"I'm a lawyer," I said. "I started out in criminal law, but most of my career has been in environmental."

She told me her name was Taylor. I told her mine was Nick.

Then she said, "I suspect I wouldn't make a very good lawyer. What do you think?"

"What do I think! I think I hardly know you."

"They say you get a sense of someone after two minutes. I believe there's a lot to that. Don't you?"

1

"I can tell you're articulate. That helps if you want to be a lawyer."

"Words, words. Everyone does words today, even if they can't spell."

"Can you spell?"

"That I can."

"Okay, now you have two qualifications."

We stepped onto the island in the middle of Sheridan Square, site of my subway entrance, but she kept going, taking a left down Seventh Avenue. Normally, I would have stopped and returned to the subway steps, but, intrigued, I went along with her unannounced detour.

She told me she was studying the relationship between the actions of statesmen and what they wrote and said before taking on leadership roles. I surmised there must be an academic cottage industry spawned by former President Barack Obama's autobiographies. It was a world away from the one I inhabited of clean-up sites, consent decrees, arguments with our counterparts at the Justice Department when they balked at suing a polluter.

"You must make a lot of enemies in your job," she said. "How does that make you feel?"

"I like to think of myself as peacemaker, but it seems I have a talent for antagonizing people that belies it."

"That tells me you don't know who you are."

After a moment's reflexive annoyance, I said equably, "I know I'm a sack of contradictions."

We crossed yet another street. She said, "Are you up for a bite or something? I know a place."

My friend and I had finished dinner earlier than usual, and Alison, my wife, had said she'd been looking forward to a rare evening on her own. That I'd extended the evening with a young woman stranger would take some explaining, but she knew how

I acted on whims.

"Okay," I told Taylor, "let's go."

"Just along here," she said, turning right.

My office shoes sent cracks against the deserted street's quiet. She must have been wearing athletic footwear because her steps landed softly. An overhead image came to me of a gray-haired man walking side by side with this young woman. In my mind's eye, she was blonde. Well, yeah. It was an image recreated from some movie in my childhood, when I'd had vision.

The couple reached a restaurant entrance, paused, turned inside. Then the overhead camera switched off. I became myself again, responding to the maître d' and sizing up the interior: small, busy but unflustered.

At the table, having declined the maître d's offer to hang up her coat, she slung it over the back of her chair. "I have to be careful with money," she explained. "Tipping to get my coat back is one expense I can do without."

I was glad I didn't have to deal with a coat. When I'd left home that morning, the air was brisk but buoyant with the promise of a spring day.

As she seated herself diagonally at my side, I said, "I have to tell you I'm kind of full. You met me on my way home from dinner with a friend."

"They won't mind. It's not like there's competition for tables right now. But I haven't eaten, so I'll be ordering something. An appetizer. That will do me fine."

I told the waiter I wanted just a decaf, and he showed no irritation. In my mind, I said I'd leave a good tip whatever we ordered. Maybe he picked it up by extrasensory perception. Sign of a good waiter.

"So," she said, sounding awkward now that we'd committed to

time together, "how did you decide on environmental law?"

"Right after law school, I did criminal defense. Then an opportunity came up at the EPA. One of those things you don't plan for that turns your life around." Catching myself thinking how much emotional territory that abbreviated résumé covered, I put on a rueful grin. "But enough on law. It's after hours."

"Oh, sorry, no more law questions. But let me ask you this. Where I come from, people blame environmentalists for jobs leaving America. I disagree, but I don't feel I know enough to have an opinion."

Our coffees arrived, followed quickly by her salad. Discreetly, I touched the tablecloth and unexceptional silverware. Sensing the space between tables would let us speak without being overheard, I decided to air misgivings I rarely admit. After all, it was after hours.

"Keeping the environment clean creates jobs, but I'm guessing the people you talk to don't want that kind of change. What troubles me more is that when we drive out the industries that cause the worst pollution, it means we're exporting it to countries more desperate than ours."

"Do you believe that? I mean, if you do, how could you continue doing what you do?"

"Before my time at the EPA, the fires on Cleveland's Cuyahoga River and death sites like Love Canal scared everyone, but those breakthrough battles have been fought and won. What's left is huge, but it can be gray. So, yes, I'm proud of the work we've done and my own small part in it. But are the results all positive?" I shrugged. "No collective human activity does unmitigated good."

"You're a pessimist," she said. "I took you for a hopeful person."

"During those first two minutes?"

"Exactly."

"I take it you're an optimist."

"See, you can tell lots of things about someone you've just met. What else do you know about me?"

I doubted the wisdom of answering, but I went ahead anyway. "You have strong opinions, but you listen to others."

"That's true."

"You're a kind person."

"I try."

"All that sounds rather basic to me," I said. "I thought this two minutes of yours was about something more subtle—more nuanced, as people say today."

"I can tell certain things about you that might or might not be subtle."

I almost groaned, having no desire to expose myself either to analysis or teasing. "Okay, like what?"

"From the quality of your suit and tie, I know you're comfortably off. Oh, forgive me. That's a visual thing."

"Are you sure about that, Sherlock? By the way, what is the feminine for Sherlock, do you know?"

She ignored my frivolity. "I was apologizing for mentioning something you can't share."

"How do you know I can't share?"

"Okay, I guess I don't know. I mean, you can know what you're wearing, of course, but I don't see how you can know what I am."

"Outside you were wearing a trim coat, not a windbreaker or something else I'd expect from a student."

She sighed. "You're better at this two-minutes thing than me."

"I doubt it." Then I said, "I don't suppose you're up for some wine. It looks like we're not leaving soon, and I feel we should pay a little more rent for this table."

"Love some. How about a half carafe of the house red or white?"

We settled on the red, which arrived with the same courtesy as before. The waiter poured.

Returning to her two-minutes theme, I said, "What else have you picked up about me, visual or otherwise?"

"I've annoyed you. I'm sorry." She touched my hand, a fleeting gesture, gone almost before I'd noticed.

"Go ahead," I said, "speculate away."

"Under that debonair exterior," she said, "I sense sadness. Maybe I'm picking up that you're lonely."

I remembered I wasn't wearing my wedding ring. I'd done so for several months after the ceremony, but it irritated my skin and Alison had graciously conceded it was best left at home. After tonight, she might think again.

Doing one of those heaving sighs that lifts the shoulders, I told Taylor, "Perhaps we'd better stop there."

She turned the subject to herself. "Would you say I'm lonely?"

"After all, you're an attractive young woman with an hour or two to spare for a man twice her age."

She answered with a halting, "Ye–es." Then she said, "What makes you say I'm attractive?"

"You act on impulse and live in the moment."

"You know me better than I know myself."

"I know you hardly at all."

"So you said. But I'm finding it fascinating how much you can know. I've never spent any time with someone who can't see. It made me a little scared."

"And tonight you decided to face up to your scare."

"If you want to put it that way."

I could have said, "Then how would you put it?" but I knew about acting on impulse. I doubted Taylor had seen me in the street and said to herself, "Time to get over that phobia." Her explanation had probably come to mind as we meandered around the West Village.

"So, Taylor, are you about to say I have super-developed perception?"

"The way you put that, I'd better not."

That brought a smile to my face, as her voice betrayed it had to hers.

After taking a sip of wine, she said, "Don't you think we're all freaks?"

"Freaks?"

"That we're all—I don't know—different. If we admitted it, wouldn't it make us more tolerant?"

Her word put me off, but it did go to the heart of what she'd been getting at.

"Tolerant maybe," I said. Then my inner trickster piped up. "But given a choice between stopping in the street to talk to someone and getting home, I usually choose home."

"Tonight you didn't."

Having made the mistake of trying to hide my amusement behind a sip of wine, I spluttered into the glass. But I recovered with what I considered aplomb. "I decided it was high time I overcame my fear of talking to women who accost me in the street."

"Touché," she said, bumping my glass with hers. "So, women 'accost' you, as you say, all the time?"

"Absolutely. But what I'm really saying is that people of all ages and genders offer help."

"Hope for humanity," she said.

"Depends on how the help is offered."

"Did I do it right?"

"Perfectly. You gave me a choice. You didn't grab my arm. You didn't ask a stupid question like, 'Do you know where you're going?'"

"Why is that a stupid question?"

"Would I be out and about if I didn't know where I was going?"

"You must experience a lot of stupidity."

"And a lot of thoughtfulness."

"So you are an optimist."

Her knee touched mine. It stayed.

"I'm not lonely in the traditional sense," she said, turning her earlier question back on herself. "But I don't seem able to settle down with one person. That's a form of loneliness, don't you think?"

"How old are you, Taylor?"

"Twenty-six."

"I was the same at your age. I mean, I found it unsettling to keep starting and ending relationships. But I also found it exciting."

"Exciting?"

"I'd long felt insecure about women's feelings for me. All of a sudden, that changed. I'm guessing you've never had doubts about your attractiveness."

"In middle school and maybe into high school. Good grades didn't make for popularity."

"Just that?"

"Okay, and I was flat-chested till later than most girls. You don't want anyone to notice at that age, but you feel lacking. And I do mean lacking. It feels like a moral failing. But it's weird that I can't settle on one person. It means I do cruel things without meaning or wanting to."

"Like what?"

"Leading guys on."

"Sure you aren't still in high school?"

"You're saying I'm immature. But I don't lead guys on to make them crazy. I get really, really involved in someone, but then something or someone else takes over."

"It's good you know you have the power to hurt."

"What do you mean?"

"There are people who think no one cares enough about them to be hurt by what they do." She couldn't know how hard-earned that knowledge was.

"Oh, I know people care."

"Well, if settling down with someone is something you hope for, it should happen. If it's only an ideal you've picked up second-hand, who knows?"

"I don't even know if I'm into women or men."

I snorted. "Aren't you being a tad too faddish?"

I sensed her knee's touch get lighter. Then to my relief, she laughed.

"I suppose I don't see a long-term relationship with a woman in my future." Her knee's pressure returned.

"Process of elimination," I said. "A start."

The half carafe yielded two smaller glasses. This time she poured.

I said, "I should be going soon. Tomorrow is another long day."

"And I've got a bunch of studying to do. I'll get our waiter's attention." As she spoke, her voice moved to the side, which told me she was signaling for the check. Then she said, "I guess loneliness is on my mind because I worry that if I'm not in a relationship after the youthful bloom has gone, I might find myself alone and left behind. In Jane Austen's day, a woman who wasn't married by my age had poor prospects."

"In Jane Austen's day, you had to follow the map laid out for you. It's sad when anyone today has unerringly followed the course mapped out for them."

"How did you avoid doing that?"

"Ah, one benefit of disability. No good maps. You've made sure you won't follow someone else's map, either."

"How did I do that?"

"By coming to New York from Kansas, for one thing. For another, by plucking a stranger like me out of thin air and sharing these two hours with him."

The check arrived. I thought about splitting it, telling her I recognized her as equal, but our finances weren't. She graciously consented to my paying the bill on condition I let her cover the tip. I hoped she honored my unspoken promise to the waiter.

"Taylor, I'm curious about the appearance of the woman I've been having this conversation with. Tell me something about yourself."

"So, you didn't learn everything about me in those first two minutes."

"I already told you so."

She proved to be "a Midwest farmer's daughter," as she put it. "Fair hair, blue eyes. Also, um, pointed chin, small nose. I have an unsightly bump on the bridge of my nose. One day when I'm rich, I'll have a plastic surgeon fix it."

Seeing me start, she said, "You disapprove of plastic surgery?"

I pushed down a memory for later. "No, I don't. Cosmetics matter."

I took the risk of touching her hair. She slightly dipped her head toward me, as if to signal consent. I brushed my thumb against her cheek, a physicality to remember her by.

Outside, I paid the price for having opted against wearing a coat that morning. The air had turned colder, sharpened by a night wind off the Hudson.

This time we stopped on reaching the steps down to my station. I considered giving her my business card or asking for her number. I did neither. I'd bragged to her that I'd followed my own map. In following it, I'd done harm. As Taylor said about herself, I hadn't meant to, but it didn't free me from culpability. At least I'd learned a lesson or two, and one was to let this brief intersection of our lives stay just that.

She, too, avoided the false promise of "Let's get together again." Instead, saying, "Thank you for a lovely time," she kissed my cheek and walked back down Seventh Avenue.

Turning to the subway steps, I gave in to the pull of the past.

PART 1

1

BRIGHT SUNLIGHT AND TEMPERING BREEZES flow through my memories of my mid- and late twenties, three decades ago. The time was the eighties, Ronald Reagan's morning in America. But I don't believe his political imagery explains that sensory quality of my memories, and I doubt the weather was unusually benign. Maybe it's just the nature of that time of life, when you've been freed from the constraints of school and haven't yet been burdened by the full weight of adulthood. It's the mistakes you make during that window of freedom that can define a life, some for the good, some not.

I came to New York City for my first full-time job on being hired by the appeals unit of the Defenders Alliance, a venerable private organization that represents impoverished criminal defendants. Although my family had moved from Illinois to a Connecticut suburb of New York when I was in eighth grade and my parents still lived there, I'd had little familiarity with the city. Like most migrants to New York, at least back then, I'd intended to live in Manhattan. However, on my meager Defenders Alliance salary I couldn't afford a Manhattan one-bedroom apartment. Because of recurring bouts of insomnia, a common byproduct of blindness, I needed a second room to accommodate guests so they weren't disturbed by my nighttime restlessness. I ended up signing an affordable lease for a one-bedroom apartment in a tiny corner of the city I'd never heard of before called Brooklyn Heights.

In time I recognized my good fortune. The Heights is a quiet neighborhood of brownstones and houses of an even older vintage, a shelter from the pulsating energy that is Manhattan. I got an adrenaline rush each morning as I rode the subway to work and a feeling of peace when I exited the station at night. Well, in those days that block of Clark Street had rowdy guys and prostitutes hanging outside Wildfire, the former topless bar, but I never felt unsafe.

My new home was on the ground floor of a rare Heights apartment building. The living room was spacious enough, but all I could fit in the bedroom was a double bed and one night-table. The dresser and other items that belonged there went, instead, into the living room. The windows of both rooms faced the street. My upstairs neighbor, Jenny, a middle manager at a local bank, called my apartment a fishbowl, but I enjoyed living at a level with people walking past, fragments of sentences hanging in the air like aural perfume.

I kept the Venetian blinds in my bedroom closed, but mostly left those in my living room open, even though I remembered a classmate back in junior high defining home as the place where you can scratch your ass. I put on no such show as I settled into the first place I could call my own.

2

JACK HAGEN, A COLLEAGUE AND friend at the Defenders Alliance, dropped by my office. Sitting in a guest chair on the other side of my desk, he said, "The supervisors are on the warpath. Lots of grim looks along supervisor row and flitting in and out of each other's offices."

He understood that, shut away most of the day with the people I hired to read transcripts aloud and my drafts back to me, I was out of the gossip loop. Against that disadvantage, Jack and I could talk freely because I had the room to myself when I wasn't working with readers. Jack, along with all the other staff lawyers, had a two-person office and little privacy.

"Why today?" I asked.

"As if they weren't already neurotic enough, they found out that someone has done a statistical analysis of indigent criminal defense cases handled by us versus court-appointed lawyers. Guess what? We cost more."

It took no guessing. Defenders Alliance lawyers were salaried, while non-Alliance lawyers were paid fixed, not exactly generous, fees per case and trial. Thus, we in the Alliance had less incentive to rush our clients through the system. Some politicians, along with many constituents, weren't happy that millions of dollars were set aside to help accused people they assumed were guilty as charged.

"So some City Council member is telling the media the Alliance's contract should be dropped," Jack concluded. I pictured him with elbows planted on his chair's arms.

I said, "It means there'll be more pressure for us to justify the City's spending on us."

"It means," Jack retorted, "the supervisors will go even more berserk."

A knock on the door was followed by Mara saying, "Hi, Jack." Mara was my reader this and two other afternoons a week. I'd hired two other readers to cover my mornings and the other afternoons.

"Hey, nice shoes," Jack said, turning in his chair.

"Don't tell him," Mara said in a booming whisper.

"Not a word."

I lowered my voice to bass. "What is it, you two?"

"Oh, nothing," Mara chirped.

"I suppose I should let you go," Jack said to me.

"Don't leave for my sake," Mara said.

"For mine," I said.

When he'd shut the door behind him, I asked Mara, "What's this about your shoes?"

"Ratty old tennis shoes. I came from the gym. We're not going to court today, are we?"

Sighing in not-quite-feigned exasperation, I handed her the trial transcript in the murder case I'd just been assigned. I told her to pick up at page 76, where my morning reader, Ray, had left off.

Robert Wilson had been convicted of killing three people and wounding two others in the course of robbing Manhattan's Serpentine Bar and Grill. The prosecutor was examining one of his witnesses. Mara read:

Q. Tell the jury what you observed about the assailant in the bar that night.

A. I watched the man as he, like, surveyed the place. He looked real calm. Then he walked to the bartender, leaned across and shot him point blank.

Q. Before that, did you notice him holding a gun?

A. Sure. I think he, like, pulled it out from under his coat when he was standing there at the door.

Q. Were you able to see his face?

A. I didn't take it in. I was, you know, scared.

Q. Are you able to say if you see the shooter in the courtroom before you?

A. I am not.

The next fifty pages went by fast, despite all the notes I was taking on my braillewriter. When we paused to give Mara a breather, she commented, "So one witness did identify him and another couldn't. Does that mean the second witness—what's his name, Heredia—was really saying our guy wasn't the culprit?"

"Whether he meant that or not, defense counsel didn't ask. He knew better than to risk getting a damaging answer."

"So it's no use to you."

"Oh, I think it will be. You get the sense that the shooter walked in the door, drew out his gun and took a long look around before starting on the spree. How can someone who had all those seconds to study the shooter's face not recognize him sitting at the defense table, unless the guy sitting there wasn't the shooter?"

"He has an answer for that," Mara pointed out. "He was scared."

"Meanwhile," I pressed on, "the witness who did identify our client says he only got a glimpse, but that it was enough. Sounds to me like one guy wouldn't be swayed by police pressure to help them close the case, while the other rushed to judgment."

"Is that what you're going to argue?"

"We don't know what else will turn up. Let's keep reading." Not that we'd finish the transcript that day or even that I'd necessarily do so with Mara.

3

I FELT I WAS PUTTING on a show when I walked into the New School classroom, and not just because of my white cane: I was wearing a suit and tie. It made me even more self-conscious that Mara was accompanying me, since my new classmates were bound to see me as dependent on her. However, I'd leave on my own, and now that she'd helped me figure out my way to the school and classroom, next time I'd arrive on my own.

Mara got me the corner desk in the front row nearest the door, best for easy exits. I didn't have to tell her. I didn't even have to own up to my anxiety about attire.

"Two other suits so far," she said softly. "See you Thursday."

I folded my cane, placed my briefcase next to the chair and sat down. When I took the bar exam, weary after two decades of school, I'd vowed I'd never set foot in a classroom again. Yet here I was, two years later, lured by a crazy urge to write fiction that the law hadn't beaten out of me.

The tapping of a pencil heralded the instructor's first words. "My name, for those of you who don't read course catalogs or who may be in the wrong room, is Albert Stern. For this course, you will hand in two original stories or two chapters of a novel you're working on, or one story and one chapter. This course is about writing. It is about imagination, but it is also about technicalities. You will quickly find out that I am not one of those free-thinking creative writing teachers who overlook grammatical and spelling mistakes. No. I pounce on them. When I do, you will feel your imagination is being stifled. You will be wrong. If you cannot write with technical proficiency, you are not communicating. Is anyone here who doesn't intend to be? Because if you are, this would be an excellent time to leave for more lenient pastures."

Another pause. No footsteps, no swish of air passing by me to the door.

"Okay, the ground rules are established."

Stern proceeded to talk about the art of writing and to read examples from literature. He contended that for the sake of cohesion, a scene must be written from a single point of view. Saying it contained examples of what he was talking about, he announced he was distributing a handout. He came near my desk and gave the pile to my neighbor, a woman, as I learned when she whispered to me, "Want a copy?"

I whispered back, "Thanks," and held out my hand. I folded the pages and placed them in my briefcase.

When Stern wished us goodnight, I opened my braille watch's crystal to find it was eight o'clock on the nose, just when the class was scheduled to end. I was about to fall in with the herd scrambling to the door when my neighbor said, "Shall we go down together?"

By the time she was at my side and I'd taken her arm, the herd had left. We didn't speak as we descended the staircase, but when we reached the ground floor, she said, "What do you think of Stern?"

"Lives up to his name—rigid, militaristic—don't you think?"

"I hope you aren't going to drop the course."

"Oh, I'll stick it out."

Outside on the sidewalk, she said, "I'm going to the right. How about you?"

"The 14th Street stop of the 2/3 train."

"It's on my way. I'll go with you, if that's okay."

The late summer's evening bordered on stifling, but it was good to be outside.

"It can't be easy to do creative writing on top of a full-time job," she said.

"The suit gives me away, I know."

"Actually, it's the briefcase," she deadpanned.

I smiled. "Well, before you ask ..." I owned up to being a lawyer, and not only a lawyer, but one who represented people who have been convicted of crimes.

"Convicted?"

"We handle their appeals. What about you? What do you do to make ends meet?"

"Oh, this and that."

I would have pursued it, despite sensing her reluctance to elaborate, but we'd reached my subway entrance.

I offered my hand. "I'm Nick—Nick Coleman."

She pressed my hand. "Caroline. Same time, same channel next week?"

Setting off down the steps, I reflected how at introductions, men say their full names while women offer only their first. If she eventually told me, it would be a sign of trust.

I'd reached the landing when she called down, "It's Sedlak. Caroline Sedlak."

Grinning, I turned and raised a hand in acknowledgment.

4

JACK AND I MET FOR lunch in my office. He asked about my writing class. After explaining my mixed feelings, I said on balance it was promising. Then I told him about Caroline.

"We walked to the subway together. Five minutes. I know, not a whole lot to go on, but I liked her."

Jack was a contrarian, and I hoped my note of skepticism would elicit something more positive. He didn't disappoint.

"Sometimes five minutes is all it takes."

"If nothing else, I'm hoping we can share a love of writing."

"With that grin on your face, is that all you're hoping?"

"I'm sure she has other fish to fry."

"Maybe you can share a love of clichés."

As paper rustling told me he was unwrapping his sandwich, he changed the subject. "This morning I got a warning about my productivity. Don't suppose it has something to do with the panic along supervisor row, do you?"

Retrieving my own Ziplocked cheese sandwich from my briefcase, I said, "I got mine last month."

When Jack and I, along with five other recent law school graduates, had arrived at the Alliance two Septembers before, Michael Flurry, head of the Appeals Unit, told us that the office operated like a law firm. "The only reason to comment is if your work is deficient. The assumption is that your work is perfect, so don't expect praise." That we weren't paid one-fifth what law firm associates got was a variable he didn't factor into the equation. We came from reputable law schools and had chosen the Defenders Alliance out of social conscience. Nevertheless, most of us had long since made the sad discovery that we weren't perfect and would have welcomed at least a little encouragement.

I was in special disfavor. Three months into the job, the supervisor assigned to review my fourth brief told me I'd overlooked a critical point.

"I thought about that issue, but I didn't think it would—"

Interrupting me, she said, "From now on, you will send along the case file with every brief you submit for review so we can make sure you miss nothing else."

She must have sent a memo around, because every supervisor afterwards expected me to attach the file to my draft brief. Although other new Alliance lawyers had also had their judgment questioned about which potential issues in a case to include or exclude, I alone was subjected to this demoralizing obligation.

I inferred the supervisors saw my dependence on readers as explaining the omission. Yet I'd gone over every page of the trial transcript, which I knew because I had my readers read every page number. When we turned to motions, exhibits and the other documents in the file, I handed them over one by one to ensure each one was accounted for. Anyway, I'd identified the issue and rejected it. I hadn't missed it.

The court wasn't impressed by the argument the supervisor had me write. The appeal was dismissed without comment. It didn't make her wrong, but it did add insult to injury.

When I'd lost my vision in ninth grade, a year after my family's move to Connecticut, I'd had to learn simple tasks all over again. Each time I accomplished something, whether typing a paper or walking on my own from class to class, I was praised. I felt ambivalent about compliments for tasks that everyone else took for granted, as I myself once had, but I found satisfaction in proving that blindness was surmountable. I'd gone on to prosper in college and law school. Now, at the Alliance, being the only lawyer not entrusted to read an entire case file, I was once again working against a presumption of failure.

Lunch over, Jack scrunched up the paper bag that had contained his sandwich, rose from his chair and fired a shot into my garbage can. "Swoosh!" he announced, marveling at his own prowess.

I scrunched up my own paper bag, stretched from my chair to the garbage can and slam-dunked it from a foot or so high. "Not as dramatic as your jump shot," I said, "but two points all the same."

5

Down on the street after the second class, Caroline asked if I was up for coffee. I avoided caffeine so late in the day, but I was happy to join her. "There's a Middle Eastern place on 13th," she said.

The restaurant wasn't fancy, which suited me fine. Even though our evening class had made me miss dinner, I thought I wasn't hungry, but mention of couscous triggered an appetite.

Once we'd settled in across from each other at a small table, she said, "I liked the way Stern read those two student stories today."

I nodded. "I was an English major in college, but this is my first creative writing course. How about you?"

The waiter arrived, and we ordered mint tea.

As if there'd been no interruption, she said, "My fourth. I take them to force me to write. But how come an English major never took creative writing?"

"I thought I needed to be much better-read, or else I'd just be repeating what others had already written."

"So now you've done all the reading you need, and you're ready to write." She spoke with a pleasantly ironic smile in her voice.

"I'll never do enough reading. I guess I've done enough waiting. I thought I was all set to let rip, but when I go to my typewriter, my mind keeps wandering."

"Luckily I have something almost ready for next week," she said.

Stern had set a schedule for each of us to hand in our first story or chapter. Mine was due two weeks after Caroline's.

"What would you folks like this evening?"

The waiter again.

Caroline said, "Should I read the menu to you?"

I turned to the waiter. "What are your couscous options?" He reeled them off. I chose vegetable. Couscous had aroused my appetite, but I still wanted something light. Caroline duplicated my order. The waiter tried to tempt us with appetizers, but we were both either too poor or too cheap.

During the pause in our conversation, I grew conscious that only two other tables seemed to be occupied.

"When I was nine," I said, lowering my voice, "the school principal published my first poem in the school rag. I blame her for my literary ambition."

"Blame?"

"I should be putting all my energy into my career."

"I wish someone had encouraged my writing," she said. "I got decent enough grades in English, but my parents had other ideas."

"What ideas?"

She didn't respond right away. Then she said, "When I was twelve, someone told my mom I should be a model. She took me around to an agent this friend mentioned, and the next thing I knew, I was showing up in ads for Stelstone's—you know, the leotard and leggings company."

"The name is familiar, of course."

"I still see posters of me around. I hate them. I hated the whole thing." She added, "It's so weird." Her tone of voice told me she shrugged.

After concealing my struggle for something to say behind a sip of now-cold tea, I settled on, "I can't imagine."

I waited, but she didn't elaborate.

I said, "Anyway, the other reason I want to shake free of this urge to write is—let's just say—I worry I lack imagination."

She chuckled. "Maybe this course will help you change your mind."

"You can tell me what you think if Stern reads my story to the class—assuming I get around to writing it."

"Oh, you will. Isn't persistence what makes a lawyer? If he doesn't read it aloud, will you show it to me?"

I realized how hard I was thinking through my answer when she coaxed, "Yes?"

"If you make the same promise."

"Okay," she said, sounding as though she had the very doubts she'd just been telling me to get over in myself.

The waiter arrived with our meals. "Okay, which one of you gets the veggie couscous?" He said it with a straight face, but Caroline and I both laughed.

•

Once again, my station was more or less on her way home. When we arrived at the steps to the subway, she said, "You're a good listener. And perceptive."

"What gave you that idea?"

"From your probing once and then not pressing when you didn't get an answer."

I smiled. Then I realized I wasn't the one who'd done or said anything perceptive. It was Caroline's observation that had been perceptive.

"I can tell you've had an interesting life," I said.

"Not so interesting to me."

"It's made you want to write."

"Writing can be compensation for a dull life."

"I'm guessing yours hasn't been dull."

"If you read my story—"

"When I read your story—"

"—you'll be the judge."

•

On the train to Brooklyn, I asked myself if I was attracted to her. But I'd already made it clear to myself and Jack at lunch. Not so obvious was why. True, her voice was melodious, somewhere between alto and soprano, and she showed no signs of baby-voice "I was like" Valleyspeak. Maybe it was an impression of fitness that I picked up from taking her arm as we walked, although I tried to shut down judgments about body type when anyone accepted my hand between arm and waist. I did like it that as we strolled along, she seemed relaxed, as if there were already a bond between us.

But beyond the physical, loss of vision meant I no longer associated certain looks with certain character traits. Not initially, anyway. I knew Caroline had a sense of humor. She seemed to have a nice awareness of herself. For two people who'd just met, she spoke openly.

Then pessimism kicked in. It insinuated Caroline and I were beginning one of those deep, sensitive friendships with women that had both invigorated and tortured me through college into law school. I supposed the women had limited our relationship to friendship for the usual reasons, but surely it was also that they feared a relationship with a blind man. They didn't own up to it, and I couldn't bring myself to confront them on it, but unable literally to watch movies, share beautiful landscapes, participate in games and sports, I was limited in a sighted world. Tellingly, the relationships I did have all happened when I was away at summer jobs or staying just a term at another school.

After my college and law school obsessions, filled with all the ardor and futility but none of the musicality of a troubadour's passion, I decided I'd exhausted my quotient of romantic love. I promised myself I'd never again idealize the beloved with an anguishing conviction that she meant everything. Wise, perhaps, but deflating.

Things improved in New York. Was it that now I had a real job? That women saw I could earn a living? Was it just something about New York women? My being older?

Whatever the reason, since my arrival, I'd had a few relationships, the longest lasting four months. That woman had long, blonde hair, a master's degree in art history and talent as a sculptor. She was delightful company when we were on our own, but she acted hostile to my friends and made my home unwelcoming. Another girlfriend was active in politics far to the left of mine, and she spent our times together attacking my "wishy-washy" views. Our parting was a fine example of separate but equal decision-making. Still another dumped me after I left her apartment in the middle of what, for me, had been an insomniac night. And so it went, with me doing as much rejecting as being rejected.

Although the two months since my last breakup amounted to no time at all, I'd already fallen into old patterns of solitude. I'd ridicule myself aloud for spilling something or misdialing a number. I'd congratulate myself sarcastically for leaving for work ten minutes late. Though I loved my apartment, arriving home could be the emptiest moment in the day. If I'd made no plans on a Saturday evening, I'd console myself that since everyone else in the building was no doubt having a good time, at least the laundry machines in the basement were free.

With my commitment to Stern's course, it didn't help that my writing was going nowhere. I was stuck in that insidious malaise from my student years: procrastination. Each time I thought of starting a story, something else became more urgent. Dishes had piled up in the sink. I wouldn't be able to settle down at the typewriter until I'd washed them. Then there was that friend who had left a message two days ago. How inconsiderate not to return calls. It all sapped what little mental energy I had left over from a day at the office.

On Sunday mornings, I went grocery shopping with Jenny, the neighbor who called my apartment a fishbowl. Although she avoided giving away her age, I put her at twenty years older than me. When I'd moved to New York, where I knew no one but for a few college and law school friends who all lived in Manhattan, she'd offered to help out. She pointed out deals and talked me through the dilemmas with which marketers tantalize shoppers: which degree of spiciness I wanted in my salsa, the unit cost of each size of laundry detergent.

There were drawbacks. "You mustn't eat too much sugar," she'd say at the frozen section. "Too much salt is bad for you," she'd observe in the chips aisle.

Sometimes it was all I could do not to scream that I was more conscientious than she made out, but experience had taught me that charity comes with self-improvement advice. The alternative was placing myself at the mercy of whichever sullen stock boy the store's manager assigned to help me find the items on my list. Though unjust to Jenny, I secretly wished I did my shopping with a woman who shared at least some of my tastes, along with my bed.

As the train pulled into my Clark Street stop, my thoughts came back around to Caroline. I hardly knew her, and yet she'd been on my mind since our walk after that first class. Was I such a sad sap that I was on the verge of succumbing once again to the myth of romantic love, to that unrelenting ache punctuated by brief flares of hope? I'd rather be unfulfilled than tormented. I must confirm, and soon, that she was, indeed, frying other fish.

6

ANOTHER SETBACK AT THE OFFICE. Jeff Stone was the supervisor assigned to the brief I'd finished drafting before starting on the Robert Wilson file. He'd never reviewed my work before, but we'd exchanged collegial greetings in the halls, and I arrived at his office without trepidation.

As I sat down in the visitor's chair, he said, "I've looked over the brief, and I see a couple of problems."

My heart did what literature teachers call a cliché, but it's a cliché that's as accurate as saying grass is green or that horns honk. It sank.

"I'm sure it's just a typo," he said, "but 'reckless' is spelled with a 'w' all the way through the brief."

If "reckless" was consistently misspelled, it was no typo. "Reckless endangerment" was the name of the statute on which the case turned. Any lawyer with sight would have read that law several times over and absorbed the spelling even if they hadn't already known it.

I sensed Jeff look up to assess my reaction. I was churning inside and knew my face had reddened, but I kept my gaze steady.

"Now, in your first point, you argue…" He proceeded to state a disagreement with my reasoning. Anything I said would be interpreted as defensive, so I sat quietly.

At last he said, "Fix up those problems and you should be all set." His tone returned to cordial, now that he'd unloaded his disappointment in me.

Walking back to my office and contemplating supervisor assessments of my job performance, I felt trapped in a vexing logic problem:

1) Blindness was entirely to blame; or
2) blindness wasn't to blame at all; or
3) blindness was partly to blame.

If blindness were entirely to blame, I'd need to accept limits I could never overcome. But if it was the analytical intelligence and a lawyer's other skills that I lacked, I had to find another career.

What that would be for someone with no special talents, except maybe for procrastination, I couldn't imagine. The murky last option, that the problem was a mélange of blindness and inadequate intellect, would mean I'd always feel limited, but unsure what to blame or what to do about it.

Then mortification morphed into anger. Why hadn't my readers noticed the misspelling? They'd read the reckless endangerment statute and seen the word was spelled with a "w" in my brief. Half a dozen years later, I would have a computer with spell-checker and a synthesized voice that reported what appeared on the screen. Back then, the only corrective action I could take was to second-guess every spelling I thought I knew.

I tried to get a grip before walking into my office, where my reader that afternoon, Louise, an aspiring cartoonist taking courses at the Learning Annex, was waiting. I told myself not to take out frustration on someone answerable to me the way the supervisors took out theirs on the staff lawyers.

"Here, Louise," I said, giving her the brief as I edged around to my side of the desk, "let's get this over with."

She turned pages. "He didn't like it, did he? What's this big red slash through 'wreckless'?"

"It's misspelled."

"Ha, so it is. It didn't hit me before."

"We have to take more care with spelling."

"What? He made a big deal out of it? Someone was bound to catch it. Just so happens he did."

I turned deadly serious. "Louise! This is a big deal. A judge will figure that if the lawyer can't be bothered to check his spelling, he won't check his facts, either."

She made the mistake of pursuing it. "That's crazy. I'm sticking to cartoons."

I suppressed an impulse to gesture at the door and order her to leave. But as annoying as she could be, she was steady and mostly kept her focus on the work. Besides, if I fired her, the Alliance might start second-guessing my hiring decisions, the last thing I needed.

"So long as you're here," I said, "you're sticking to correct spelling."

It shut her up.

•

That evening I went to the opera with Jack. He'd been urging me to join him for months, but I'd put it off until doing so one more time would have been offensive.

"I have two tickets on Thursday, and Elaine can't go," he'd said.

It was to be *La Bohème*. If I had to suffer through an opera, it might as well be *La Bohème*. When I'd heard excerpts on WQXR, the orchestration sounded lush and intense.

After a light meal across from Lincoln Center, we entered the Met's lobby and joined the throngs of opera-goers, with their expensive scents, cultivated accents and melodramatic surprise when acquaintances encountered each other. I grew conscious of the plainness of my suit and my no-nonsense haircut. At the Defenders Alliance, extravagance was out of place, but Jack, on the surface a self-effacing man, was living with a woman, Elaine, who had inherited wealth and I suspected he'd dressed up to fit in with tonight's crowd.

As the performance started, I discovered we were a long way from the stage, on the whole a good thing because when the singers belted out their arias and recitatives, my eardrums didn't break and the orchestra's sound was balanced. At dinner, Jack had taken me through the plot, and during audience applause, he would lean across to tell me which scene was coming up.

"This is where they're going to sing about how they love each other," he announced during an early pause in the action.

"But they just met."

His howl of protest at my bovine sensibility was cut short as the applause ended.

During intermission, as we paced up and down a carpeted hallway, I owned up to "wreckless."

"Ha!" Jack exclaimed. "I'd never have guessed what 'reck' without a 'w' means, but I'd know right away that 'wreckless' with a 'w' has something to do with destruction. What's wrong with that?"

"Jeff saw a lot wrong."

"We all have words that defeat us. Mine is 'anonymous.' I always want to spell it with three n's. I'm sure if I'd made that error, Jeff would have laughed and moved on. Everyone makes mistakes."

"No big deal, as Louise said."

"I bet Louise feels pretty bad about it."

"It didn't show."

Well into the second half, Jack leaned across the chair arm and whispered, "This is going to be 'Sono Andati,' the aria I rhapsodized about."

I nodded. Mimi and Rodolfo, reunited, were to sing of the old times and their love while the other bohemians were out pawning their valuables to pay for medicines for the consumptive Mimi. She would die sometime after the duet, and I waited for some sign that she'd succumbed.

A loud sigh from her, an Italian cry of anguish from him, and I knew the moment had arrived. Jack had warned me it always brought tears to his eyes. He stayed quiet the rest of the way.

When the performance ended, he clapped with gusto. "Got me again," he said happily.

7

DESPITE MY RESISTANCE, THE OPERA had transported me to a world where poverty was redemptive, tedium had meaning, and tragedy was beautiful. Odd to feel uplifted by Puccini's ethereality while going home in a subway train, with its air of rancid sweat, the tunnel-compressed roar drowning out conversation, and an urgent-voiced beggar snaking along the aisle. The promise of transformation held out by art was no more trustworthy than the dreams of romantic love. Yet I believed in it.

Back home, despite the late hour, I had an urge to prove Caroline right about a lawyer's persistence. Engaging with an artistic work, even opera it turned out, inspired me to create my own. I rolled a sheet of paper into the typewriter, placed my fingers on home row and willed them into action.

It was a late winter's afternoon, sunlight about to evolve into reds and golds.

Atmospheric, at least. A start. I kept going.

Memory of that beauty turned him inward. If with friends, he'd know the sunset had begun because he'd sense their mood change under the talk, even their laughter.

"Whoa!" I yanked my hands away from the keyboard. Where had that come from? How depressing.

But I had an inkling. My mind's synapses responded to sad stories, end-of-love songs and the second movements of classical symphonies. I was drawn to the andante. Not tragedy. Vicarious anguish at Mimi's untimely death was an experience I happily did without. The andante was pretty and touched the heart. Tragedy was grim and gouged the soul.

Yet what I'd written wasn't andante at all. It wasn't pretty, and it didn't touch the heart. It wasn't even tragic. It was pathetic.

Where did I go from here? If I hated or despised my character, it could have been okay, but I disliked him the way I would ill-fitting clothes. If anything worthwhile could be written about an uncomfortable pair of pants, I had no desire to be the one to do it.

Stern's insistence on writing from a single point of view was getting in my way. What if the narrator was blind? Visual description was so much a part of fiction. If my character couldn't see beyond recalling a generic sunset, how could I establish a setting in a reader's mind? How to get the reader to picture my characters?

I could make up a narrator with sight, but I hadn't seen in a decade and a half. The world had moved on. Fashions had changed. New buildings had been erected. My world was populated with people I hadn't known when I had vision. I didn't even trust myself to describe anything I did recall, because crucial details eluded me. So even if I did use a sighted narrator, how could I create authentic images of a setting and the people in it?

This was the morbid, unhelpful way I tortured myself when overly tired. I'd get no more writing done tonight. But antsy as I was, I wouldn't sleep. I should settle myself down by doing some late-night housekeeping. Nothing like manual tasks to take me outside my head.

Turning off the electric typewriter, I thought how there was something andante about Caroline. It contributed to my curiosity about her.

8

Ray, my reader three mornings a week, wore his Republican heart on his sleeve. I found it disorienting because, a Jack Kemp devotee, he got as excited talking about how to solve problems of poverty and inequality as an old-fashioned leftist, no matter that his solutions were diametrically opposed.

This morning, we were progressing through the testimony of the prosecution's witnesses in the Robert Wilson triple-murder transcript. There were only a few dozen pages to go, indicating the defense hadn't put on any witnesses. Undoubtedly, defense counsel's contention would be that the prosecution had presented insufficient evidence for conviction. And with good reason. All the evidence had been in the form of identification testimony that was riddled with contradictions.

But now, as the attorneys argued before the judge at a sidebar, the transcript revealed that Wilson had been arrested at the scene of another armed robbery six weeks after the events at the Serpentine Bar. No one involved in that incident had been shot. However, the ballistics evidence that the police gathered at a shooting range after this second incident indicated Wilson had displayed the same gun the Serpentine Bar shooter had fired.

Defense counsel contended that allowing the prosecution to bring on testimony about the later robbery might induce the jury to convict him on an unproven pattern instead of the Serpentine Bar evidence. The judge agreed. But he ruled that the prosecutor was entitled to bring out that Wilson had been arrested while in possession of the Serpentine gun.

Defense counsel didn't challenge the ballistics evidence. I contemplated making a claim that his decision amounted to ineffective legal representation, but it had made sense. Fighting a losing battle would have run the risk that the judge would allow the prosecutor to counter by bringing in yet more damaging evidence.

The judge got the two attorneys to work out the wording of a statement, which the prosecutor read to the jury:

> Defendant's attorney and I, with his Honor's approval, have agreed to the following stipulation. Six weeks following the robbery at the Serpentine Bar and Grill, the defendant, Robert Wilson, was arrested and determined to have in his possession the gun used in the Serpentine Bar robbery.

Ray paused in his reading. "Who needs ID evidence when they have this gem up their sleeve?"

"You sound happy, Ray."

"I'm happy to see justice being done. You were beginning to make me think this case wasn't open and shut. I should have known better."

"I don't jump to conclusions. Let's finish the transcript, and then we'll talk."

Despite its length, the entire case hinged on just those two factors: the identification testimony and Wilson's possession of the gun when he was arrested six weeks later. In his summation to the jury, defense counsel said:

> The prosecution would have you convict my client on the identification testimony of just one witness, even though it's contradicted by a second witness and confirmed by none of the others who were at the Serpentine that horrible night. Now, what other evidence does the prosecution present to you? Right, just one

item. The gun. Ladies and gentlemen, I ask you to ask yourselves this question. What would anyone do with a weapon used to kill three people? It's impossible for any of us to put ourselves in the shoes of someone who could commit such a heinous crime, but I submit to you that even the stupidest and most jaded criminal would get rid of that thing at the first opportunity.

The prosecutor's summation followed. He talked about the terror and shock the Serpentine's patrons had felt that night. That most witnesses refused to risk making a wrong identification is a testament to their integrity. That one who felt more certain had come forward and pointed to the defendant in this courtroom showed both integrity and courage. As for the gun being found on the defendant six weeks later, I visualized the prosecutor spreading his arms wide as he opined, "Ladies and gentlemen of the jury, why accept defense counsel's invitation to speculate when the fact speaks for itself?"

Ray and I sped through the judge's instructions, where I detected no errors. In a few flat sentences, the transcript captured the afternoon's hours of waiting in the courtroom, followed by the foreman's announcement of the guilty verdict, the polling of the jurors to confirm their unanimity, and the judge's courteous words as he dismissed them. He bound the defendant over for sentencing.

"So, Nick, I can't wait to find out how you manipulate the evidence to this dirtbag's benefit," Ray sneered.

"You aspire to be a lawyer. Test your brain's right-wing hemisphere by coming up with your own argument."

"But, Nick, I don't have your talent for twisting logic to save these slime buckets from the consequences of their actions."

Behind his harsh words he was grinning, as I realized so was I.

He posed a question he liked to put to me from time to time. "By the way, how many cases have you won so far?"

"Considering the odds against our clients, you should be impressed we get any victories at all."

He snickered. "The odds being that society really doesn't like murderers, thieves and rapists."

"People also don't like it when innocent people get convicted or the Constitution you love so much is violated."

"Have it your way, Nick. Time for me to head for class."

I put on an enraptured expression. "My favorite moment of the day."

"See, Nick, we have something in common." At the door, he paused to add, "See you tomorrow."

•

Jack settled into the armchair Ray had just vacated. "Our opera got a good review in the *Times*, although the reviewer found the death scene over the top. He obviously doesn't get opera."

"Obviously," I grunted.

Jack pretended to ignore my sarcasm. "Well," he said, "any developments with—um—?"

"Caroline?"

"You read my mind."

"Fortunately, I can't. But I don't want to tempt fate by talking about her."

"I take that as another good sign. In that case, how's the writing course going?"

"The course is going fine. My writing is going nowhere. I wrote a first sentence."

"A start."

"Then a second and third. They were so bad, I left them in the typewriter and went to clean the bathroom."

"Metaphorically speaking."

"And literally. It was very satisfying."

9

"WAIT WHILE I HAND IN my story," Caroline said when our third class ended. She darted among the students milling around Stern to drop her manuscript on his desk.

On the sidewalk she said, "Up for a drink? I need one."

She took me down to a bar on Sullivan Street, where I discovered she was a celebrity. Making me sound like a long-time friend, she introduced me to the crowd that pressed in on us. Reggie drove long-haul trains, and Caroline said he was a regular whenever he stayed in town. I'd never met a locomotive engineer before, and I tried to draw out of him the romance I felt for the railroad.

"I drive freight trains," he said. "You're talking to a dying breed. One day freight trains will run by themselves. Maybe then I'll get a gig driving passenger trains. Management would be too afraid of lawyers like yourself to run those trains without someone in the driver's seat. I just hope there'll still be enough people who want to ride them."

"I wish trains hadn't passed their heyday," I said, feeling the effects of the beer that had been shoved in my hand. It would have helped to have eaten something first.

"It isn't like you can drive a car, right?" Reggie's laugh was somewhere between hearty and cautious. For some people, the way to deal with disability was to inject edgy humor. I put on a grin I remembered from the silent movies—smile not quite wide, eyebrows suggesting bewilderment as much as amusement.

I said, "I used to love trains—those whistles disappearing down a valley, the chug-chug and clanking metal as a train pulls into a station. Cars never did that for me."

"The only reason for cars," Reggie said, "is so people can drive themselves and we can stay beholden to Big Oil."

Unwilling to get into politics with a stranger, I again played the grinning mute.

Someone tapped my arm and told me in a gruff voice his name was Gavin. "Where do you live?"

When I told him, he said, "Oh, nice down there. Great views of Manhattan. Not that they mean much to you, but you know what I mean."

I did know what he meant, so I did my grinning mute routine.

He continued, "Pity there isn't enough work there for me. I'm in construction. The best I can hope for in that neighborhood is renovation, and you have to go through hoops with Landmarks Preservation to get even renovation projects approved. I stick to the Bronx and northern Manhattan."

As we talked, I overheard Caroline saying something about catering. Was that how she made a living?

"Finished?" a third guy said, taking the glass from my hand. "Here, give this man another whatever he's having on me," he said to the bartender. Moments later, I had a filled glass in my hand.

I said, "Next one on me."

No reply.

I found myself in a conversational lull, despite all the talk going on around me.

A voice said into my ear, "I overheard Gavin saying how pretty Manhattan looks from Brooklyn Heights."

Caroline, I realized. Her breath smelled of beer. It was oddly pleasant.

Seeing she had my attention, she added, "Show me some time."

"How about tonight? You get the view with all the lights."

"Let me finish this drink," she said. "How are you doing on yours? Oh, you've just started."

"Won't take a minute."

Chugging beer isn't very smart. Fortunately, the resulting need wasn't urgent, and I spared myself the horrors of the bar's bathroom.

On the sidewalk, I sighed at being released from the noise and the crowd. Caroline said, "Which subway?"

"The A is just around the corner. We can take it to High Street, first stop in Brooklyn. The Promenade is three or four blocks from there."

"Let's go," she said, seizing my hand and pressing it between her arm and side. We set off around the corner for the West 4th Street station.

In the Heights, as we walked along Orange Street, I gestured to the right. "That's Plymouth Church, where Harriet Beecher Stowe's abolitionist brother was a preacher." At the next corner, I pointed in the direction of the yellow brick house in whose basement Truman Capote once lived. Caroline made noises of interest, but although she lived in the neighborhood that had spawned a folk movement that already felt like a relic of the past, I could tell historical significance didn't do it for her.

I backtracked. "Funny how famous names and history lend allure to a place. We're hardly breathing the same air as Preacher Beecher."

"Just as well," she said. "Horse shit and food spoiling in summer heat must have smelled really bad."

When we arrived at an entrance to the Promenade, she exclaimed, "Oh, wow."

I'd often imagined the vision that had just enthralled her:

dazzling skyscrapers, one after the next, beaming power and wealth. I'd never looked at Manhattan from this vantage point, but I'd seen it from other angles on a vacation from Illinois and on trips into the city after we moved to Connecticut, even as my vision was fading. Then again, my most formative images might have come from photographs. We continued on to the railing that marked the top of the cliff for which the Heights was named.

She said, "The Staten Island ferry is leaving the Manhattan terminal."

Curious that she thought to mention that detail. It got me thinking how movement can become the focal point in an image that ought to be beautiful in itself. In music, a chord doesn't touch the heart if struck alone, with nothing before or after. Something else to keep in mind as I wrote: A story needed to move.

She suggested we find a seat. There were benches all along the Promenade, but she turned at the next entryway where, in the evening, the seating area was more secluded.

"It's lovely here," she said when we'd settled on a bench. "So peaceful."

It was peaceful if you pretended the Brooklyn-Queens Expressway traffic wasn't a constant roar on two lower levels below the cantilevered Promenade, and also if you ignored the mosquitos that found us, now that trees blocked the breeze from the bay. But yes, I did feel at peace, happy to be in Caroline's company. I leaned into the bench's back slats.

The next I knew, she'd rested her head in my lap.

"Hey, what's this?" I said.

"I feel like lying down for a minute. Do you mind?"

For answer, I stroked her hair.

"Auburn," she said.

Emboldened, I ran the backs of my fingers against her cheek, then spread my palm out to mold against the side of her head, and she turned into it.

After a while I wanted to move my hand, but wasn't sure where. I rested it at her waist. Time passed.

"Don't be afraid," she said. "I want you to know what I look like."

I let her words go unanswered for a minute or two, or more, or less. Then I said, "Tell me about your other coloring."

"I have a fair complexion, like you, but my eyes are a paler blue."

"Okay, how tall are you?"

"Five-eight. About like you, so you can't look down on me."

"I'm looking down on you at this moment."

I ran my hand along her side, then over her stomach. Down to her hips, back to her stomach. I jumped to her chin and explored her face with thumb and forefinger to find she had nicely defined features. I told her. She stayed expressionless.

I said, "A bump on the bridge of your nose."

"They always airbrushed it out when I modeled."

I moved my hand down to her neck, back to her stomach. Then back to her chin, but this time gliding over her breasts. No protest. No change of expression when I touched her face again. I returned my hand to her left breast and traced its bra-molded shape, then her right one.

"How are you doing?" I grunted.

"It feels nice."

"I hope no one's watching," I all but whispered.

"Who cares?"

She didn't live here, so yes, why should she care? But I did live here. I'd probably never know if I'd made a spectacle of myself, but if I was doing just that, I would be encountering people around the neighborhood before whom I wouldn't know to feel embarrassed, which could make me feel embarrassed before all.

Flexing to a sitting position, she said, "Shall we walk some more?"

Standing up, I was shaky with arousal. We returned to the Promenade and walked to the southern end, where I projected the Statue of Liberty standing far ahead of us in the harbor. With her arm pressing my hand even more firmly against her rib cage, I sensed her shoulders pushed back in a posture of well-being.

It was the consequences of the beer that induced me to invite her to my apartment.

"Want to see my etchings?" I said.

"You're an artist, too! Oh, you're being funny."

Fortunately, even though I'd considered the chances that we'd end up in the Heights, let alone my home, next to none, I'd given it a quick clean that morning. If my few years with the law had taught me nothing else, it was to prepare for all outcomes, however improbable.

But what could be less romantic than showing a woman into your home and telling her she has to wait while you take a leak? At least, as I unlocked my door and turned on the hallway light, I had the presence of mind to ask if she wanted to go first.

She responded to my nightcap suggestion by asking, "Postum? What's that?"

"A non-alcoholic, non-caffeine, five-calorie hot drink that C.W. Post created as a healthy alternative to coffee."

"Are you a paid spokesman? You don't have anything to eat, do you?"

"I was wondering the same thing myself. I'm pretty sure the cheese is in date."

As I foraged in the refrigerator, she strolled around the apartment. "A Haddon College rocking chair. Is Haddon where you went?"

"Yes. My parents bought it for me. Rather small, don't you think?"

"I see that. It doesn't invite being sat in."

"Where did you go to college, Caroline?"

"I didn't. Oh, so this is the story you're going to submit?"

She'd reached the desk. I cringed on remembering I'd left the first page in the typewriter. "You'd be better off not reading that."

"Too late. I like the opening sentence."

"That's the part I thought I liked, too." I came to the kitchen entrance so I didn't have to shout.

"The rest doesn't sound like you. Hm. 'Memory of that beauty turned him inward . . .'"

Oh, it's me all right, I thought. Just not a side I like to show the world.

"What's the story going to be about?" she asked.

"I have no idea." I went back into the kitchen as the kettle whistled into action.

I brought the mugs of Postum into the living room. She took a seat on the couch, and I handed them to her. I had neither end tables nor a coffee table to rest them on.

I said, "Put mine on the floor for the moment. Your side, so I don't kick it over."

Returning from the kitchen, I handed her a plate of cheese and crackers. Then I closed the Venetian blinds. This wasn't a time to keep the fishbowl on display, least of all at night with the lights on.

I sat down beside her. She handed me my mug, and we wolfed down the cheese and crackers on the plate between us. Finished, I put the plate on the floor and my mug to the side.

I turned toward her and stroked her hair. Now that she was sitting, rather than lying on the bench, I took pleasure in how it fell back to her shoulders. I put my arm around her, and she rested her head on my shoulder. We were going to sleep together. The knowledge quieted my nerves, though hardly my excitement.

10

FRIDAY EVENING, ON THE TRAIN for a long-overdue visit to my parents, I had an idea for a story. It would be based on an incident in my life that distressed me even ten years later. How to turn an experience I'd mostly kept to myself into a story would be something to think about through the weekend.

Mom and Dad met me on the platform in Greenwich, Connecticut. During my childhood, there had been few demonstrations of affection, but as they'd been doing lately, they each gave me a hug that made me feel loved, but also sad.

Once I got into the back seat, all the conversation I'd rehearsed on the way up drained away. Mom might be eager for news of my friends, but Dad's indifference usually won the day. Neither ever showed any interest in my criminal defense work. Dad had wanted me to go corporate, and Mom no doubt found the whole subject sordid. I didn't want to talk about my writing class, never mind the writing itself. There may have been other subjects at least to test, but their apparent preoccupation with themselves and their world had the effect of shutting down my mind. Maybe they lived in fear of saying the wrong thing. Not without cause. Sometimes the way they'd responded to things I said seemed so inadequate that I'd reacted with undisguised irritation.

From the driver's seat, Dad said to Mom, "See the blue house over there? They've made progress on the addition."

"So they have. Maybe they'll actually finish it one of these days."

The car sped on.

I thought of something to say. "Jack and I went to *La Bohème*,"

I called from the back.

"Oh, yes?" Mom said.

"How was it?" Dad asked.

"The music was gorgeous."

"Puccini had a knack for a good tune," Dad said.

Cute, I thought sarcastically, but didn't say aloud.

Through a labyrinthine process of association, the thought of the opera's impoverished bohemians took my mind back to my summer internship at a Tennessee legal assistance center and the weekend my parents flew down to visit me and do some touring. Seeing my threadbare apartment, they found accommodations they deemed more acceptable and persuaded me to sign a lease. But I refused their offer to cover the difference in rent, though it was twice what I'd been paying. While earning an income during the summer, however small, I was determined to pay my own way. Refusal to accept their financial help had been a step in my separation from them. They'd also seen it that way, and I'd sensed it hurt them.

"Here we go," Dad said. The car slowed and turned as we entered our driveway.

Yes, "our." Though I had my home in Brooklyn, I also thought of my parents' home as "ours." That's how they wanted it, too. Mom had floated the idea that I get licensed in Connecticut, move into the former carriage house on the property and hang my shingle there.

I carried my overnight bag up to my room, where Mom and Dad had put a four-poster bed. It hadn't been my choice. I feared hitting my chin or forehead on one of its posts. Extending my forearm crosswise before me, I located the one at the near corner before tossing down my bag and sitting on the bed.

Each visit to my parents had me exhausted almost before I

stepped inside the house. Why? Why did I feel I couldn't be myself around them? Why did I feel I could never spark unguarded interest in the events of my life? I lay back and summoned up the same memories I'd gone over so many times before.

I'd had a contented boyhood in Illinois. Although happy to stay inside and read and make model planes, I also enjoyed playing outdoors with friends. Dad often worked late at the office, while Mom was active, in her understated way, in charitable activities around town. They naturally grew alarmed on learning that my vision was deteriorating, but I initially took it in stride. There was nothing I could do about it, and it didn't interfere much with my life.

After our move to Connecticut, the decline became inescapable. No longer able to participate in sports with other kids, and then finding reading more and more difficult, I did a lot of gazing into space. Changes were made. My parents read school texts to me and took dictation for my essays. An itinerant teacher came to our house to introduce me to braille and a mobility instructor to teach mobility. I was given a talking book player.

I can't isolate the moment when I went from having some sight to having none. There were several days when my vision seemed gone, only to revive the next morning. So the day it didn't return, I'd already made so many adjustments that I must not have recognized it as the moment. When not seeing came to stay, I could accept it.

Mom and Dad kept their distance during that phase, perhaps feeling they couldn't be soft if I was to be strong. Their focus was on keeping me afloat in school, their love expressed through practical assistance. I might have wanted it that way, too. They certainly sacrificed, to use that contemporary cliché. Mom cut back on her public life in order to dedicate her afternoons to my needs.

Dad still worked long hours, but sometimes he assisted after dinner in the project that was me, if with an exhaustion-driven short temper.

Before, they hadn't been overly protective, although a boy doesn't notice just how much his parents do for him. But through high school, there was no escaping my dependence on them, and not just for getting work done. If I returned home from a party complaining about how I'd been mostly on the sidelines, Dad would click his tongue in sympathy and Mom sigh. I needed that brief expression of understanding.

But then I went away to college and acquired a whole new base of support. Mom must have felt she'd lost her reason for being. It was the only way I could explain something new in her, a sullenness mixed with fatalism. An instance from a later time came to mind. One evening after I returned from Tennessee, as we prepared to sit down for a game of cards, she put a mug of tea in front of me and said, "I put soy milk in it. Let me know what you think."

I was a prude when it came to food and drink, balking at anything new. After tasting the tea, I said, "I'm sorry, Mom, but I don't like this soy milk." She grabbed the cup and stormed out of the room.

"You know how upset she gets," Dad admonished me from across the card table.

Well, sometimes she got upset. Usually, she was patient with my fastidiousness. I took Dad's rebuke not only as his way of saying I didn't appreciate her enough, but also that I didn't appreciate him, a sentiment impossible for him to admit except indirectly.

My perspective was, of course, subjective. Maybe all my speculation about empty nest syndromes was self-serving exaggeration. Maybe by college, I'd become an opinionated prig. I suspect my parents saw that in me.

Mom got a job as an assistant in a local women's clothing store. I had a hard time imagining her answering to anyone except possibly Dad, let alone a stranger, but she needed an activity. Like me, it seemed she also needed a little autonomy. Dad didn't resist, even though they didn't need the extra income. I respected the way he supported her after bad days at the store.

In recent years, their hugging me felt like an effort to recover our former emotional, if not demonstrative, closeness, even as our inability to talk easily got in the way.

Back downstairs in the kitchen, I found Dad fiddling with the boiler, which we'd been told was as ancient as the house. Mom was making her patented stew. Well, it deserved to be patented. The aroma made me hungry and nostalgic.

I took my accustomed seat at the kitchen table and waited, hiding my discomfort at having nothing to do. After losing my vision, if I'd offered to help around the house, I was told it wasn't necessary. Back then, I'd been happy to be spared chores. Now I wished household chores were ingrained habits instead of tasks that betrayed my incompetence.

Dad reached a point in his fiddling and turned to announce, "Right, drinks." He poured his usual bourbon, I asked for my usual gin and tonic, and Mom got her usual glass of water.

In the dining room, as we started in on the stew, Dad asked me, "So, how's the office?"

"Difficult, but worth it."

Mom said, "How's Jack?"

"Doing fine. He really loves his opera. This is delicious, Mom."

"I wasn't sure about the turnips. I thought I'd boiled them too long."

"No, they're just right."

If Mom ever felt pleasure at being complimented, it was

imperceptible. Like my office's head, her minimum standard as homemaker was perfection. But I'd come to realize that compliments meant a lot to her. The difference showed when no one thought to offer praise and she'd go quiet for the rest of the meal.

"Anything happening at your office, Dad?"

"We closed a small deal last week. I had reservations about the income statement, but they gave satisfactory explanations, so I signed off and we went ahead."

Beyond polite questions, talking about his financial world, like mine of criminal law, was off-limits because it had political angles, and Dad saw political discussion as leading to heated arguments that changed no one's mind.

Entrees finished, Mom collected the dishes and left for the kitchen. Dad proceeded to give me a detailed synopsis of the movie they'd seen the night before.

Mom returned with more dishes and dessert.

"Are you telling him the whole thing?" she said to Dad.

That angered him. "What else am I going to talk about?"

We played our customary rounds of cards. All the talk was about the game. No dancing around forbidden subjects. Our play was lighthearted, and I was as happy in their company as I remembered from the best moments of my childhood.

Next afternoon, we hugged as the train pulled in, then Mom dashed onboard to find me a seat while Dad waited outside, ready to signal the conductor to hold a moment. I shrugged off embarrassment about other passengers observing this show of dependence because I was touched by my parents' solicitude and amused by our little theater. Besides, it made finding a seat easier.

"Right," Mom said, placing my hand on the back of the seat. "See you soon."

11

BACK IN MY APARTMENT, I yanked the page with my failed story attempt out of the typewriter. My first impulse was to trash it, but maybe one day I'd find a use for that opening sentence, so I tossed it in a drawer. Then I sat down at the desk and wound in a fresh page. I centered and typed the title: "The Portrait," then my name and the date. After that, words flowed.

•

I look back with detached awe at how my younger self managed in those pre-computer days. When attempting a story, I'd do only a single draft, have a reader recite back what I'd written, and then dictate handwritten revisions. I didn't have enough reader time, let alone time of my own, to have it be read back as I retyped it. Today, I am so accustomed to editing over and over again on my speech-synthesized computer that I can't compose even a note to a friend without making wholesale revisions.

On Monday afternoon I asked Mara how she'd feel about reading back to me what I'd written so far. "Only if there's time left after we've done with Alliance work and if your four hours aren't up," I added.

"Okay."

I sensed reluctance. "I know it isn't the kind of work I hired you for."

"I can stay late, if it would help."

This time a smile in her voice. Faint, but enough to reassure me she was willing and maybe even interested.

Half an hour before we normally left for the day, we turned to the story. As she read, only a few corrections occurred to me, and she found only three or four typos. Years later, I had a reader from another generation record all my stories so that I could transcribe them onto my computer. I destroyed the original drafts, but although I've made numerous revisions to "The Portrait" in the years since, the essential story remains the same.

I

"You look like you're sleepwalking," Amanda said as I entered the artist's studio after philosophy class, which met way too early in the morning.

I leaned on the counter that angled into the room, tucked my white cane under my arm and tried to squeeze dopiness out of my expression. Her husband, Len, mumbled something from behind his easel. I knew its location from the previous times I'd come here to meet Amanda.

"What are you working on, Len?"

"An abstract based on one of your fellow freshmen. I think you know her—Cheryl DiFrancesco?"

"She's friends with my suitemate, Peter." Well, more than friends, but no need to get into it.

Len said, "Amanda has a proposition to put to you."

"Oh?"

"Amanda will tell you."

Outside, morning sunshine had skimmed the chill from the early spring air. Amanda and I walked across campus to the library, where the college had set aside a room for my readers and my reel-to-reel tape recorder. She read to me for two hours each on Tuesdays and Thursdays.

Like her husband, she was an artist, but she was taking a break. "Len's residency means a nice sabbatical for me, as the workers around here call vacation."

I said, "Doesn't this weather make you want to paint?"

"I seem to have suppressed the urge for now. It isn't false modesty to say Len's the one with the gift."

"I'd never let myself even think that."

"You're still so young, Terry."

"So what's this proposition, Amanda?"

"Len wants to paint you."

"Well, I'm afraid I don't take off my clothes for anyone but a woman, and then only one woman at a time." My bluster entertained me.

"He wants to do a portrait—you know, your head."

"I'm flattered." I was skeptical.

"Not flattery. Tell you what. Let's get your work done, then we can talk about it."

At the end of our session, I brailled Auden's "Musée des Beaux Arts" as she read it aloud so I could study it afterwards on my own.

She said, "It's a little strange to read about a painting, even in a poem. A painting speaks for itself."

"Doesn't mean you can't talk about it and get even more out of it." I recited, "'The sun shone as it had to on the white legs disappearing into the green water.' The painting can't say, 'as it had to.' That's Auden, the poet."

"What do you think the phrase means, Terry?"

"Something like life is tragic, but life goes on."

"The painting says that, too. Breughel was an artist of ideas." She paused. "But talking about a painting is like trying to explain a Beethoven symphony. Explanation helps, but what matters with music is the sound, and what matters with painting is the canvas. I guess I'm saying you can't really appreciate paintings, not being able to see. I hope you don't mind."

I shrugged. "Few things are all or nothing."

I took her arm. As we trotted down the library's front steps, she said, "How about we take a swing by the athletic fields?" We turned away from the quad and set out across gradual slopes of grass.

I said, "What exactly does Len want me to do?"

"Sit around for an hour."

"Without moving?"

"Not like a statue. Len likes to have a model feel at ease so he can capture their expressions, not just some self-conscious photographic still."

"I'd freeze up."

"You soon forget yourself."

"You've modeled for him?"

"We all modeled for each other in art school."

"The face is revealing," I said.

"Sure is. More than the body."

Caught up in conversation, we'd picked up speed, and I tripped on the edge of the asphalt path to the science building.

"I'm so sorry," she said. "I should have warned you. You know, sometimes I forget you don't see. Is that a horrible thing to say?"

"My own fault. Don't make such a fuss, Amanda."

We headed over more lawn to the ridge overlooking the fields.

"Do you have any notion what Len sees in me?"

"A mobile, expressive face. Most people are more guarded or bland."

"When I start writing a poem, it's usually because I'm interested in someone or something, but I always need to move on to some larger idea."

"Just like Breughel. But for me, there doesn't need to be a big message with painting. Painting is about the artist's look on the world and viewers opening their eyes to it. It's about perceiving."

"I'd like to think about it overnight."

"There's no hurry. We're not pressuring you."

That was as far as I'd gotten in the story. When Mara finished, she went quiet. Some instinct told me to wait.

At last she said, "Did this happen? Tell me if I'm being too nosy."

"Some of this did happen, yes."

"Someone wanted to paint your portrait? How did it turn out—in real life, I mean?"

"Let's wait for the next installment. Maybe it will contain the answer, maybe not. If it doesn't, I'll tell you."

12

PROFESSOR STERN DIDN'T DISTRIBUTE COPIES of student submissions, and when he read one aloud to the class, he didn't identify who had written it. But when he announced the title, "'Colombia'—that's with an 'o' not a 'u,'" Caroline tapped my wrist. I turned slightly and slightly nodded, hoping she'd see but that no one else would notice.

Her story began with a young woman covering her ears against the noise of a single-engine plane as it flies low over boundless stretches of barren land. There are also the pilot and another passenger, a man the young woman apparently knows. A town appears, consisting of multitudes of huts and narrow roads. Further on are more substantial, Spanish colonial buildings that the woman takes to be the town's center. The plane turns and eventually lands on a rough airstrip, where it is met by a crowd of disheveled men. Nearer the perimeter, men carry rifles.

The men in the crowd organize into a line. Hunched over in the plane's hold, the pilot and the other passenger sling several boxes, one after the other, to the first in line, after which each box gets passed from hand to hand until it ends up in the back of a truck. They have manufacturers' labels, but the woman isn't close enough to see what they say—not that there'd be any relationship between label and contents. When the plane is emptied, the reverse process commences: boxes are transferred from the truck to the plane.

The woman tells herself she knew, or should have known, what this trip had been about, so she wonders why it wasn't until now that she's felt afraid. But she doesn't seek assurances from her companion.

The stream of boxes peters out, and the line of men disperses. The pilot climbs into his seat, and the other passenger gets in beside her. Neither he nor the pilot has said farewell to anyone. Other than the chattering of the men in the line, hardly any words have been exchanged. The plane takes off.

The woman asks herself how the other passenger—her boyfriend, we infer by now—got into this insanity. Had he been told to in order to implicate himself? Were they both now, God forbid, caught in a web from which there was no escape? The story ended with those questions unanswered as next morning they arrive at the airport in Bogotá for a flight back to New York.

Caroline could write. I felt tense, as though I'd lived through the trip, and as Stern read the story to its end, I was left with a sense of dread.

Stern opened the floor for comment. The first guy talked about the strength of the writing and how scary the story was. Another expressed his skepticism about the woman character's motivation. Yet another doubted the likelihood that these events could have taken place in real life.

It frustrated me that Caroline had to stay silent. I would have liked to hear her defend her work. But Stern said the only way we'd find out how our words were received was to listen to a critique. Right or wrong, it always told us something. If a class of readers missed an important point, the author could go home and make it harder to ignore in the next draft.

Eventually Stern gave us his own reaction. "This is a slice of life. Not everyday life, of course, but a discrete moment. I think the author does a credible job of bringing the reader in, as some of you have commented. I trust the author. I find the situation itself believable." He didn't address the motivation question. Maybe characterizing the story as a believable slice of life neutralized it.

Had this been a story I'd found in a book, I might also have questioned the woman's willingness to take such a risk. As she admits to herself, she had to have had some idea of what the trip was about. But the story contained a great deal of convincing detail, and I was sure it came from Caroline's own experience.

In my apartment that night, I uncorked a bottle of wine in the kitchen and brought it into the bedroom, along with two wine-glasses. The first time, Caroline had told me she liked a glass of wine after making love. I hadn't had a bottle on hand then, but I'd brought one home the next day. She sat up when I held out the glasses, and she poured.

"I guess Stern liked my story," she said, putting the bottle on the floor as I pulled the covers over our laps. She'd fended off my praise as we left class for the Sullivan Street bar, but now it seemed she was ready to talk about it.

"Is it based on experience?" I asked.

"Mostly. Well, yeah, all of it."

"Who was the guy? Or do you want me just to think about it as a story?"

She went quiet. At last she said, "The guy I was seeing."

"The guy you were seeing was a dealer of some kind?"

"Small time."

"But big enough to be sent to—where?—Medellin?"

"Medellin must be scary, but it's a real city. I don't remember the name of this place. It was a dump, a shanty town. He said it was an adventure."

"To persuade you to go along?"

"I guess."

"He'd done it before. Sounds like they wanted to hook him, as the story's narrator speculates."

"That's what I told him, after we got back to New York. But he's stopped doing it, and they haven't hunted him down. He's too far gone to be useful, and he doesn't really know anything."

"Where is he now?"

"In my apartment."

During the years my vision was deteriorating, I'd been told over and over to protect my head against knocks and violent movement, and so I'd taught myself to stifle spontaneous reactions. That ingrained habit kicked in now. I limited myself to asking a question.

"Does he know . . . ?"

"Does he know I'm here with you? He doesn't notice a whole lot anymore. So long as he has his supply and a roof over his head, he's okay."

"Then you don't really have a home."

"Oh, I don't mind him being there. Trouble is, I also wouldn't mind him not being there."

I almost asked if they slept in the same bed, but we hadn't placed conditions on each other. Besides, when she wasn't with me, where else could she sleep in her "microscopic" apartment? Then again, for all I knew, there were other guys in her life. Maybe

I'd even met one or more of them at Sullivan Street.

"Does that sound weird to you?" she said.

"A little."

"I guess it is. I've been living with it for so long, I've stopped giving it any thought."

"How are you doing on your wine?"

"Finished."

"Another glass," I said, "or should we call it a night?"

"I think you need to sleep for work tomorrow."

"Today, actually. And yes, I ought to. Do you think we could get together on a Friday or Saturday night so we don't have to get up early?"

"I don't see why not."

I rinsed the glasses and put the wine away, then got in bed and snuggled up to her.

I was on the point of dozing off when she said, "How did you lose your vision, Nick?"

The same old question, but ever new to new people. All I wanted was to sleep, but saying we should talk about it later would only heighten the melodrama that inevitably colored the subject.

Our first night together, I'd had to explain that I wore painted lenses over my cataract-clouded eyes that I couldn't keep in through the night. I'd been fitted for the lenses during law school. I hadn't known or even thought about my eyes' appearance until a friend bravely told me how their all-white aspect troubled him. I'd wondered since if it had contributed to my difficulties with women. Maybe it explained the change more than all the other factors I credited with my move to New York.

Caroline had taken it all in stride, as had my previous New York girlfriends. When she saw me without the lenses, she said, "Don't feel you have to keep those things in for me." She hadn't

asked more questions; for the time being, it seemed we both wanted to know just enough about each other. The rest would come out
when we were ready. Now we were. At any rate, she was.

I yawned before answering, "A medical condition called retinitis pigmentosa. It causes deterioration in vision starting anywhere
from age ten to forty. Mine took a tailspin when I was a teenager."

"Retin—? I've never heard of it."

"Retinitis pigmentosa," I repeated, "RP. One by one the retina's
photoreceptor cells shut down until they all stop working."

"Do you read braille? I've never seen you."

"Slowly. I started learning too late to become fluent, though
God knows, I've practiced and practiced. I use it for notes. My
bottom desk drawer is stuffed with them."

"Could I learn?"

"But then you'd be able to read my secret diary."

"Oh," she said, taking me seriously.

"Of course I'll show you."

"Losing your vision must have been traumatic."

"It was a long time ago."

"I had a traumatic experience when I was ten. My parents and
I went out shopping for Grandpa. When we got back to his house,
my parents were loaded down with bags, so they told me to unlock the door. I walked in to find he'd shot himself in the head."

Anything I said would be even more feeble than what people
said after they'd asked about my loss of sight, but I had to say
something. "That's horrible."

"Like you said, it was a long time ago. I still think of him, though.
He was a dear man."

"Did he have some awful sickness?"

"Cancer. Don't ask me what kind—I don't remember. He was
pretty much immobile by then, which is why Mom shopped for

him. This time Dad and I went with her. I'm sure Grandpa told himself his son-in-law would walk in first. Not good thinking, I know. But he wouldn't have wanted me or Mom to see him like that. I think he was so desperate to escape his body that he convinced himself we'd be spared."

I squeezed tight to let her know I felt for her.

I woke up around two and felt as alert as if it were eight. I slipped out of the bedroom without disturbing her, or so I thought. But soon after I settled in to read in the living room, she came out to sit beside me.

"Can't sleep?"

"I'm in one of my insomnia phases."

"You go through this often?"

"A lot of people who can't see do. When light doesn't reach the retina, your biorhythms can go haywire. It's like jetlag. And it's cyclical. Several weeks on, several weeks off."

"That's terrible."

"Terrible for you if I keep waking you up. I do see light, by the way—all the time, though not from outside. It's caused by neural activity in the surviving part of the retina. It's there even if I'm not always noticing it, like the hum of a refrigerator."

"I never think of you as being in the dark."

I smiled at that. It felt like a compliment. "It's a pity people assume blindness and darkness are the same. I suspect most blind people see some form of light—I mean real light perception, not just my neural activity. For the rest, I'm betting it's an unawareness of light. I don't think that's darkness, either."

She went quiet. At last she said, "Listen, have some wine. It will help."

In the kitchen, she poured a glass for me and one for herself. The wine did make me drowsy.

"Come back to bed," she said.

I slept another two hours. It got me through the day.

13

CAROLINE'S STORY MADE ME IMPATIENT to get back to my own. It wasn't out of competitiveness, but like the itch I'd felt after my night at the opera, she'd reawakened my craving to be engaged in the work of creation. Next evening I raced home from the office, heated a frozen dinner, gobbled it down and at last sat before the typewriter.

//

It felt odd arriving at Len's with no plans to meet Amanda. As he was finishing up his previous task, I stood just inside the echoing studio and marveled at the notion of my features being transformed into something that might one day be deemed a work of art.

At the far side of the room, Len said, "I'm ready for you." As he directed me by voice to a seat, I felt him staring at my movements. Finding I was looking down, I raised my head. I folded up my cane, dropped it underneath the wooden chair and sat down.

How to sit? I felt as if I were in my high school yearbook picture session all over again, when I'd wondered what to do with my hands. I found a position with my back straight and hands folded between my knees, which were slightly apart. I didn't ask if the pose was acceptable, and he didn't say.

Where to look? It had to be in Len's direction, but he wasn't talking. Fortunately, the methods of his trade involved rustling noises and the hardwood floor tracked the movements of his feet.

When he broke the silence, his voice carried the length of the room.

"Amanda told me about Icarus's white legs disappearing into the green water. You were wondering if paintings need to express ideas. Amanda and I disagree. I believe ideas belong in painting, though they aren't always easy to articulate. Take Impressionism. Impressionism involved colors, natural light, and reflections. It was born and worked out in the paintings. It wasn't intended for words, but out of it came lots of words."

My mind drifted, and I'm sure expressions drifted across my face. Once, I noticed the direction of my eyes had strayed to the far-left corner of the room, following some trail of thought.

I crossed my legs. A few minutes later I found my left hand clasping my shin. God knew what Len would make of all this, but I felt comfortable, which Amanda had said was the important thing.

Amanda might be the first adult who acted as if we were equals, though I was half her age. Well, most of the time. Her "you're still so young" still nettled.

Feeling at ease with the posture I'd assumed and gazing casually in Len's direction, I felt less the absurdity of someone wanting to paint me. If anyone was suitable for painting, then why not me? I all but said it aloud. Why not me?

"That will do for today," Len said, banging something.

I took a deep breath and stretched. "I'd almost hypnotized myself." Unfolding my cane, I headed for the exit. I was curious about the painting. But what could I ask—"What have you done with me?"

"Goodbye," Len said. "Oh, and thanks. Let's do a second sitting next week."

Back at the dorm, I lowered myself into our scratched-up

wooden armchair and told my suitemate, "Peter, I can't decide if sitting for a portrait is normal or weird."

Turning from his desk to face me, he said, "A lot of normal things are weird, my friend."

"How does Cheryl occupy her mind when she's with Len? It has to be even weirder with no clothes on."

"Cheryl doesn't talk about modeling. I've asked, but nada."

III

Amanda waited until we left the library before saying, "Len was pleased."

"Have you seen what he's done?"

"You can never tell which way he's going. I can never tell with my own work."

Outside the entrance to my dorm, I leaned against the wall and she sat on the end of the stone banister. I pictured her with one leg swinging.

"What are you thinking about?" she said.

"Sorry. I didn't mean to go all quiet on you."

"That's all right. I was thinking, too."

"About?"

"About what an idyllic place this campus is. I'm distrustful. It's like you put Adam and Eve in a garden and they fuck up."

"So to speak."

"Right. I mean, here we are in paradise, and all I'm thinking is where we used to live, Detroit, with all its crime and grime, was more—I don't know—trustworthy."

"I don't trust this either," I said. "I almost wish I owned it, so I could be sure of keeping it the way it is."

"Terry, you sound like one of those people who buy Vermont

air in a bottle. Uncap the bottle and it all escapes. This is one time I'm reminded how young you are."

Second time in two weeks, I was tempted to point out.

She touched my forearm, prelude to, "Gotta go. I have to fix up the house for a dinner party. Would you join us one evening? Len and you could get to know each other better."

When Mara finished reading, she said, "So you did go through with it. I couldn't stand being under such minute scrutiny."

"I felt I owed Amanda as a friend and because of all the reading she did for me as a volunteer."

Mara said, "You'd just graduated from high school. What a lot to take on."

"Well, the story is about to take a darker turn. You may change your mind. Thanks for doing this, Mara. Talk about brave—reading someone's creative work back to them."

"I just hope I don't blow the lines and spoil it for you."

I shook my head. "Any flaws are solely the responsibility of the author. Now, let's get out of here. It's eerie being the last ones to leave."

"We usually are," she said, handing the pages back to me.

Outside on the sidewalk, I had an impulse to ask her to join me at a nearby bar for a drink. I was grateful and wished to show it. But I reminded myself she was an employee. I couldn't put her on the spot. Saying "Goodnight," I turned for my 2/3 train and she for the Lex.

14

THE EVENING BEFORE I WAS to make the oral argument in a case I'd briefed some months earlier, Mom surprised me by calling to announce she planned to come down to see me in action. Dad and she had been to all my school events, from grade school races, where I demonstrated my lack of athleticism, to law school graduation, but neither had evinced any curiosity about my court performances. Nor had I encouraged it. Pleasing my parents had no place in the best interests of a client, which, to my rigid way of thinking at the time, made it unseemly. But all my ethical qualms fell away at Mom's show of interest.

Her timing was good. After two years and at least a dozen oral arguments, I'd overcome much of my early nervousness. I'd learned to modulate my voice to be loud but not jarring.

I'd filed the brief for the appeal a couple of months ago. The case's name was *The People of the State of New York* v. *Joseph Waddle,* as if the entire population of our great state was against this lone man. I never ceased to find "The People" presumptuous. What if he'd turned out to be innocent? Wouldn't the people be rooting for him? Besides, his name in the caption sounded so formal, which the D.A.'s office reinforced by calling him "appellant" throughout its brief. Part of my job was to give my client touches of humanity.

"Mom," I said on the phone, "to make a couple of things clear, when a case goes on appeal, the party filing the appeal is called 'appellant.' That's my guy. At the trial, he was called the defendant. The party opposing the appeal is called 'respondent.' That's the D.A.'s office. Sometimes they call themselves 'The People.'"

"I'm sure I'll figure it out," she said, sounding impatient.

"I'll be speaking for ten minutes at most. The justices already have the briefs and everything else, so it's my chance to answer any questions they have."

The next day Mara and I arrived early at the Appellate Division, First Department, on Madison Square, so we could claim aisle seats near the front and I'd be able to walk on my own to the lectern. Alliance colleagues spoke in awe of the courtroom: rows of upholstered chairs facing the judges' elevated, carved bench under a dome whose windows let in light from the sky. Mom would be impressed. As the room filled, I visualized her gliding in, head lowered in the unobtrusive way I remembered from watching her as a boy, and finding a place near the back.

My case was third on that afternoon's calendar. Usually I was happy to sit through several arguments to observe how other lawyers performed, but I was glad Mom wouldn't have to wait long for my turn.

When my case was called, my stomach did its familiar lurch. I never would overcome the terror of the transition from private self to public speaker, but I'd taught myself to get past it. Mara tapped my elbow by way of wishing me luck.

I unfolded my cane and walked up to the left lectern. My opponent from the D.A.'s office would be heading for the right one. I took three brailled index cards out of my suit jacket pocket and placed them before me. Then I looked up toward the five justices, turned my gaze left and right, and returned to the middle. I might not be able to make eye contact, as advocacy instructors taught, but I could show the justices they were in my field of mental focus. Then I spoke the opening formula: "May it please the Court."

I was challenging the trial court's ruling that upheld the lineup where my client had been identified. Like trial counsel, I felt it had been rigged, though I didn't put it that way. I said it had failed to satisfy the minimal standards developed in *People* v. *Wade* and later cases.

I argued to the justices before me, "The witness told the police that the perpetrator was slim and medium height, but what did they do? Put Mr. Waddle in a lineup with five people who didn't match that description. One was the same height but much heavier.

Another was slight but taller. The others resembled him even less."

"They were all Caucasian, were they not?" Justice Robinson broke in.

"Yes, your Honor."

"All six, including the defendant, were wearing Yankees caps, were they not?"

"Yes, your Honor."

I waited a beat for him to list any other common factors. He didn't.

"Your Honor, I submit the least the police could have done was find a few men who matched Mr. Waddle's build. Then we wouldn't be faced with this lingering doubt."

The justices said nothing, a bad sign for me. I thanked the court and sat down. Whatever my opponent was about to say, I wouldn't have an opportunity to rebut, but I'd tried to anticipate the points he'd be making.

The A.D.A. picked up with Justice Robinson's rhetorical questions and went on to conclude, "There is no doubt lingering in anyone's mind, except, it would seem, that of appellant's counsel. The trial judge certainly had none, ruling that the witness's identification was admissible, and the jury took no time to convict."

The prosecutor was asked no questions, a good sign for him.

I stood, turned and briefly rested my hand on the back of the chair to set my course back along the middle aisle. Rising to intercept me as I passed her row, Mara gave me her arm, and together we made a graceful exit.

We didn't have to wait long for Mom to join us in the anteroom. Hugging me, she said, "You were really good."

I was annoyed with myself. I should have anticipated the A.D.A.'s parting shot that the jury had taken no time to convict. They'd done so exactly because the suggestive lineup guaranteed the identification that tipped the balance against my client, the very harm that the court in the *Wade* case had sought to prevent.

I wanted to explain to Mom the flaw in my presentation. But how narcissistic. Besides, she was responding to my court demeanor rather than the strength of my argument, which she would have been the first to say she was unqualified to judge, and I was touched by her pride.

"Mom," I said, "let me introduce you to Mara. I'm glad the two of you are finally meeting."

"He speaks about you all the time," Mara said, as she shook Mom's hand.

I silently thanked her for this gracious exaggeration. Mom probably did, too.

Outside on Madison Avenue, Mom said, "Well, you two, I have to go uptown to do shopping. I know you have lots more work to do."

As I more fully appreciate today, she'd set things up so that she placed the least demand on my time. When she asked which subway line she needed, I urged her to take a cab. My suburban mom had never negotiated the subway. She gave in, and Mara helped her flag one down.

As Mara and I headed back to the office, she saw I was dejected. "Your mom was right, you sounded really convincing."

"The operation was a success, the dog died."

"I think," she said, "the dog was dead on arrival."

15

IT HAD BEEN AN EXHAUSTING day—court days always were—but after five-thirty, even though Mara sounded as tired as I felt, she read back the next two sections of "The Portrait."

IV

"Hey guy, knock knock. Can I come in?" It was my suitemate, Peter, standing inside my bedroom door, pretending it wasn't open.

"Haven't you already come in?"

"That doesn't stop me from being polite, does it? Or would you prefer I just act like there ain't no door here and walk in and out whenever I feel like? Huh? Huh?"

"Blow it out your ear, Peter."

He sat down. "Mind if I sit down?"

"Is that like asking if I mind your coming in?"

"You just don't appreciate good manners. Speaking of blowing, mind if I smoke?"

"Are you telling me I have a choice?"

"You have a choice."

"Go ahead, light up." I stood and raised the window as high as it would go.

"You make a guy feel real welcome." Peter sucked his cigarette into life.

I sat down on the bed, but didn't lean against the wall as I usually did. I could tell he had something he needed to get off his mind.

"I spoke to Cheryl," he said.

"I'm glad. I mean it would be tragic if there weren't a verbal component to your relationship."

"Len's finished the painting she was sitting for, so she's done with modeling."

"I'll be happy when my own stint is over."

"She went back to look at the finished painting and to pick up the check."

"That's a point. I'm not getting paid." I was doing it as a favor to Amanda. Then again, she wasn't getting paid for the reading she did for me.

He made his sucking sound with the cigarette. "So while she was there, she saw the painting Len's doing of you."

"Can't be too abstract."

"You're recognizable all right."

"Don't make that sound like such an atrocity."

"She noticed your eyes are closed in the painting. The only time I've seen you with your eyes closed is when you doze off in class."

I thought back to my session with Len. "Funny. I didn't remember my eyes being closed. I did notice at one point that my gaze had wandered off to a corner of the room as my attention drifted. But most of the time I was looking right at him."

As I tried to take it all in, Peter made a sucking sound. "Terry, he's painting you as a blind guy."

V

Cheryl stopped by the next evening. I let her in and told her Peter had called to say he'd be ten minutes late. She sat at his desk.

Returning to the armchair, I said, "Cheryl, I'm glad you told Peter about the painting Len's doing of me. I know the two of you are on your way out to the theater, but could we talk about it some time?"

"I don't know what there is to add, but sure." She suggested we meet the next afternoon.

As I approached the library on Saturday, she was waiting halfway up the front steps, not knowing if I'd be coming from inside or out. Calling to me, she descended to the sidewalk, and I took the arm of the woman I couldn't help but think of as an extension of Peter.

We walked to the ridge overlooking the fields. On this side of the hill, narrow stone steps had been cut into the slope, and there was a landing every fifteen steps or so where ledges made solid seats. At the second landing, she suggested we sit down. She had a view over the fields and back up toward the college's southern buildings. The wind gusting through the trees gave me a feel for the expanse of landscape. Had Amanda known how much I visualized my surroundings, she might have been less worried about discussing Breughel with me.

"I think the place to begin," I said, "is by telling me about the painting."

"Well," she said to the woods in the distance, then stopped. In that one syllable, I heard her reluctance to say something difficult to someone she hardly knew.

"Well," she repeated, "There's a tinge of red in the top half of the canvas, and the lower half is in shadow. He's caught the shape of your face, and there are hints of what he'll do with your hair and mouth, but he was clearly concentrating on your eyelids and brows and the bridge of your nose."

"And my eyes are closed." Slumped forward, hand supporting my chin, I surrendered with a shiver to the chill in the air. Had my mother been here, she'd be correcting my posture.

"Do you mind my asking what upsets you about that?" she said. "I mean I guess it's obvious, but maybe it isn't."

I straightened my back. "I suppose I thought he was painting me for myself."

"And what would that be, do you think?"

"I know lots of things I'm not—scientist, athlete, party organizer."

"How about poet?"

"Much too grand," I said, though it brought a telltale smile to my face. "How about a work in progress?"

"If Len got to the truth of who you are, that would be something, wouldn't it?"

"I refuse to accept the truth about me is blindness, but when Len paints my eyes closed, that's what he's saying. It's how he sees me."

"One way he sees you."

"But the way he chose to represent me."

"And that upsets you because?"

I recalled a moment from the time when my vision was fading. I'd closed my eyes, held a leaf and traced its moist undulations with a fingertip. Then I'd opened my eyes and observed the even tinier striations and gradations of green. Sight discerned the millimeters that touch glided over. Did it mean those features of mine that Len had dabbed on his canvas were truer than those I knew?

There was a poem here, if I were capable of writing it: The window on the soul gone blank, lights out, curtains drawn. I could work in Aristotle's aphorism that the soul never thinks without a picture. Was vision essential to humanness, the poem would ask. I'd say no, and the sentiment would be genuine. But there on the hillside, making wild surmises about Len's painting, I felt marginalized in a world where a single picture speaks a thousand words.

I'd been dishonest with myself. Len hardly knew me. I offered only one subject for him. The shut eyes confirmed it.

I burst out, "You know what, Cheryl? It wouldn't matter what else he does with the portrait. What I already know about it would obliterate everything I want to be."

"What do you mean, Terry?" She sounded frightened.

"I mean that if Len paints me as blind, that's all I'll be. I'll cease to be a poet, or student, or whatever else there might be in me."

"I think I understand."

Quiet fell between us.

"Okay," I announced, "enough on the painting." I racked my brains for something else to talk about, but my mind was a wall.

She said, "Shall we head back?"

Nodding, I rose stiffly from the cold stone ledge.

16

THE WEEKEND HAD ME ON the horns, so to speak, of a dilemma. I would have liked to spend it all with Caroline, but I had to finish the story for Tuesday's class, which meant by Monday so that Mara could read the last sections back to me.

Caroline came over late Saturday afternoon, and it wasn't long before we were in bed. She was about to put her diaphragm in when I asked, "Can I do that?"

"You need to know exactly how it fits, or it won't be safe."

"Want to bet I don't?"

She squeezed a little Ortho into the middle of the device, handed it to me, lay back and parted her legs. I eased the half-folded diaphragm inside her, then let it open again. With my fingers freed, I probed. There it was, the cervix—what I thought of as an upside-down chimney. I positioned my fingers at the diaphragm's edge and slid it into place.

"Done, I think." I pulled back to let her check.

I was pleased at my cleverness, although cleverness felt wrong for lovemaking. My ambivalence vanished the moment she said,

"You should have been a gynecologist." In her appreciation for a skill I had no intention of taking to a professional level, I felt we'd moved on to a more secure intimacy.

After making love, we lay together and talked before realizing it was almost past dinnertime. We hurried over to the Old Hungary, a second-floor restaurant since replaced several times over in a building on Montague Street, the Heights' main drag. Tablecloths graced the room, the service was remote, and I could afford the prices. Relaxed still further by a dry Hungarian white wine, we devoured the heavy Central European fare.

It was good to wake up with her on Sunday morning, even though the demands for domestic comforts promptly began.

"Why don't you have a coffee maker?"

"When I want my coffee, I want it instantly."

It turned out she had reasons of her own to leave before lunch. I hated to have her go. My place would feel empty without her. And yet, while I'd churned out a number of pages before she arrived on Saturday, I had more to write before the story was finished. I accompanied her to the station, my exercise for the day.

Back at the typewriter, a mug of instant coffee at my side, I waited for the aura of Caroline to fade and the drive to create to reassert itself.

VI

When I arrived at Len's studio, he greeted me cordially. I leaned an elbow on the counter near the room's exit.

"Come around and take a seat," he said, dragging a chair across the wood floor toward me. We sat down facing each other.

"The painting you're doing of me," I started.

"Yes?"

"I understand you're showing me with my eyes closed."

"Ah, Cheryl." He spoke down, as if to himself. Then he looked back up at me. "Does that upset you?"

He knew it did. Why else would I bring it up? "I thought from Amanda that your interest had to do with what you saw as my expressiveness."

"It does."

I recognized the trap I'd set for myself. Expressiveness and blindness weren't incompatible. My mind clamped shut.

He sat silent, clearly waiting for my next move. He no doubt guessed the cause of my concern, but he wasn't going to say it for me.

I opted for stubbornness. "I didn't realize you were going to paint me as blind."

"I could tell you, Terry, that I'm not painting you as blind—"

"Despite my eyes being closed." I stared, eyes open, at him.

"But as a young man in repose," he finished.

"That's what eyes being closed means?"

"I said I could tell you that, but I didn't. To be honest, I'm not sure where the painting's going. You suggest certain images to me and, because of the kind of painter I am, certain ideas."

"One of which is blindness," I said.

"One of which is, yes, blindness."

In my intentness, I'd been sitting forward. Exhaling, I leaned back.

"May I ask why that upsets you?" he said, echoing Cheryl. Except now I felt under attack.

"Because," I said, "blindness is so sensational, that's all people will see."

"See blindness," he mused. "Maybe that's the point. Telling

people not to look away from blindness. Not to treat it as something secret and shameful, like a scar or a family tragedy."

"That's your intention?" I said, with a belligerence I hadn't meant.

"I'm thinking aloud. Although I'm a painter with ideas, a painting can't be just an idea. It's not a static thing. A good painting keeps moving in the artist's mind, as it should in the viewer's."

"Len," I said, leaning forward again, "can't you understand? I'm the only blind student—only blind anyone—at this college. A picture of me with my eyes closed will forever mark me as the epitome of blindness. Years from now, my classmates will see my photograph in a newspaper, and their first thought will be, oh yeah, the blind guy."

"You're planning on being famous?" he said. "There's every reason to think you will be."

"I was giving an example. More likely they'll see me waiting to catch a bus."

"Let me put this to you," he said. "Cheryl is that rare woman, a true blonde. Everyone is drawn to her hair. Does that mean that's all she is?"

"That's my fear: that for all the talk around here about the life of the mind, we're Pavlovian dogs before images."

"You're a freshman, aren't you?"

"Young, as Amanda keeps telling me. What's that got to do with it?"

"What you're saying ...." He cut himself short. Then he said, "Terry, what you're doing is reducing human relationships to the bare-bones physical, which is what you're accusing me of doing, isn't it?"

Once again he had me. I valued the life of the mind. I believed image wasn't everything. Even so, I wanted to protect mine. I could live with the contradiction.

"Terry," he said, "you're telling me you want me to stop. That's it, right? You feel I misrepresented what I planned to do."

He was asking too many questions. It allowed me to latch on to the easy one. "I'm not saying you misrepresented."

"Amanda told you I saw you as expressive. You made certain assumptions from that."

He sighed loudly, stood up and walked to the back of the studio. "I'll tear it up as soon as you leave."

I sat speechless. I wanted to tell him not to destroy it, but hadn't that been my objective, even if I hadn't admitted it to myself? Okay then, I should thank him. But I was overwhelmed.

I stood, located the counter and, following it around to the corridor, said, "I'm sorry."

"Don't be."

VII

Outside, the texture of the brilliant sun, the aromas of grass, stone and earth and intermittent breeze made a layered landscape for my mind's opposing factions. I'd told Amanda I'd like to make this place my own, but would I really? I knew nothing about managing property. It would fall into ruin. Except as I'd also said, few things are all or nothing. I might not do it perfectly, but ruin wasn't the only possible outcome.

Just now I'd taken a stand. It had gone badly, but maybe the next time I asserted myself, I'd do better.

By prearrangement I met Peter at the cafeteria. He got coffee for us and chose a table out of hearing range from the other morning-subdued students.

I owned up to my misgivings about my confrontation with Len. "If I'd had antennae coming out of my head, you know he would have worked them in."

"But you don't go around with your eyes closed. It's not who you are. That's what this is about."

I gulped coffee and crashed the cup onto the saucer. "Okay, so that's what this is all about. Now what do I say to Amanda?"

"Leave it be. She's not scheduled to read until tomorrow, right? Let Len explain and wait for her to bring it up when she's ready. Piss-poor position to be in, but that's how it goes."

We parted outside the cafeteria, Peter for class and I for the dorm. The phone was ringing as I unlocked the door to our suite. It was Amanda.

"I'm going away for a week, maybe longer," she said. "I think you should find a replacement. I'm sorry about this short notice. It's a family emergency."

Palm pressed against Peter's desk, I struggled for words. In the end, I said, "I hope it isn't too serious."

"I just hope you find someone better."

"'The End,'" Mara recited. Then she said, "What a bitch!"

"Amanda? What choice did she have?"

"She set you up—I mean Terry—for this. She should have accepted responsibility."

"Maybe it was Terry who didn't accept responsibility."

"How was he to know what he was getting into?"

"How was anyone? Len says that at the end, don't you think? Len couldn't know where his painting was going any more than Terry could dictate to him what it should be about."

"Is that how you feel—about yourself, I mean? This is how it happened, right? You blame yourself for Amanda deserting you like that?"

"Kind of." I paused. "Yes, I blame myself. I let her down."

"You believe art justifies everything?"

"Lots of artists do. And critics."

"But you don't."

"No."

"Wow, this is so weird. I can't believe I'm upset."

"I'm sorry."

"It isn't—it's—I don't know—it's life."

I got up, went to her side and touched her shoulder. Trying for a light tone, I said, "It couldn't have been so bad if I'm here to tell the tale."

"I think it's one of those days when I'm just upset," she said.

"One of those days? This is the first time I've seen you like this."

"So much for appearances. God, what a scene." She lowered her shoulder and sniffled into a handkerchief. Then she looked up at me and said, "But, Nick, why be unkind to yourself?"

"I wasn't trying to be. But as I was writing the story, I realized that in college I'd gone through an identity crisis and that I didn't handle it well."

"We all went through that," she said. "I'm sure everyone handled it badly. Look at me. I graduated and went to work for the family business. How lame is that? This incident here"—she tapped the pages of my story—"didn't stop you like it would have me."

An involuntary smile betrayed I was flattered, just as Terry's revealed how much he wanted to be a poet, but I stayed on track. "Terry—let's call me Terry for now—saw himself as so special that he considered himself entitled to impose his will on everyone else."

"He had a right to protect himself, didn't he?" she said. "Politicians and movie stars spend their entire lives controlling their images."

"That's how Terry justified it to himself. And as he says, there wasn't anyone else around with his disability. He had to figure everything out on his own."

"Peter helped, didn't he?"

"I don't know where I would have been without the friends behind the Peter character. They got me through it, but they were going by instinct and decency, not experience."

"And," Mara said, "I guess Len and Amanda had no experience to guide them, either."

"I feel bad for them. As adults, they probably felt they should have done better by Terry—by me. I'm guessing, though, that they came to hate me, but who knows?"

Through my fingertips on her shoulder, I noticed she flipped her hand across her forehead, as if to shift hair away from her eyes. Strands of fine hair splayed on her cotton sweater.

"You, Nick, never saw them again?"

"No."

"Well, it's quite a story. Definitely makes you think." She blew her nose. Then she said, "Would you let someone paint your portrait today?"

"I doubt it. A year ago someone asked if I'd be willing to be photographed in my lawyer's suit walking on a street with my cane. They wanted to put it on the front page of some local rag for an article about disabled people entering the work force. I refused."

"So you're still controlling your image." A smile came through in her voice.

I shrugged, which she would have sensed through my fingers. Standing there and touching her shoulder had become awkward, but removing my hand might dispel the moment.

I said, "I haven't figured it all out yet. This story is really the first time I've attempted to write about it or even talk about it."

She looked back up at me. "I never knew you had all this going on in your head."

"It makes me see how defensive I can be. Is that how I am around the supervisors? Is that my real problem here?" Thinking of my past relationships with women, I added, "And with all this confusion in my head, should I be involved with Caroline—with anyone?"

"Caroline?"

"I met her in the writing class."

"Describe her."

At last I returned to my chair. "Oh, auburn hair—"

"That woman sitting in the desk next to yours?"

"You remember from just one glance?"

"I'm from a big family, remember. In a big family, you learn to notice people. Nick, everyone's confused. Why should you be any different? I bet she's confused, too."

17

A LAWYER WHO HAD BEEN at the Alliance for four years wangled a job at a small private firm, and several of us took him out for a farewell lunch. No supervisor joined us; he'd made his unhappiness with them loud and clear.

I found myself sitting next to Wendy, a colleague who had started at the Alliance the same time as Jack and me.

"I'm wearing the sweater I just knitted." She extended her arm. "What do you think?" She'd told me before that knitting was the activity that kept her sane.

Tracing the lower sleeve, I said, "So smooth."

"It came out well."

"Maybe one day you'll make a second career of knitting."

"Maybe that day is coming soon."

"Oh," I said, "give the law more time."

"I'm willing," she sighed. "I'm just not sure the law is."

Like me, Wendy was in the supervisors' doghouse. Still, her

flagrant pessimism irritated me. Perhaps my own unhappiness with the Alliance made me too close to it.

Near the head of the long table, Frank, who had come to the Alliance from a law firm, tapped his glass. Having gained our attention, he boomed, "A few words for our soon-to-be ex-colleague, Bob. I'd like to say we wish he weren't leaving, but that would be selfish. I'd like to say I wish him greener pastures at Gluckman Schultz, but some here would say that goes without saying."

He went on in that vein, voicing his colleague's dissatisfaction with the Alliance and yet not exactly endorsing it. After all, he'd made the reverse transition, from private firm to here. He understood the disillusionment around him, but also the perks, above all, more rational hours.

The farewell lunch didn't last long. Perhaps we all knew it would be one of many in the months, never mind years, to come.

Jack and I returned together to my office, where he parked himself in the armchair.

"I found Wendy crying in her office this morning," he said. "Her brief got slaughtered."

"I'd never have known. She had her act together by lunch."

"That's Wendy for you." Then he said, "I should swear you to secrecy, but that would be unnecessary, right?"

"For the record, I won't repeat whatever you're about to say."

"By the way, I believe your story is due tonight. Did you get it done?"

"Mara and I finished reading it through last night. Speaking of keeping things to ourselves, don't tell anyone that she and I are working on non-office material, even though it's after hours."

"Mum's the word. Speaking of Mums, what did your mom think of your court appearance last week?"

I went along with his tangents. He knew perfectly well I was impatient to find out what he'd really come to say, but I wouldn't give him the satisfaction of showing it.

At last he said, "Anyway, I was saying Wendy got reamed out again. Meanwhile, of course, Frank got another ringing endorsement. By the way, do you spell 'reamed' and 'ringing' with or without a 'w'?"

Seeing my scowl, he chuckled. "Frank is pretty easygoing," he continued, "and there's no end to the love people in public interest law have for someone who deserts the law firm ranks for ours. But he feels they're being unfair to Wendy. He suggested they draft each other's next briefs. He'll pretend he wrote hers, and she'll pretend she wrote his."

"He what?"

"I was dumbfounded, too."

"What does Wendy think?"

"She said, 'Why not?'"

"You're kidding. She agreed to go ahead?"

"Already begun. They've asked me to look over the briefs before they hand them in. I've read other ones they've written, so I should pick up telltale signs of authorship."

I had mixed feelings. I was curious how the experiment would turn out. On the other hand, it was, putting it starkly, dishonest. For all the ill-repute in which lawyers were held, integrity was rated highly within the profession. For false claims of authorship, they could get fired and, for all I knew, hauled before the Appellate Division's Disciplinary Committee on ethics charges.

"It's a big risk you're all taking."

"That Wendy and Frank are taking. They wouldn't rat me out."

"It takes a month to draft a brief," I said. "You think their courage will hold up?"

18

BEFORE CLASS STARTED, I ASKED Caroline to hand in my story. She walked over to Stern's desk, where I heard him mutter, "Thank you." I tracked her footsteps as she returned. Amazing how the male brain can process even a pattern of footsteps as an aphrodisiac.

Stern began the class. "Sometimes we read a story together to see how things are done right. Sometimes the objective is to analyze why it was done horribly wrong. The story I'm about to read is an example of the latter—an object lesson. We're here to learn. The author of this story will learn more than anyone."

Mercifully short, I guessed five or six pages, it depicted some guy walking on a beach and reflecting on a past love affair. Stern had a field day mocking the absence of a plot, the failure to develop the narrator's character, the poor choices of words. He said nothing about the story's sentimentality, for which I gave him credit. The author might have heard it as mockery of his, or possibly her, emotional maturity.

I enjoyed the rest of the week, free from the necessity to write a new story hanging over my head. The Robert Wilson brief was enough of a worry. But by Thursday it was rolling out of my office typewriter.

Although I'd muted my enthusiasm when talking to Ray, I was charged up. The questions we typically raised on appeal went to fairness, the prosecutor's conduct, the length of the sentence and other factors critical to notions of justice, but rarely guilt or innocence. In this case, although Wilson had a history of robbery and other crimes, he'd never killed or injured anyone before. To me, it seemed unlikely he'd committed such cold-blooded murders.

Ray, Mara and Louise were reading installments back to me,

handwriting my revisions, cutting out paragraphs and taping them back in where they better fit the argument. The painstaking process created ample opportunity for miscommunication. I'd complain they hadn't followed my instructions, and they'd answer back that I hadn't been clear. Tension mounted, usually handled with humor, always forgiven, though not always right away.

On Saturday, Caroline met me at the entrance to her subway station for a walk through the Village. The October air produced a lovely clarity of sound, as I recalled it did of vision, a memory which, that day, brought on a pleasant nostalgia. Encountering a street fair, she told me what each stall had to offer and brightened when something caught her fancy. She'd hand it to me to judge for myself. Each time her enthusiasm promptly waned, with one exception.

"That pair of earrings you called delicate back there," I said, pointing to the left. "Let's have another look."

She told me all over again about the design and color, and I said I would buy them.

"Sure?"

For answer, I handed the stall owner the cash.

Playing records that evening, I was delighted to find we had musical tastes in common. Under the stereo table, I had a long row of LPs, each with a tiny braille label I'd stuck on its cover. I pulled out one LP after the next. The one she particularly liked was Manfred Mann's *Chance.*

I hadn't liked their version of Bruce Springsteen's "For You," but she asked me to play it again, and then again. By the third time, I was hooked. Most of the lyrics eluded me, but I caught a reference to "Bellevue." The singer loved the woman, but something was very wrong with their relationship. Then as now, I listened to music for what the sound evokes in me rather than the lyrics. Still, I would afterwards wish I'd drawn Caroline out about why the song moved her.

Soon enough I found myself in class and trying not to make it obvious that she was the north to my magnet. But when Stern began the session by reading my story, a sunstorm of gratification sent my compass haywire. Then he came to the passage calling attention to my discomfort at being the subject of a painting, and I experienced a heart-stabbing recognition that I'd revealed too much. As the revelations kept coming, I made my face expressionless.

Reaching the end, Stern opened the floor for comment. Students who speak first in class are a different breed from mine. They may not be the cleverest, but they're definitely the bravest.

A youngish guy said, "It's a really interesting depiction of how art and life battle each other."

"Which one wins?" Stern shot back.

"Um."

A woman I guessed to be in her thirties answered from the back. "Life. Because the artist promised to tear up the painting."

"It isn't life, but humanity. Humaneness," yet a third student offered. "As the Peter character says, the artist should have told Terry what he was up to."

"Really?" Stern urged.

A young woman got the hint. "That's crazy. You don't ask permission to do a work of art. Art is about freedom—freedom of expression."

That woman always sounded forceful. One who sounded gentler said, "I wanted to know Terry better. I wanted more context for why the painting bothered him so much. I understood why it did, but I wanted to feel it, really be inside his head. I'm not sure how to get there—maybe weave in another memory."

Someone sitting diagonally opposite me at the back said, "Something that hit me was 'brailled'—not typed, not wrote. I mean it isn't just that this guy reads a different way, he also writes a different way. It feels, I don't know, kind of isolating."

Stern said, "Interesting, too, which you couldn't know from listening, that the word is written with a small 'b.' I assume the author writes it the way it's supposed to be. I guess Louis Braille isn't around to protect his name with the zealotry of a Xerox." Then, apparently nodding to someone else, he said, "Yes?"

A middle-aged man who had admitted to being a lawyer, probably one of the two other suits Mara had noted, said, "That's what interests me, how the story reveals what it's like to be blind. You hear it in the conversations. They feel like they're in a vacuum, removed from physical space. It's obviously how a blind person experiences life."

Sitting in my corner, acting as if I weren't the author even though I was the only blind person in the room, I tried to hold back from showing I'd taken a personal, not just artistic, hit. My story had been meant for a mainstream audience, but this guy was saying a blind person's experience could never be mainstream. If Stern's etiquette had permitted, I would have asked which scene or scenes he had in mind. I thought I'd adequately hinted at the art studio's layout, and elsewhere I'd given indications of the college grounds, the dorm room, the cafeteria. Despite my fear that I wouldn't be able to incorporate the visual into my writing, I thought I'd succeeded. Where was the vacuum? I wished Stern had asked him to elaborate.

An earnest young man took up the theme. "I was wanting descriptions of the characters. I didn't hear one. Okay, his roommate's girlfriend is blonde, but that's it."

The woman in her thirties at the back responded, "That's what

I find so fascinating. I pictured each of these characters—most of them anyway. Like, Len is a wiry man, not tall but with lots of presence. Amanda is an attractive woman, maybe dark brown hair, like mine, or with a reddish tinge. Peter is full of suppressed energy. I see a lock of hair falling over his forehead, and he has a compact frame. Terry? We sense he's insecure because of how he feels about being painted, but the other characters are drawn to him. We do know he's expressive."

"That's funny," said a woman sitting diagonally way back from me, "because I see Amanda as tall with short, blonde hair. Peter is tall and slim with dark hair and a Mediterranean look. Until we learned Cheryl was blonde near the end, I saw her as dark and buxom."

The class tittered.

The lawyer raised his voice. "We're imposing our own biases on the story. Who knows what they really look like."

The woman who'd started the exchange laughed warmly. "It's a story. There's no 'what they really look like' about it."

The earnest young man had reconsidered. "She's right. It's like when you read a novel and then you see the movie. The actors hardly ever look like I imagined the characters did."

The forceful woman spoke up. "It bothered me how Terry is always looking at things. Like, when he arrives at the studio to begin the portrait, he's looking down. Then he's wondering which way to look. Later he claims he was looking right at Len. But blind people can't look. That's what it means to be blind—they can't see."

In the story I'd taken care to avoid the word "see" in its literal meaning to preempt just this kind of criticism. "Look" was different. While it often meant the act of seeing, it could also suggest taking in something or someone while turning in that direction.

I waited in vain for another student to make this point. Instead, her comment emboldened the young man who had just admitted that actors don't always look the way he'd imagined the characters in a book did.

"I remember what I meant to say earlier," he began. "I don't really agree with the comment someone made that we find out from this story what it's like to be blind. I mean, he lives by sounds and smells—right?—but there aren't a whole lot of them in this story."

Here we go, I thought. A room full of sighted would-be writers is going to tell me what my experiences ought to be. But the same woman took exception, thank God, because I was on the verge of violating the rule that we take our punishment in silence.

"I think you do learn a lot about what it's like," she began. "Terry knows where the artist is standing from the noises he makes. There's that passage where aromas and temperatures mingle with his thoughts after he leaves his suitemate in the cafeteria. I find it interesting how he experienced distance and how he translates so much else into visual images. And you see—if I can use that word—how he reacts when people act too nice or helpful. You get insights into how he, you know, sees himself and sees how the world sees him."

Stern asked, "Is it broader than that? Listen again to this passage." He recited three paragraphs:

I burst out, "You know what, Cheryl? It wouldn't matter what else he does with the portrait. What I already know about it obliterates everything I want to be."

"What do you mean, Terry?" She sounded frightened.

"I mean that if Len paints me as blind, that's all I'll be. I'll cease to be a poet, or student, or whatever else there might be in me."

"Yeah," one of the guys said, "I noted that part. He's speaking for everyone who's ever felt pigeonholed."

"Which suggests," Stern said, "that this story might be about even more than a blind man and his run-in with art."

At last Stern had spoken for me. Yet such was my excruciating sensation of exposure that I cringed at "blind man." It felt like a reductive cartoon. But any other way of referring to Terry would be convoluted and only end up saying the same thing.

A response to Stern's pointer came soon enough from a guy who hadn't made an impression on me before. "Why does Amanda end her working relationship with Terry? I mean I don't see how it figures in a story about art and blindness and pigeonholing."

A younger woman, who made interesting comments on the rare occasions she spoke, said, "It fits in because of what this story is really about: isolation. Amanda tells Terry she's going away for a week. Being on a small campus, which I think this is, she couldn't say that without meaning it because Terry would find out she was lying. So it sounds like she's getting away not only from him, but also from her husband. I don't get a sense that Terry and Amanda were involved—romantically, I mean—but there is something between them. They and the husband are in a triangle, and when it falls apart, each of them is left alone."

I hadn't thought about this triangle before, but it was obvious when pointed out. I took a deep, meditative breath. Maybe, if I'd just let myself listen, Stern's method was working.

A woman who appeared to be sitting next to her said, "That's interesting, but I think of a triangle as involving some kind of sexual thing. I think ultimately this story is about something simpler and yet maybe even deeper. I think it's about how sad it is to lose a friend."

Murmuring followed. She'd struck a chord. But then she added,

"I wonder if it would be even more compelling if we knew more about the painter. I'd like to have some insight into why he was painting Terry with his eyes closed."

The lawyer piped up again. "Screw the painter! We know too much about him as it is. This story feels like some judge's balancing act. If the author has something to say through Terry, say it. I mean, if this were about racial discrimination, it would focus on the victim. But this story wants to give both sides equal time. Well, like I said, screw the other side."

Trust a lawyer to promote one-sided advocacy.

"Okay," Stern said, his tone indicating he was taking over. "A few things. There are parts that should be deleted or shortened, like that 'Adam and Eve' scene."

A student had the nerve to jump in. "I thought that set up Terry's innocence and naïveté."

Though interrupted, Stern refrained from crushing him. "Right, like his thinking of his mother reprimanding him for not sitting straight. But it goes beyond what's needed to get that point across, and I'm not even sure it's relevant to the story."

Stern stopped speaking, but he wasn't done. "Now," he resumed, "for the point of view. Obviously the story is written from Terry's perspective. I agree with those of you who said the author is trying to do too much. I feel like I'm reading, 'On the one hand this, but on the other, that.' As if that weren't complicated enough, the author is writing about both the responsibilities of artists and what it's like to be blind in a visual society. That's one hell of a lot to stuff into—what?—fifteen pages."

Class ended an hour later, after discussion of a second submission. As the other students passed before my desk to the exit, I imagined them glancing at me out of the corners of their eyes. I'd revealed my soul to them, and they'd commented bluntly on that revelation, but now, to maintain the pretense of anonymity, no one said anything. Caroline retrieved my manuscript and we left the way we always did—quietly, apparently unnoticed.

It wasn't until we were in the street that she said, "That was fantastic."

We walked down to a café on MacDougal. It gave us the space to talk that we wouldn't have at her Sullivan Street bar. We chose an outdoor table, an island in the currents of tourists, bridge-and-tunnelers and NYU students plying the vehicle-free street. At the other tables, people debated with an urgency that said all the world's major decisions took place right here. Caroline entered into that spirit.

"But you do put a lot into a story," she said.

"You're saying I should make a novella or even novel out of it? But length wasn't the point. I was being told to write about the morality of art or about blind people, but not both."

"If it's too complicated, no one will read it. Great work, no audience."

"A black writer can write about jazz and being black, a suburban-ite about a swimming marathon and living in the 'burbs. A blind person's life isn't just about being blind—least of all about that."

"I get that. You know I do."

I did, but I was intent on my argument. "I ought to be free to write about anything from the point of view of a blind charac-ter—art, bowling, traveling through Mongolia—anything. When the class commented on your story, they didn't wonder how the woman perceived things. They didn't want you to describe every single character. They praised the quality of your writing, as they should have."

"Someone did say I didn't explain my character's motivation."

"But Stern didn't endorse it."

"He doesn't have the time to comment on everything the class says."

"I feel like I can't write a story without someone criticizing my lack of description, then someone else complaining they don't know how my character sees things, then someone else demanding to know every character's motivation, then everyone saying I'm doing too much."

"It's a lot for you to take in, that's for sure," she said. "It took me a while to take in everything they said about my story. I'm still figuring it out."

I nodded.

What burned the most was that lawyer's remark about my scenes taking place in a vacuum. In college I'd been trained to read the story for itself, to focus on what was said and not said. But that asshole lawyer was telling me people would read my work with their preconceptions intact.

I should have brought my cassette recorder with me. I'd thought about it, but I wouldn't have used it in class. Even so, I could have been recording notes here and now, while the comments were fresh in my mind. Fortunately, I trusted my memory. I'd write down everything I could remember when I got home.

I said, "There was something no one thought to raise in class—what Terry's eyes looked like. I avoided that issue in the story because I feared it would take over. Or maybe I'm too sensitive about it."

"Completely understandable."

"I didn't have my lenses then, so, if Len had painted my eyes open, they would have been clouded over and blindness would have been obvious. It just occurred to me that by painting them closed, he might have been protecting me."

"You think so?"

"I have no idea. But if he had been, I think he would have enjoyed the irony, despite the awfulness of that confrontation. He was that kind of man."

I let my thoughts wander some more. Then, pausing my cup mid-lift, I said, "Okay, I'm done."

"I have you back now?"

"I'm back. Let's finish our coffees and head for your bar."

She said, "I'm wearing the earrings you gave me. See?" I reached out my hand as she tilted her head.

19

CAROLINE AND I SPENT TUESDAY nights together and at least one weekend night. Sometimes she'd call as late as nine or so to say she'd like to come over. I liked her free-floating ways. I begged off just once, on a night when I had to make an argument in court the next day. Preparing for a ten-minute presentation had me practicing in the evening and getting up early to start all over again.

When she came on her own, she did so by cab. I didn't know how she could afford the fare. She had a copyediting job at a small firm in the West 20s. "It's kind of erratic, depending on when the work comes in and my schedule," she'd told me. Such an irregular job couldn't possibly leave much over after rent, food and other living expenses. In fact, I had to come out to give the driver cash more than once.

Besides, even in those days, her subway trip would have been not only easy, but also safe—at least as safe as a ride in a cab. In a cab, she never remembered how to tell the driver the way from the Brooklyn Bridge to my street. When she was on her way, more often than not, she'd end up calling from a public phone booth for help.

I'd bring up the subway option, but she always deflected the idea. I thought of typing out a set of directions for the cab rides, but she would have lost them. I'd decided she was playing some kind of game. I couldn't get annoyed.

One evening I asked her about catering. "I overheard you talking at Sullivan Street about it."

"Copyediting is boring. I've helped out friends who cater, and I'm thinking of setting up my own business."

"You should incorporate."

"And pay all those taxes? No, thanks."

"Better than having someone sue you for food poisoning and taking you for everything you've got. I'll help out with the taxes."

"If you say so."

"I've never done an incorporation. We'll need to find a book on it, and you'll have to read it to me."

"Okay."

Not exactly a resounding endorsement.

Bringing up incorporation was premature. It was the lawyer in me, anticipating how Caroline would need to protect herself, but all it did, I'd tell myself afterwards, was present her with another obstacle.

"What else do you do to make ends meet?" I said.

"Oh, people are always wanting things done. And my parents help out."

Her parents were vague figures in my mind. Both were civil servants, but I couldn't remember exactly what they did. Maybe Caroline hadn't said.

We were sitting side by side on the couch. She was wearing a thin shirt and a corduroy skirt.

"Same old skirt," she said when I ran a hand over it.

"You don't have any others?"

"Clothes haven't been a priority."

"If you're going to start a business, we'll have to get you fixed up."

Was I pushing this notion of starting a business too hard? Maybe she'd mentioned the idea just to divert me from my interrogation. As with her living arrangement, how she kept financially afloat seemed to me a private matter that I had no right to examine, at least this early in a relationship, although it wouldn't be good for me as a lawyer to be associated with someone doing anything illegal. I leaned toward believing she wasn't. That Colombia trip had spooked her.

As I undressed to join her in bed, she said, "Spank me."

"I'm sorry?"

"Smack my ass."

"Why would I want to hurt you?"

"It's not about hurting."

"What, then?"

"I don't know."

I sat on the edge of the bed and reached across to her. Naked, she was lying on her front. I ran a hand over her buttocks as I contemplated defiling their shapeliness.

Molding my palm around her right buttock, I said, "You mean it?"

She nodded, which I detected through the muscles in her rump. I raised my hand, paused in wonder at myself, then brought it down. The slap jarred against the boxed-in quiet of the small room.

"Other side," she said from deep within her. "Harder."

In my head, dark music played from an S&M soundtrack I'd overheard somewhere.

"Caroline, this makes me uneasy."

"Do it."

I hit the other side, harder this time.

"Again," she rasped.

I smacked both buttocks.

"That hurt. More."

I felt a surge of power at having Caroline in total submission to me. I gave her two vicious smacks.

She groaned. I waited. She sighed. "Now turn me over and fuck me."

20

MY BRIEF IN THE ROBERT Wilson case was assigned for review to Howie, the supervisor who had warned Jack about his productivity. I'd been surprised about that. Not about Jack's productivity. He saw so many angles to each problem that he had difficulty honing in on what was central. We'd spent whole lunch hours debating the fine points in his cases. No, what surprised me was that it was Howie who had given Jack the warning. He was a dedicated advocate for our clientele, but in every other way a pussycat. It pained him to dish out criticism. He also couldn't cope with his very angry, not-yet-ex who phoned him so often that Michael Flurry, the office head, had instructed our long-suffering receptionist to intercept the calls.

When I sat before Howie to discuss the brief, he said, "You make a good argument for the prosecution's failure to prove the defendant's guilt."

I heard a "but" coming.

"Did you read the parts about the upset juror?"

After the first day of trial, in which the prosecutor had vividly described the scene of destruction in his opening statement, a juror called from home to say he was too upset to continue. Nevertheless, next morning he showed up and took his place in the jury box. At a sidebar, defense counsel urged the judge to question the juror about his fitness to continue. The judge refused, saying the juror had told a court officer he was "done being upset" and was ready to do his duty.

Howie said, "Trial counsel made a good record."

Of all the supervisors, I felt Howie would listen, so I explained myself. "I don't think this juror issue is a winner. If we had a weak case, I'd throw it in, but it could detract from our best argument—that the prosecution didn't prove guilt beyond a reasonable doubt."

"We can't let an issue go that has such a complete record."

We did all the time, but his mind was made up.

I threw myself into the task of making the juror issue compelling. I even convinced myself, sort of.

When Ray finished reading it back, he said, "A juror has a bad moment, and just for that you want to hold the trial all over again? We've all had moments like that, Nick."

"It would have been no skin off the judge's nose to question him. I can imagine a juror being so rattled that he'd vote for conviction to be on the safe side, regardless of the evidence."

"You can imagine it, but I see nothing to support it."

"That's because the judge didn't dig deeper."

"Why waste an hour of court time? The guy came back the next day. What more do you want, Nick?"

21

"I FINISHED READING THE DRAFT Frank is writing for Wendy this morning," Jack said, "and this afternoon I work on the one she's writing for him."

A week later, we were talking in the diner we liked at the corner of Church and Park Place. I was enjoying my tuna sandwich and, guiltily, the chips on the side.

"How was Frank's?" I asked.

"I had to pencil out some corporate-sounding phrases here and there. They'd be a dead giveaway that Wendy had gotten some help, and from whom."

"I can't believe they're going through with this."

"Believe it. Wendy is nervous, but she hasn't wavered."

To fill a lull in the conversation, I asked about his girlfriend, Elaine. He told me she was fed up with her job at a publishing firm and thinking about moving on. "Those editors are always changing jobs. By the time they're thirty, they've worked at every publishing house in the city."

A strange thing about Jack and Elaine: they never fought. They didn't seem to have any problems at all. Yet I found Elaine remote and no-nonsense, seemingly an ill-suited companion for the outgoing Jack. Opposites were said to attract, but in their case, the cliché seemed all too apt. It must have meant that I hadn't brought out the best in her. Jack was always citing her advice, talking about the books she worked on, telling me about the parties and artistic events they attended. She made him happy.

He inquired about Caroline. "Still going well?"

"I've never had a relationship go better. I trust her, and she trusts me. We have interests in common. I like being with her."

"I do miss the *Sturm und Drang* of your old love life."

The smile behind his words showed he knew he risked hitting a nerve. I did feel his remark trivialized the suffering I'd endured for love and confided in him at other lunchtimes. I'd long harbored a suspicion that Jack was, unbeknownst even to himself, a moralist. Looking back, I wonder why he put up with my lamentations at all. But then, people in their twenties do indulge their friends' morbid angst. After all, it's sincerely felt.

"Maybe it's going too well," I said. "I'm not ready to make a commitment. Everyone else got it out of their system by law school."

"Sowed their oats, you mean."

"Since I came to New York, women have been banging down my door. Part of me hates to miss my moment."

"So humble."

"Boasting borne of long disappointment."

"Does Caroline know?"

"We've made no claims on each other. And …" I hesitated. "She's living with someone."

"Say again?"

"You heard me. I'm sure it's over, but he isn't in any condition to move out. He's a drug addict. It seems his brain is addled."

"His apartment or hers?"

"I think hers. Yes, she refers to it as hers."

"Is she an addict?"

"I don't know about the past, but she isn't now. She hasn't taken drugs around me, and I don't see it in her behavior."

"Could this explain your reluctance to commit?"

"It might make me look better if it were so."

I changed the subject. "Howie approved the Robert Wilson brief and agreed I should ask for twenty-five minutes at oral argument. He seems as convinced as me of the case's merit."

"That's unheard of. The longest I've asked for is fifteen minutes, and I didn't use up my time."

"You, Jack, couldn't fill up fifteen minutes?"

"Those Appellate Division justices aren't as indulgent as you."

Then he jumped so violently, I felt it through the table. "Oh, shit. Wendy. I'd better get back."

22

COCAINE MAN (I NEVER LEARNED his name) moved out of Caroline's apartment.

"How did you manage that?" I asked her when she mentioned it, seemingly offhand. We were walking down Columbia Heights, the street that declines sharply from the Promenade to the bank of the East River as it opens out into New York Harbor.

"He has other friends," she said.

That was all she told me. I never knew if she threw him out, although with Caroline, it was unlikely. It would have required severity. Maybe she'd explained her new situation to him, and he'd taken the hint. But I found that implausible, too, based on his long dependence on her. However she arranged it, whoever had taken him on, that was some friend.

It strikes me now how accepting I was of Caroline's mysteriousness. I think I saw her as a real-life Holly Golightly from the film, and so I was content to take her the way she presented herself, just as the people at the Sullivan Street bar seemed to. Besides, the last thing I wanted was to play Colombian cop and interrogate her, or even cross-examine her like the New York lawyer I was. I'd read enough trial transcripts to imagine what that must be like for the witness. For the time being, all I cared about was that Cocaine Man was gone.

She said, "I'm glad you don't do drugs."

"I'm glad you don't, either."

"I used to. That's how he and I got involved and how I ended up on that plane in Colombia."

"No craving?"

"The only craving I have is to stay away."

"So, you have your apartment to yourself."

"All mine."

"You'll have to introduce me."

"I mean it's mine, but it doesn't feel mine yet."

Even this far into the fall, remnants of summer stink rose from the river as we reached the foot of the hill. We sat for a while on a bench on the nearby pier, where I projected out to Manhattan, staring down at us from across the East River, and the Brooklyn Bridge, a short walk upstream. Then we strolled into DUMBO, at the time a rundown area of knitting factories, printing presses and artists' lofts.

I said, "Your second story's due in a couple of weeks, isn't it? What are you writing about this time?"

"What should I, do you think?"

"It's got to come from you."

"That's the problem. Oh, someone's moving out of the house up ahead. Can't blame them, living among all these industrial buildings."

"How do you know they're moving out?"

"My great detection skills. They're heaving furniture into the back of a U-Haul. How about we hang around in case they can't load it all and decide to give some away?"

"You're looking to furnish your apartment, now that it's all yours again?"

"I was thinking about your place."

"Where would I put anything?"

"You'd replace what you have, silly. Like your vinyl couch."

"My parents are very attached to that couch."

"I bet they gave it to you after they bought a new living room set and had nowhere else to put it."

Time was when I would have taken offense at such a casual dismissal of my parents' feelings. Even now, I caught myself frowning as a primeval protective instinct briefly revived. But Caroline meant no malice.

The couch, one of my parents' first purchases, an ungainly thing colored two shades of gray, went all the way back to my childhood. It later migrated from the living room to the den, which became my study during high school. After delivering it to my Brooklyn home, Mom and Dad did buy a new couch for the living room and moved the one it replaced into the den. So Caroline was more or less right, but still unjust to them. The old couch undoubtedly reminded them of when they were young and poor. Now I was young and poor, and they'd known that the cost of a couch was an expense I could do without.

Exchanging hi's with the movers, we sidled between the U-Haul and the piles of possessions and kept going. Although Caroline had talked about hanging around, she wasn't one to circle like a vulture.

Turning her head for one last look, she said, "Probably roach-infested."

"Caroline, what were you saying about not having anything to write?"

"I've run out of ideas. I don't think I'm meant to write."

"Of course you are. Your Colombia story was great. Write something about this guy finally leaving your apartment. If nothing else, it would give people in the class some tips."

"On how to end a relationship that's died?"

"I was thinking more about getting an unwelcome guest to leave."

23

IT TURNED OUT CAROLINE HAD been thinking about upgrading my apartment for some time. Next weekend she had us explore the furniture stores off Park Avenue South that huddled together like a bedraggled therapeutic support group of decades-old survivors. The sales assistants were either unhelpful novices or wizened old guys who had long ago lost interest.

At last we stepped inside a place where a man I guessed to be the owner gave us an enthusiastic tour of his wares. Caroline was immediately drawn to a black couch, but I felt it would look like a monolithic slab in my living room. Saying "Spots will show," she ruled out a white one I liked for its textured fabric.

She turned to the assistant. "How about that blue one over there?"

"What kind of blue?" I asked.

"A nice blue," she said. "It will brighten up your apartment."

The assistant said, "It's on the light side. Call it sky blue."

I wondered if he was deliberately putting me off, saving that item for another customer, but I leaned toward believing he wished me to have an accurate impression. Either way, "sky blue" decided it for me.

"Uh-uh," I said, "too garish for a couch."

Our choices narrowed down to one: a convertible brown love seat. I figured brown wouldn't dominate my apartment, and it answered Caroline's spot concerns. Some other colors, such as blues and greens, were woven into the fabric, so it wasn't boring. Also, it felt prickly in places, giving it what I thought of as character. And it was under $400, with tax and delivery.

"The only problem is that a love seat will mean one less place to sit," I said.

"Your apartment is too small for a full couch. And the love seat opens out into a bed for when you have guests, which your couch doesn't."

As far as I was concerned, we were done, but Caroline wanted me to add a coffee table. "You don't have anything for guests to put glasses and cups on. Even with this love seat, you won't have room for end tables."

The coffee tables were fully one-third the price of the convertibles, which made no sense to me, but I didn't like to think of myself as inhospitable. The one I chose had legs that curved into the top, so if my shin hit a corner, it wouldn't be too painful. That, I realized, had been my objection to coffee tables.

With taxes and delivery, I was up to $550.

Mentally balancing my dwindling bank account on the subway home, I suffered a bout of buyer's remorse. Then I reminded myself that with Caroline's help, I was about to put my stamp on my home. Everything except my desk and desk chair was a castoff from my parents or something they'd bought for me.

The psychological shifts I was making between parsimony and enthusiasm apparently brought changes to my expression.

"What are you smiling at?" she asked over the train's noise.

"My inner accountant and homeowner are battling it out. It isn't pretty."

"Did I make you spend too much?"

"You made me do something good."

Next afternoon, when Caroline had left, I called my parents. Mom was on the kitchen extension and Dad on the one in the living room. I asked if they would like their couch back.

"But we gave it to you," Mom said.

"It's kind of big for this apartment. I saw one yesterday that would fit nicely, and I can afford it." I gave them a description, but I couldn't bring myself to say I'd already bought it.

"Do whatever you need to," Dad said. "It's your place." I heard no edge in his voice.

"Your dad's right," Mom said. I did hear an edge in hers.

The delivery came the following Saturday. Caroline stayed over on Friday night to do the inspection. While we sat waiting for the delivery guys, she said, "Are you going to have them take away the old one?"

"I know you said this place is too small for a couch, but I've been thinking that with both this old couch and the new love seat, there'll be seating for lots of people. We could have a party."

"It will get really, really crowded in here."

After the delivery guys squeezed into my apartment's narrow entrance, she watched them remove the covers and tape. Then she examined both items for flaws.

"They look good," she assured me.

I had the guys move my old couch along the window wall and put the new one where it had been. The coffee table went in front of it.

I thanked them and gave them the tip that took the price of the transaction close to $600. So much for my under-$400 couch. Well, love seat, but it was meant for relaxing and socializing, not romance. Why couldn't they call it a minicouch or two-thirds couch or two-seater, or something else less provocative?

•

The decision to get rid of the old couch came to me two weeks later during a sleepless night when I'd succeeded in leaving the bedroom without waking Caroline. She was right, there was no space for it. But having refrained from asking the delivery guys to take it with them, I convinced myself I had to remove it myself. The timing would never be better. The Sanitation Department's weekly furniture pickup was scheduled for later that morning, and the doorman didn't come on duty until eight, so I wouldn't be making a spectacle of myself. I resolved to do the deed then and there.

I'm guessing the couch was seven feet long, with a straight

back and rounded arms, all vinyl. I removed the cushions so they wouldn't fall off in the hallway or lobby, but the couch was still heavy. Without its wheels, it would have been impossible for me to handle.

I first had to push it across the living room floor to my apartment's narrow entrance, then out to the hallway. Once in the hallway, I'd need to drag it to the foyer, where I'd have to turn it ninety degrees and maneuver it down two steps. Ahead of me at that point would be two sets of glass doors, both closed. On the sidewalk, it would just be a matter of finding a wide enough space at the curb.

Wheeling the couch across the living room presented no difficulty. I steered it into the passageway leading to the apartment's entrance, where I climbed over it to open the door. Only then did I realize that the couch was too long to push on its wheels into the narrow hallway and turn. I needed to stand it on one end to ease it over the threshold. I'd then have to turn it around and lower it in such a way that it didn't scrape a wall.

I should have known then, if not from the outset, to abandon the whole idea. Looking back, I see another two sides of myself vying with each other. On the one hand, the law had taught me to anticipate the consequences of every action. On the other, living with a disability had taught me there was always a way. That morning, befuddled by insomnia, I ignored my legal brain and acted on the dubious lessons of experience.

Clambering back over the couch, I raised it by the end. Vertical, it was more than a foot taller than me. It just passed under the top of the doorframe, a potential deal breaker I also hadn't anticipated. Holding the couch's back and twisting this way and that, I edged it over the threshold.

Now the couch was in the hall, but standing precariously. Its bottom faced across the way and threatened to crash through my neighbors' door. Still gripping the back, I turned the bottom to face back along the hallway so it could land safely on its wheels. However, now I was trapped inside my apartment, facing my neighbor's door but with the couch pressing down to my right. The angle prevented me from maintaining complete control, and I worried about the couch's front rubbing against the opposite wall. But I couldn't retreat back inside without losing control altogether.

Using all my strength, I commenced lowering. Then I felt, more than heard, metal scrape something. My neighbors' door. Later, I would run my hand under the couch at the front and discover a metal flange at either end.

Gravity kept pressing, and I couldn't pause the descent; I could only try to keep turning the couch. At last it landed on its wheels. No one emerged from my neighbor's apartment.

I negotiated my way over the couch's arm, which still blocked my doorway, and pulled from the front end. Once in the foyer, I'd have enough room to turn the couch toward the steps leading down to the entrance.

"What are you doing?"

I froze. Then I took in the voice. Caroline.

Turning, I said, "Getting rid of the couch."

"At the crack of dawn? By yourself?"

"No longer. You grip the couch by the arm at your end and I'll lift it from the front so we can get it down these steps."

"Hold on while I go get my jeans."

"Be quick."

She was. With her help, managing the steps was easy. Now we confronted the building entrance, consisting of two doors, one after the other. The couch had to go vertical again. I did my routine of pushing one side forward, then the other. Caroline simplified the maneuver by holding open the first door. She complicated it by voicing dismay: "Nick, you'll never make it!"

I eased past her and shifted the couch over the first threshold. God, it had better not fall here. All around was glass. Probably unbreakable, but I didn't know if unbreakable encompassed being slammed by a flailing couch.

Now the couch stood between us and the final door. I twisted it some more to make room for Caroline to squeeze by and open the door. The couch wobbled, succumbing to gravity again. I hung on tight, all the while concealing panic to forestall Caroline from renewing her anxious commentary.

She made it to the door. "Hold on. Now go ahead."

The couch and I edged over the final threshold. She closed the door, and together, we lowered the couch to the sidewalk.

"Along here," she said. She piloted from the front and I pushed until we got the couch to a clear space facing the street. Relieved, I sat down on the couch and let my feet dangle over the curb.

Caroline sat beside me. "I didn't know you were so crazy."

I gave her a mock-puzzled glance. "What crazy? This is furniture pickup day. You told me the couch had to go."

"Is this something I'll have to get used to?"

"Moving furniture? Are you kidding? I'm the most incompetent person the world has ever known."

"I see that, but it doesn't seem to stop you."

The birds that hadn't yet retreated south began a ragged dawn chorus over the distant roar of BQE traffic. No cars drove down the street, and no one was out walking.

Caroline changed the subject. "I've got to get my act together. I feel kind of lost. I don't have an education. I don't have a career."

I saw the couch escapade had interrupted something she'd been thinking about when she'd woken. For me, it was good news. I'd worried about her seeming inclination to drift along.

"Do you have an idea what you'd like to do?"

"That's another thing I don't have—direction."

I tried to draw her out by bringing up catering.

"I like the idea," she agreed. "I like cooking. I like entertaining. When I've helped out friends who cater, I got to meet people from all walks of life. I just wish I felt more confident."

I pictured her holding court in the Sullivan Street bar. Such a woman was unsure of herself? The woman who had brazenly rested her head on my lap on the Promenade bench?

"You, of all people, lack confidence?" I said.

"It doesn't do any good to show you doubt yourself. But I'm talking about ambition—a goal, something to aim for."

I got it. She wasn't talking about attractiveness, intelligence or any other outward manifestation. It was about taking control of her life. I held her hand and tried to communicate through it that I realized she was telling me something important.

In the fresh air of first light, I was feeling closer than ever to her. Yet by identifying her lack of direction, she'd reawakened concerns that nagged at the back of my mind. I had to say what had become clear to me since my lunchtime talk with Jack, more so now that Cocaine Man had moved out. I couldn't have her believe in a myth I might be creating as much through neglect as by words and action.

"Caroline, I'm not ready to make a commitment yet. You know that, right?"

"Sure," she said. But she didn't say she wasn't, either.

At last she said, "I'm tired. Let's try to get an hour's sleep before the alarm goes off."

I tapped the couch and said goodbye, sad to think of it as a step in a long farewell to my mother and father.

In the hallway I pointed to my neighbor's door. Caroline cried out. Yes, I had scratched it.

"Keep it down," I hissed.

Before returning to bed, I gave her my spare key so she didn't have to leave when I went to work. So much for non-commitment. But one of us, at least, should get the sleep we needed.

It happened that all the building's doors were repainted soon afterwards, and my conscience was allayed. For some things, all it takes is not being caught.

24

IN THE MIDDLE OF READING the transcript of a judge's instructions to the jury, Louise was interrupted by a knock on the door, followed by Jack asking if he could talk to me alone for five minutes.

"What's up?" I said when she'd closed the door behind her.

"Frank and Wendy got their briefs back."

"With comments?"

"None on what the supervisors believed was Frank's. Wendy got lots of finicky edits and a sarcastic general comment and was told to submit hers again."

"Even though Frank was the ghostwriter." I swung my chair back and forth, taking it in. "I can't say I like having our suspicions confirmed."

"Wendy doesn't, either."

"Even though the brief she actually wrote proves she's good? How about Frank?"

"Frank just shrugged. He feels bad for Wendy, but he isn't surprised. Makes me wonder why he suggested this experiment in the first place."

"He can't like it that he has to rework the brief."

"Wendy will do that." Jack sighed. "Anticlimactic, isn't it? They can't go and say, 'Gotcha,' because the supervisors would be so angry they'd fire them on the spot and make sure no one ever hired them again."

I nodded. "Now we know, and the supervisors don't know that we know, and they don't even know they're doing it. Pathetic. Lawyers against injustice can't defend against injustice to ourselves."

Jack got to his feet and left without a parting shot, which showed how rattled he was.

25

AT THE SULLIVAN STREET BAR, Caroline introduced me to Doreen. I never got clarity about Doreen's story or even how they'd met. She just appeared, although I sensed this wasn't her first time in Caroline's life.

"Sure I can type," Doreen told Gavin, the construction company owner.

"I'll see what I can do," he replied.

I inferred Caroline had hatched a plan to get Doreen a job. I wasn't sure Gavin's heart was in it, but Caroline's definitely was.

"You'll have people knocking down your door just to spend five minutes with Doreen," she told him.

I felt sure Gavin could believe it about Caroline. I wondered why she didn't finagle a job like this for herself.

To me, she said, "Doreen has a legal question."

"Oh yeah," Doreen said, "it's like this. My uncle died two years ago. The lawyer told me he named me in his will. I think I'm supposed to get $20,000. Not a whole lot, but it would make a difference to me."

"It would make a difference to me—to anybody."

"Well, the estate has been tied up in what you call probate, right, ever since. I think my uncle's sons—my cousins—are trying to cut me out. Should I hire a lawyer to represent me?"

"Can you afford one?"

"If I had the 20k, I could."

"There's the rub," I said. "I don't think lawyers take on this kind of case on a contingency basis."

"What's that?"

"Where they don't charge anything up front, but collect a portion of your winnings."

"Ambulance chasers."

"So you'd have to pay by the hour, and pay even if you don't get anything."

"What would it cost?"

"Maybe two or three hundred dollars an hour. That's just a guess. I'm sorry, Doreen, I don't practice in this area. Call the Bar Association and speak to someone who does. An initial consultation is free."

But she was hung up on one of the figures I'd mentioned. "Wow! Three hundred dollars an hour? No way."

"Otherwise, write to the estate lawyer for an update. He's already notified you that you're named in the will. You could even write to the judge in Surrogates Court to say you can't afford a lawyer but feel your interests are being hurt by the delay. Worth a try. Worst that can happen is your letter will be ignored."

"What's Surrogates Court?"

"In New York, that's what they call probate court. Haven't you received any notices about the case?"

"They don't mean anything to me."

"Caroline and I could go over them with you. Something might occur to me."

The conversation left me feeling inadequate, but my offer to read the papers did seem to appease her.

Gavin said, "You follow politics, right?"

"You're asking me?" I said.

He tapped my arm. "What do you think of these accusations about Koch giving favors to developers?"

"Guys like you, you mean."

"I'm small fry. If I draped my coat over a puddle for the mayor to walk on, he wouldn't even notice. But where would the city be without us?"

To humor him, I said, "With a lot more unemployed people."

"And a lot of people without homes to go home to. So why do environmentalists and such block our industry everywhere we turn, and why is the liberal media all over us? Do they want everyone thrown out on the streets? Before you know it, half of New York City will be living on planks of wood and floating up and down the Hudson and East Rivers. And guys like me, how are we supposed to stay afloat?"

"It's a sink-or-swim world all right," I said.

I thought of my clients. They also considered themselves victims, even when they couldn't deny having committed a crime. Then again, I thought of myself as a victim of supervisor bias at the Alliance. Everyone was a victim.

Except Caroline. Whether over Cocaine Man or money matters, I hadn't once heard her cast blame.

26

CAROLINE LEFT FIRST THING THE next morning, saying she had to spend that day and the next conjuring up her story that was due on Tuesday and complaining more vehemently than ever about my coffee. I took the opportunity to call my parents.

"Your couch has gone to the great living room in the sky."

Dad chuckled. "You did the right thing."

"Yes," Mom added, this time with no edge, "it's your place to fix up the way you want."

I was tempted to say the way Caroline wanted, but I hadn't yet mentioned her to them.

27

"MAY IT PLEASE THE COURT."

I was standing at the lectern to argue the Robert Wilson case before the five justices hearing appeals that afternoon. Because I felt this appeal had a chance, I would have welcomed a show of strength from my Alliance colleagues, but with our big caseloads, we rarely gave each other that kind of support. This afternoon was to be no exception.

Almost all the other lawyers waiting their turn would be from private firms engaged in one or another area of commercial law. They'd all know I was from the Defenders Alliance or some equivalent organization whose mission was to represent the otherwise defenseless. They'd respect my place in the legal tradition of *Gideon* v. *Wainwright*, the Supreme Court decision that established the rights of poor people to legal representation in criminal cases, but I felt sure they assumed Wilson was just one more loser, guilty as charged.

In a law firm, I'd still be taking an associate's back seat to a new partner's middle seat. For a young lawyer, handling a case from start to finish was an allure of the Defenders Alliance. But gravitas didn't come with youth. How could the worldly men sitting behind the bench take me seriously? Looking back, that awareness must itself have been, well, a handicap.

Howie hadn't gone over the oral argument with me. For some reason, the supervisors never did. So I decided not to clutter my presentation with the upset juror argument. If the justices liked it, the point was driven home in the brief, and then some. I also wouldn't talk about Wilson's childhood of orphanages and foster homes. I'd written that part of the brief in all sincerity, but judges had heard all the sob stories before. They'd rely on the reaction of the trial judge, who had read the probation reports and seen the defendant's demeanor in court. None of it had stopped him from imposing the maximum.

At the lectern, I launched into a recital of the evidence. Unlike many appellate courts, this one had jurisdiction not only over whether the law had been correctly applied, but also to review the facts of the case.

I told the justices, "Only one witness identified Mr. Wilson, another said it wasn't him and the rest didn't know."

I pressed on, waiting—hoping—for them to prod me with questions. Surely they, too, had misgivings. They stayed silent. The whole room was silent, but for my voice, sounding to me like a prolonged drone. These few minutes were about the next two decades and more of a man's life, really his entire life. If I was failing to provoke the five men before me into seeing injustice, I wasn't doing my job.

I gathered up my braille index card notes and stuffed them in my jacket pocket. Then I took a step back, untethering myself from the anchors of my preparation and the lectern. "The only other item of evidence was the gun found in Mr. Wilson's possession six weeks later."

I heard outrage in my voice. Maybe it would shake up the justices enough to engage with me. Maybe it would help my client.

"Not something to dismiss lightly, wouldn't you say?" said Justice Callahan.

"Even a halfway rational person would have ditched it, so odds are that the man who had the gun six weeks later wasn't the Serpentine Bar shooter."

Justice Klegg spoke up. "Counselor, are you suggesting juries should be instructed to give—what?—a presumption of innocence when a defendant is found with the murder weapon?"

His mockery gave me the opening I'd wanted. "No. I'm saying that in this case, where the main evidence is conflicting identification testimony, his possession of the weapon was disproportionately significant."

Justice Callahan spoke up again. "Then you're saying the judge should have excluded that evidence."

"No. It was properly admitted. I'm saying that its outsized importance to the fact-finding process demonstrates the insufficiency of the evidence to convict."

No more reaction. I sensed the justices, momentarily roused, settling back in their chairs and getting impatient for a contract dispute or medical malpractice case—anything but a vicious murder case where the defendant was a career criminal.

Long before my twenty-five minutes were up, I thanked the court, stepped forward and reached for my chair. I'd feared becoming disoriented, but my hand met it right away, and I sat down.

The prosecutor wasn't asked any questions.

28

CAROLINE AND I HAD AGREED to spend Thanksgiving apart because we hadn't met each other's parents, so she decided to host a small pre-Thanksgiving celebration to be held in my apartment.

She'd been inspired by my offhand mention of a party. Despite the pretext, there'd be no roast turkey, stuffing or the other accoutrements.

"Just food you can put on small paper plates and hold in your hand," she said.

"You're going to cater it?"

"Maybe I'll make a dip, but your kitchen's tiny."

She'd already invited Doreen, Gavin and Reggie (the train engineer) for the coming Saturday night. A couple of other Sullivan Street regulars might join us. Their ticket, she told them, would be a bottle.

I asked Caroline to give me an idea of what Gavin, Reggie and Doreen looked like.

"If Gavin were a character in a novel," she said, "he'd be called pugnacious. Actually, he isn't short, like you might think from that word, though he isn't unusually tall, either. He's got a good build, a wide smile. I think it's his narrow eyes that bring pugnacity to mind. It feels like they shoot beams at you."

"Wow. Ever thought about doing creative writing?"

"Reggie is six feet tall and really slim. He's no Sidney Poitier, but he's magnetic, and there's always a smile on his face or waiting to come out."

"Sidney Poitier? You're saying he's black?"

"You didn't know? I assumed you could tell."

"Like I can tell blondes because they sound stupid?"

"You must think I'm blonde."

"You're super temperamental, not stupid, which makes you a redhead."

"Auburn."

"I know."

"And I don't think I'm super temperamental."

"You're not." Then I said, "I can't always tell if someone's black. Besides, I've only spoken to Reggie once, and that was in your very noisy bar."

"As for your real object of interest," she resumed, "Doreen is nice-looking—kind of pretty. She has thick, curly, dark brown hair that she sometimes lets stay unkempt so that it blows all around. Mostly she keeps it in place with a ribbon, a clip or even a piece of string. She's shorter than me. Has a good figure."

I'd never hosted a party before. I wasn't exactly doing so now; that was Caroline. Still, it was my home. I thought hard about whom I would invite. I couldn't imagine Jack bringing Elaine to an occasion where a bar crowd would set the mood. I also couldn't see my bookish friends enjoying a party with the likes of Gavin and Doreen, let alone the political activists and nondrinkers. But I did ask Ray. He'd confided that he'd broken up with his girl-friend. His placid surface hadn't changed, but underneath he was upset. What that had to do with my inviting him is a mystery to me now, but I did, and his gratitude surprised and pleased me.

Caroline arrived in the afternoon with Doreen in tow. We'd agreed beforehand to go over the paperwork in her uncle's estate. When Caroline had finished reading aloud the documents, I saw more was involved than her cousins' antagonism or greed. Several debtors had claims on the estate, leaving me to wonder if any-thing would be left over for the will's intended beneficiaries.

"The lawyer handling your uncle's estate looks like he's doing his best against some determined creditors," I told Doreen.

"When will I get my money?"

"I don't know. Ask him. Maybe he'll look at spending a few minutes with you as part of his fiduciary obligations." I explained "fiduciary."

She didn't thank me. I think she saw the law as a secret society that kept her looking in from outside. All I'd done was show her a glimpse. Based on what I'd told her, someone else might have accepted the need to let go and move on. If a settlement came through a year or a decade from now, treat it as money falling from the sky. But Doreen needed the money now.

I handed Caroline some cash, and then Doreen and she headed out to buy alcohol, food and paper plates. On returning, Caroline added the finishing touches to my apartment cleaning job.

"You never remove all the spots from the counter," she called cheerfully from the kitchen to me in the living room.

"I can hear you."

After scrubbing the counter, she turned to food preparation, which meant that afterwards she'd have to scrub it clean all over again. She cut up raw vegetables for crudités without letting even Doreen assist, never mind me. Doreen did help out with the dip, and they both set out plates of deli sandwiches. I retreated to the bedroom to read. That didn't stop Caroline from issuing decrees that implied yet more complaints about my domestic arrangements.

"We have to get you nicer bowls for the chips and dip," she called through to me. "Oh, and Doreen, put the sponge cake in the refrigerator before the whipped cream melts. I think Nick left just enough room on the top shelf."

She was almost done when Gavin and Reggie arrived.

"Reggie just drove a train back from Pittsburgh," Gavin told us.

"Cold out there," Reggie said.

"You can tell even inside the cab of a locomotive?" Caroline said. "I'd have thought it was roasting in there."

"I stick my head out the window."

I suspected he was toying with us.

Gavin said, "Doesn't your head get whacked by tree branches?"

Reggie laughed. "They clear trees away from the tracks."

Gavin replied with grim satisfaction. "Environmentalists must hate you, almost as much as they do me."

"Environmentalists love me, man. My freight train and I use less fuel than a few hundred trucks carrying the same load. We're great for the environment."

When Ray showed up soon after, Caroline commiserated over what it must be like to work for me. "He'd never hire me," she told him. "He hates the way I pronounce things."

The day before, I'd teased her for butchering "mischievous," as if there were an "i" after the "v."

"He hates my opinions about defending murderers and rapists," Ray countered.

Caroline turned serious. "You don't think he does good work?"

"He does some good, I'm sure."

Ray's attempt to say something conciliatory sounded smarmy.

"Enough on me," I told them. "Ray, what are you drinking? We have beer, wine, scotch, gin."

The food ran out quickly, but we had more than enough alcohol. Caroline took charge of the stereo, knowing what I'd choose might get sad. Over the music, Gavin and Reggie debated infrastructure spending, Caroline got Ray to talk about himself, Doreen hummed to the songs and I sat back and listened to them all.

Caroline addressed everyone. "Nick has a set of dominos. Who's going to play?"

Only Doreen declined. She seemed content humming to the music.

We moved the coffee table out of the way, dragged the folding dining table before the couch, and placed mismatched chairs around the remaining sides. Caroline put a tablecloth over it, despite my protests at the delay.

"How are you going to know what dominos you have?" Gavin asked me.

"The dots are raised." As I took the top off the box, I told the room, "When you put one down, tell me what the numbers are."

"That's cool," Reggie said. "You're going to keep all that in your head?"

Sitting next to me on the couch, Caroline tapped my temple. "He keeps everything in his head. See the stuffing coming out of his ears."

Ray said, "He doesn't remember everything. That's what he hired me for."

"I hired you," I retorted, "for comic relief."

"I'm the one who's always laughing," he said, which was true.

Five people is too many for dominos, but with the alcohol already in us, no one cared. Every so often Doreen would make a tour of the table and look at each player's set. "He's cheating," she'd announce. She'd act serious, but she had no idea how to play the game. When she rested, she took up residence in the rocking chair at the side of the stereo. I was glad someone found it comfortable.

By 10:30, Doreen had had enough. "Okay, you guys. Make room for me." She reached across the table and swept all the dominos onto the floor. Gavin thought it was hilarious. Reggie's reaction was muted.

"I'll pick them up," Ray said, jumping down from his chair. In line with my preconceptions of smug men, he gave the impression of width over height, so his agility surprised me.

We all got down on our knees around and under the table, more getting in each other's way than gathering up the pieces, and all the while giggling. As I got ready to stand, I bumped my head on the table. Doreen found that funny, which set us all off on a fresh wave of loud cackling.

Doreen yelled, "I see lots of empty glasses. Where's our gar-kon?" That was how she liked to pronounce *garçon*.

Gavin retrieved the current wine bottle, since that's what most of us were drinking, and did a *garçon*.

"Whoa, there!" Reggie protested. "You're pouring more onto the table than in my glass."

"*Pardonnez moi.*" Gavin's accent was as horrible as Doreen's.

I squeezed Caroline's knee to convey my gratitude that she'd had the forethought to put the tablecloth on. She'd long since given up going through my records for something different to play, and now WCBS-FM was broadcasting oldies to the room.

I have no idea where the conversation went from there. I'm sure it would have made no sense to any sober person. We were all drunk, and so it all made perfect sense. That is, I think it did. It also got rowdy.

There was a knock on the door.

"Someone wants to join the party," Gavin declared.

"Bring 'em on," Doreen yelled.

Caroline, sitting between me and the entrance, stood to let me pass.

When I opened the door, Mike, the doorman that evening, said, "It's getting very loud in there."

"Thanks, Mike. We'll tone it down."

"Loud, very loud."

"Got it. Thanks," I repeated, as I closed the door.

"What kind of building is this that you can't have fun?" Doreen asked.

"Not my kind of building," Gavin said, which he wouldn't have if sober.

"I guess we are being pretty loud," Reggie said.

Caroline lowered the volume on the stereo, but I doubted we

made much less noise. Even so, Mike didn't knock on the door again.

Midnight came and went. Reggie sang an old song about a hobo on the railroad to us. Gavin, on discovering he had a fellow conservative in the room, drew Ray into raving about Reagan, "the best president this country's ever had."

"This is why I'll never work for you," Caroline cheerfully called to Gavin.

"I can take liberals, sweetheart," he replied. "I mean, I live in New York, don't I? So can't you put up with a little balance in your life?"

"Balance? You call yourself balanced?"

"Oh, I'd say I'm the most balanced person here."

"You're forgetting me," Doreen cried out. "I'm the most balanced person in this room. I'm the most balanced person in this building, in this street, in this city, in this state, in this country, in this hemisphere, in this—"

The next I knew, the tablecloth had slipped out from under my resting hand. Glasses, bottles—everything—ended up on the carpet.

"In this whole fucking world," Doreen finished.

We all sat in bewilderment, except for Doreen, who stood up and paced triumphantly.

Once again, the first one to pull himself together was Ray. "I'll clear up the mess."

Caroline rushed around the table to the kitchen. "I'll help."

Ray, Caroline and Reggie got back on their knees to do what they could with a couple of brushes and one dustpan. Accepting that I'd only get in the way, I stayed seated.

"Shit." This was Reggie. "I cut myself on this damn glass."

"You'd better wash it so it doesn't get infected," Caroline said.

"Yeah, yeah, wash your sins away," Doreen chanted. "Wash your sins away."

Sitting across from me, Gavin, who had also decided to stay out of the way, said, "I bet you've never had a party like this before."

After everyone left, Caroline said, "What are we going to do about all this spilt beer and wine and whatnot?"

"We'll deal with it in the morning."

Later that Sunday, it turned out she knew all kinds of cleaning techniques. We applied seltzer water and baking soda and I don't recall what else, and she said the carpet looked better. "I mean better than it did when we went to bed," she qualified.

Next weekend we walked down to Atlantic Avenue and bought a new area rug and a new supply of glasses. As after the couch removal, I didn't hear a word of complaint about the party from my neighbors.

29

I NEVER FOUND OUT THE subject of Caroline's second submission for Stern's class. When I asked, she grew evasive—"I just put some thoughts together and called it a story." She refused to show it to me, which had me wondering if she hadn't submitted anything. Would she lie to me? But such speculation was unfair to her. It sounded like what she submitted was incomplete. If she had finished the story, Stern would surely have presented it to the class— her writing was that good. He didn't.

I thought back to our talk on the old couch on the sidewalk, when she'd owned up to her fear that she lacked direction. In that light, her Colombia story was all the more striking for being something she'd completed.

There was another possibility. Stern might have felt he'd

showcased enough good pieces and that we needed more object lessons. That was the function my second submission was to serve.

A novel had been taking shape in my head, and I'd written the first chapter, based on an event from my late teens. Weeks-long training for a volunteer position at a suicide intervention hotline had culminated in a 24-hour "encounter session." It was an artifact of the time we call the sixties, although the year was 1971. Participants coughed up their deepest secrets and submitted to various touchy-feely activities. One was the "blind walk."

In the novel, I was Terry, as I'd been in "The Portrait." I'm pleased I named the program's director Max; it fits my memory of him. He took me aside and admitted, "I guess this is nothing new for you." He had me participate anyway.

We were divided into pairs, one partner being blindfolded and the other acting as guide. The guide took the blindfolded partner through a zigzag course on a large estate that its owners let us use for the day. When the pair reached the end, they switched roles and went back through the course.

Max assigned a girl named Hillary as my partner. She and I had become friends in the training process, which Max had clearly noticed. After laying out this background, I wrote:

Hillary took on the role of guide first. I rested my hand in the crook of her elbow, and we set off. We walked down a steepish slope, then hung a right. From time to time my arm brushed against what I took to be a guide rope. After a while, the route went uphill and the ground switched from lawn to boards. We appeared to cross a small bridge.

"Be careful," Hillary said, "there's no barrier at the side."

I shifted so that I was walking more behind than to her right. After a few yards we returned to grass. Only then did I ask if we'd crossed a stream or something.

"Just a dip in the ground, but that's what Max must want you to think."

We turned in a gradual circle that involved ups and downs, presumably designed to throw off the blindfolded partner's sense of direction.

"Are you okay?" she asked.

"Great."

We reached the end, where Max greeted us. "The two of you are naturals. Now, Terry, how do you feel about taking Hillary back through the course? There are ropes on both sides to give you direction."

I said I was ready, and Hillary said she was ready for me to guide her.

After Max blindfolded her, I turned the way we'd come and opened out my folding cane. Max placed my hand on the rope suspended at my left. It meant holding my cane in my right hand, which was my preference anyway. Hillary took that right arm.

"Don't be thrown off as I move the cane back and forth," I told her. "I'll try to keep my upper arm still."

"Okay," she said, voice strong.

I set off, feeling the slight tension of Hillary's hand above my elbow.

"That's good," Max said, keeping in step behind us.

Thanks to the rope, which kept me on course, and occasional cane-taps of the ground before me, I figured the only danger would be tripping, at least until we got to the makeshift bridge. As we approached left turns, I slowed down, knowing she'd need to walk an extra step or two on the outer curve. At right turns, I eased my arm inward so that I'd be a little bit farther ahead and she'd know to compensate. If my cane alerted me to an upcoming dip, I told her so. In her place, I hadn't asked for such information, but I thought I should concede that much to her newness to being guided.

I became aware of her footfalls on the springy grass ground. I sensed her adjusting her walking pace to mine. I, too, must change my pace when walking with someone, as opposed to when I walked with my cane.

"You're both doing great," Max said just behind us.

Making sure to keep looking forward so as not to confuse Hillary, I called back, "I thought this was about Hillary and me learning to trust each other."

"And I can see you do."

I shook with silent laughter that must have traveled through my arm, but Hillary stayed focused on walking.

"Now," Max said, "the bridge is coming up."

"I know," I called back.

"Okay there, Hillary?" he said.

"I'm doing great."

"I'll slide my cane along the edge so I'll always know where it is," I told her. "Don't let go, but come a little more behind me. That's it."

My cane made a grinding noise as we traversed the bridge. I didn't slow down, nor did I feel any extra nervous tug on my arm. My cane's tip found grass before the board gave out, and almost immediately I touched the guide rope.

"We're about to step back onto grass," I told Hillary.

"Nicely done," Max said, still just behind.

"Sounds like you were anxious," I called back.

"Not at all. Not at all."

This time Hillary laughed, too.

Down a slope, left, and soon up a slope back to the beginning. "Here we are," I said, squeezing Hillary's hand as she released my arm.

"This was fun," she said, head bent as she untied the blindfold.

"How was it being on the other end?" Max asked me.

"It gave me a huge sense of responsibility. I liked it."

Stern read my submission to the class straight through without comment, but when he finished, he didn't open the floor for discussion. Instead, he announced, "Nice dialogue, interesting subject, but it's purely descriptive. We know too little about the narrator, the girl and the director."

Agreed, I thought, which is why their characters will develop chapter by chapter. His object lesson ground on, with me chafing in my chair.

At the end of class, while the other students filed past my desk, no doubt glancing at me with pity, I said to Caroline, "Let me know when the crowd at his desk thins out."

"Why don't we walk over so he sees that you want to talk to him?"

We put on our coats, and I slung my briefcase over my shoulder. Then I unfolded my cane and tracked the desk fronts until he was at my right. I turned to face him and waited, Caroline standing loyally at my side.

At last Stern looked up and spoke my way. "Yes?"

I inferred he was addressing me. "That story you just trashed wasn't a story. It was the first chapter of a novel. It says 'Chapter 1' at the top."

"Oh."

That was it. No apology. Next week he said nothing about it

to the class. I suppose his demolition job had been an excellent object lesson, even if misdirected. Still, since everyone knew I'd written it, an acknowledgment would have been nice.

Voicing anger on my behalf, Caroline floated the idea that we stop attending his class. I was tempted. But we'd learned a lot from him and hoped to pick up yet more. So, even though neither of us was taking the course for credit, we stayed on to the end.

Afterwards, whenever one or the other of us read a flawed story, we'd say, "Must be Chapter 1."

30

IN MY PHONE'S EARPIECE, ALEJANDRO Diaz introduced himself. "I was defense counsel at Robert Wilson's trial."

"It's good to hear from you," I said. It was the first time we'd had contact of any kind.

I'd just arrived at the office and was half asleep, so I opened the window, hoping the winter air would blow away the cobwebs. The door opened and Louise murmured, "Hi." She shut the door behind her and tossed her things into the spare chair.

Diaz said, "I saw in the *Journal* that the case was set for argument on appeal last week. How did it go?"

"I'm not optimistic, even though I'm convinced the prosecution didn't prove his guilt."

"Me, too. You know, for a trial lawyer, it was the worst kind of case. I liked the client. He was smart and by his rights, fair, but also hard. In the courtroom that was a problem—an intimidating-looking black guy. Not huge, but muscular, and he didn't soften his expression for the jury. But I'd gotten to know him. That exterior came from a childhood of being passed around from orphanage to foster home and back again."

"I saw that in the probation report. What happened to his parents?"

"Same old story—father abandons mother while she's still pregnant, she dies before boy is old enough to remember. Prosecutors keep reminding me lots of guys come through that kind of experience intact. But a lot don't, and either way, no one knows why."

I grunted my agreement.

Diaz continued, "The judge ran a fair trial, but he got an eyeful of Wilson for a week or more and didn't like what he saw. Besides, the crime was horrendous."

"Assuming Wilson committed it."

"That was my assumption, too."

"Why the past tense?"

Diaz paused before answering. "Wilson isn't totally bereft of family. A cousin came to see me toward the end of the trial. She adores Bobby—that's what she calls him—and wanted to help by testifying about what he'd been up against in life and the good things he'd done. I was excited because, until then, I'd had no way of showing Wilson's sympathetic side to the jury."

"You could hardly put him on the stand," I said, to signal I'd followed his strategy. "The prosecutor would have brought out his priors on cross."

"And, don't forget, that arrest six weeks after the Serpentine robbery. Hey, I bet you questioned my decision not to fight the ballistics evidence."

"I figured it was solid and you didn't want to reinforce it in the jurors' minds."

Diaz's relief came through in his voice. "Anyway, the cousin was so well-meaning. One way she tried to convince me Bobby is basically a good guy was by telling me how bad he felt after what happened in the Serpentine."

Diaz heard my gasp. "Yeah, exactly. He came by her crib—her

word—a day or two later and cried about it. He told her something had gone wrong."

I wished Louise, sitting across from me, weren't witnessing any part of this conversation. I thought of asking her to leave, but I couldn't take the chance that she'd talk to anyone else before I'd warned her to keep what she'd heard to herself.

Diaz was still talking. "No way I could put the cousin on the stand after that. It also meant I had to be real careful in my summation. As an officer of the court, I couldn't claim he was innocent because she'd as much as told me he'd confessed."

I thought over Diaz's closing statement to the jury. He'd held back from endorsing his client, but he'd passionately dismantled the evidence against him.

"You did a great job of exposing the holes in the prosecution's case," I said.

Diaz must have heard something in my voice that wasn't there because he said, "Maybe you wish I hadn't called."

"I'm glad you did. I never want to get jaded, but I also don't want to be naïve."

He laughed mirthlessly. "I struggle against cynicism every day of my professional life."

"It must be hard when you get to know a client. Maybe it's good for my mental health that I hardly ever do."

"So you've never met Wilson?"

"The office won't approve expenses for client visits."

"He's far, far away, that's for sure—up by the Canadian border. Anyway, now you see why I waited to call until you'd done the argument. It wasn't like I had anything to add."

When I hung up, Louise asked, "Something wrong?"

I went over in my mind what she'd overheard and decided I hadn't repeated anything about Diaz's meeting with the cousin.

"Just some things about Robert Wilson's background that are kind of sad."

"Mind closing the window?" she said.

31

As Jack and I set off for our Park Place diner, I felt gloomy at being unable to see the Christmas lights and displays downtown, even though I knew they weren't as glamorous as the midtown ones I remembered from childhood. And though I no longer cared about displays of elves or toys, walking through the streets with no holiday distractions, I felt only the cold wind. But it didn't take long for Jack to pull me into the minutiae of his current case. He was still going on about it as we waited to be seated, as we took off our coats and laid them on a spare chair, as we contemplated the day's specials and even after we'd given the waitress our orders. True to form, he didn't reach any conclusions, but at last he exhausted the subject.

Then he asked, "What do you think of Elaine and me getting married?"

"Is this your way of making an announcement? It has the Jack Hagen signature—avoidance of a simple statement—so I'm guessing it is."

"I suppose—well, yes, I suppose it is."

I stuck my hand across the table, managing not to knock over glasses and condiment containers, and we shook. "Mazel tov."

I'd first heard that disarming Yiddish phrase from Jack himself.

"It's not definite," he said.

"I thought you just said—"

"We talked about it, and Elaine said she wants to."

"Yes?"

"And I said, 'Let's give it one more day.'"

"Why?"

"So I could get your opinion."

"You didn't tell Elaine you wanted to talk to me first, did you?"

"I did. You and one or two other friends."

"Jack, sometimes you display the sensitivity of a slab of concrete. The last thing she needs is your busybody friends helping you decide whether or not to marry her. She must want to kill me."

"Elaine isn't like that. We've circled around this for three or four months. Now it's out in the open, I need just a little more time to think. It's a big decision."

"The rest of your life," I acknowledged.

This was when the waitress, a middle-aged woman who liked us, brought us our orders.

"Everything okay, guys?" she said.

I inferred Jack looked pained. "Jack's agonizing over a decision, but don't worry. He's never happier than when he's agonizing."

"I see," she said. "Well, enjoy your lunch, gentlemen."

She left, and I pressed on. "What reasons do you have to hesitate?"

"She might come to hate me in a year or two."

"Or you might hate her."

"Doubtful." Then he said, "And I'd be defining myself."

"You mean you'd be defining yourself differently. Now you're an unmarried guy who lives with Elaine. If you marry her, you'll be her husband."

"You're saying it's semantics. Well, maybe it is. Nothing changes if we get married except we'll have more legal obligations to each other."

"Till death do you part."

"If you want to be morbid about it."

As I was about to take the first bite of my sandwich, he said, "So, what do you think?"

I put the sandwich back down on the plate. "I think it's wonderful news."

"You think it's wise?"

"If I said it was, you'd remind me only fools rush in."

"You're saying this isn't about wisdom, but love."

"Why sound so miserable when you say 'love'?"

"It's a gooey concept."

"May I ask if you talked about having children?"

"Now you're suggesting marriage is merely a practical proposition."

I feigned exasperation, although it wouldn't take much for the real thing to emerge. "I'm not saying it's practical or gooey, to use your charming words. Jack, how do you ever put one foot in front of the other? That brain of yours must come up with hundreds of reasons against taking the next step."

"There might be a hole in the sidewalk," he acknowledged, "or that fallen leaf might conceal a mine."

"Jack," I said, "do you have any good reasons not to marry Elaine?"

"No."

"Any good reasons to marry her?"

"Too many to list."

"Then I say again, mazel tov."

32

THE NEXT DAY JACK TOLD me the wedding was on and said he and Elaine hoped I'd bring Caroline. She was coming over that evening, a Friday, to begin what had become our regular weekend together.

As we sat on the love seat, I told her, "My friend at the office, Jack, is getting married. He and Elaine have invited me, and they're hoping you'll come, too. It won't be a church thing. A judge is conducting the ceremony in her chambers."

"Wow. Have they been together a long time?"

"Since they were undergrads, and they've lived together ever since Jack came to New York—same time as me."

"So why now?"

"Elaine is ready to have children. So's he, I'm pretty sure."

The record we'd been listening to came to an end, and the arm returned to its slot.

Caroline's fingers brushed my cheek. "Do you ever think about being a father?"

After too long a silence, I said, "I should have discussed this with you before."

"It never came up." She spoke gently.

It never came up, I told myself, due to my refusal to commit. But by staying with her, commitment or not, I was abetting her biological clock against her. It was only fair she knew I had doubts about fathering a child.

Acknowledging her kindness with a nod, I blundered on. "Well, my eye condition is genetic. I'm what they call 'a mutant,' the first member in a family tree with the defective gene. But now it's on my limb of that tree, chances are fifty-fifty I'd pass it on. It's what geneticists call 'dominant.' Not all RP—retinitis pigmentosa—is, but in my case . . ."

Then, to the silent stereo across the room, I said, "I'm not sure it would be right for me to help bring a child into this world."

"But think of what you've accomplished. I see you as happy."

Here was my conundrum. I felt mostly good about things and about myself. I was glad to be alive. So why question the quality of life of a child who might, but might not, share my disability? I had no good answer.

Turning to face her, I said, "How about you? You'd like to be a mother?"

"Oh, one day. I'd need a little more stability in my life, don't you think?"

"You'll know when the time is right."

What a cliché. Pure evasion.

I proposed we go into Manhattan the next day to take in a Midtown Christmas, and she leapt at the suggestion.

33

ON FIFTH AVENUE, I WAS uplifted by the cheeriness of the sidewalk shoppers and the aroma of roasting chestnuts. I even sensed the glow in the air. Going from store to store, Caroline helped me look for gifts. In Saks, she found some for her parents and helped me select others for mine.

"I'll wrap them for you," she said. "I'm the world's best gift wrapper."

Friends and family spoken for, I said, "Shall we look at dresses?"

"So I can be respectable at Jack's wedding?"

"No, Caroline."

"Because I couldn't really go in my old rags. But clothes are too expensive here in Saks. Bloomie's is the place for bargains, if you know where to look."

Inside Bloomingdale's, Caroline took us unerringly up several escalators to a particular women's clothing department. I kept in step beside her as she flipped through the racks. From time to time I'd check out a dress, all the while imagining disapproving eyes on me.

After picking out three dresses to try on, she asked, "Are you sure about this?"

"We got gifts for everyone else. Now it's your turn. Where shall I wait while you're in the dressing room?"

"Come this way." We walked into an open area where a saleswoman greeted us.

Caroline told her, "I'd like my friend to accompany me inside so he can give me a second opinion."

I turned hot with embarrassment.

"You can show him out here."

I was carrying my cane folded up.

"He can't see," Caroline said. "It really would be too awkward."

The woman said, "I'll see what rooms I have available." When she returned, she said, "You can take the large room. I think you'll be comfortable there."

We walked into the dressing area as I did my best to become invisible. After closing the door to our room, Caroline whispered, "You're blushing."

"I'd have to be dead not to."

Why do women love buying clothes? It's such an operation, especially in the winter. Caroline had to hang up her coat, remove her boots, then take off most of everything else before at last selecting a dress to try on. I sat down, grateful that stores put chairs in dressing rooms.

At last she turned to me. "What do you think?"

I stood to trace her shoulders and arms, then crouched as I followed how the dress fell to her knees. "It has a nice line on you."

"I think so, too."

She liked the two black ones. I told her we'd get both.

"We only came for one. Are you sure?"

"They're gifts for both of us. I like how you look in them."

We also got a couple of skirts and tops. I was amazed when I learned I'd get away with under $500—a lot for me at the time, but much less than I'd expected. Caroline knew what she was doing stylewise and pricewise. Still, between this and the furniture, my savings account was fast depleting. I'd need to economize for a month or two.

Back in my apartment, she swirled around the living room in each of her new dresses and outfits and made me check them out all over again. This time I felt freer to take pleasure in how they flattered her body.

As she was taking off the second dress, she said, "Come for Sunday brunch with my folks tomorrow."

"In Riverdale?" I said, as if the location explained my reluctance.

"You can decide which dress I wear."

"Isn't this a bit soon?"

"No time like the present. Come on, Nick."

The subway trip to Riverdale, an affluent section of the Bronx near the end of the 1 line, is convenient, involving just one simple change, but long. I was lulled into my own thoughts, and Caroline was also quiet. But I was shocked into wakefulness when we got out at her parents' stop, where the tracks ran above the street and the winter wind blew unobstructed. We hurried downstairs for the relative warmth at ground level.

"Your name is . . ." Mrs. Sedlak said when I stepped into her house's hallway.

"Nick."

"Oh yes, Nick. I'm Rena Sedlak."

"Hi. Ed Sedlak." Caroline's father let his hand meet mine for a handshake in which mine did all the shaking.

"Well, brunch is almost ready," Rena Sedlak said.

On the way to the dining room, Caroline gave me a few hints about layout. "The living room's on your right, and you can hear Mom going into the kitchen."

"Okay, okay," I snapped. I hated drawing attention to my need for special clues the first time I met her parents. But she was being sensible and thoughtful. And what would her father, a step or two ahead of us, make of my irritability?

Mr. Sedlak and I sat at the dining table as Caroline and her mother chattered away in the kitchen. I didn't initiate conversation because he was so quiet that I couldn't tell exactly where he was sitting, and I hated to speak to someone while looking in the wrong direction.

"I think Caroline said you're a lawyer."

He'd spoken softly, but I had him now.

"I am. And she tells me you're an engineer with the Port Authority. Is that a good place to work?"

"It pays the mortgage."

Caroline came back, chirping over her shoulder to her mother and then asking her father to take a serving dish from her. Mrs. Sedlak followed. The two women sat down, and we all dug into pancakes and bacon.

To me, Mrs. Sedlak said, "Are you with a firm? The city?"

"It's a hybrid organization—private, but we carry out government mandates to assist poor people."

"A worthy cause, I'm sure."

To complete the round of job descriptions, I said to her, "I understand you're a psychologist in the school system. You must see a lot of heartache."

"There are some real head cases out there, that's for sure."

She left it at that, and I wished I hadn't put my question so negatively.

Caroline reminded them that we'd taken a writing course together.

"Caroline is a fabulous writer," I said.

"So are you," she said.

Her parents didn't react. At any rate, they didn't say anything.

Desperate to get conversation flowing, I told Mrs. Sedlak, "I was thinking of a career in psychology before deciding on law school."

"I'm sure you made the right choice," she told me.

Caroline engaged her mother in talk about fashion. Mr. Sedlak and I ate in silence. I sipped slowly to make my glass of water last.

Caroline cleared the table and joined her mother in the kitchen. Mr. Sedlak vanished to another part of the house. Although unhappy at being left alone, I was relieved the torment of stop-and-start conversation was over.

At long last we were at the front door saying our goodbyes. Caroline's parents thanked me for coming and invited me back. I was tempted to ask why they thought I'd want to. I hoped I didn't communicate it through my handshakes.

After the claustrophobia of the house, I luxuriated in fresh air as Caroline and I walked to the subway. The December sun touched the back of my neck, sparking a memory of a streaky sunset sky.

With a woman's gift for chatting uncomfortable moments away, she talked about renovations her folks had done to the house and how her mother had been complaining about the distance she had to walk to the train to work. She didn't ask for my reaction to the brunch, which I gladly took as a cue not to share it. I felt sure she knew it hadn't gone well for me, but ambivalent as she seemed toward her parents, she might still be upset if I said so. I didn't want us to get into a hurtful argument where neither of us was right or wrong.

I came up with what I hoped was a safe subject. "You and your mom like to talk about clothes. I'd never have guessed."

"She used to think fashion would be my ticket to the big time.

Remember, I was a teenage model for Stelstone's."

"Oh, of course, the leotard company. I forgot I was sleeping with someone so famous."

I expected her to thump me in disgust, but she kept walking and changed the subject.

After such a grueling experience, I wanted time to myself, but Caroline assumed she was coming back to my apartment. Once we settled in, I was glad our day together hadn't ended with that brunch. She sat at my desk and set about wrapping the presents we'd bought.

From the love seat, I said, "Mom and Dad will wonder how I've suddenly become adept at gift wrapping. I'll have to tell them about you."

"You've been keeping me a secret?"

It hadn't occurred to me that my reserve with my parents might be hurtful compared to her seeming openness with hers.

I said, "I'm never sure how my news will register with them, so I tend to keep things to myself."

"Really? I thought you talked to them regularly. And didn't your mother come down for your court appearance?"

"I do a lot of listening."

Maybe one day she'd meet them and see what I found too complicated to explain.

She left the desk to sit next to me and handed me a package. "I made this for you."

I opened it with care, admiring the exactness of her wrapping. Inside, I found she'd fashioned a diminutive portfolio out of board, padding and hard paper.

"You can put your private correspondence and bills in it when you take them to the office for Ray and Mara to read to you."

"It's the nicest gift you could have given me."

34

MARA AGREED TO WORK THE day of Christmas Eve. When we finished, I'd be going to Connecticut.

We began with the mail she'd picked up on her way in. One item was a notice reporting the decision in the Robert Wilson case. Judgment affirmed, no opinion, no dissent.

She looked up. "Not a word of explanation. How can they not justify their decision after all the effort you put into it?"

"That we all put into it. Par for the course, though."

In my mind, I reviewed the next steps. We'd file an application for leave to appeal to the state's highest court, even though the Court of Appeals wouldn't second-guess the verdict and the upset juror question wasn't strong enough, as even Howie was likely to agree. Assuming the application was denied, I'd have to write to Wilson that nothing else could be done. It would lead to an exchange of letters in which he blamed me, if only because who else could he blame?

I said, "Let's move on." Mara shifted in her chair, fabric brushing against wood, and then resumed going through the afternoon's mail.

Before we began that day's main project, I put a question to her that I'd been dreading to ask because it would mean her doing a favor for me outside her job responsibilities. Worse, I should be able to do it by myself, in theory at least.

"Are you going home on the Lex when we're done?"

"I'm taking the Lex, but not to my apartment. Why?"

"Would you mind stopping off at Grand Central to help me through the ticket lines? They're chaotic on holidays. We'll leave half an hour early, so I won't make you late for any plans you have."

"I'm also seeing my family," she said, "so I'm going to Grand

Central, too. I'm surprised you didn't figure that out. I take the Hudson Line. You take the New Haven, right? We'll get tickets together, and we'll find your train. No problem. How about leaving an hour and a half early for a Christmas drink?"

I shook my head at how complicated I made things.

She knew a quiet place on 42nd Street. We had to come out of the Terminal, walk down 42nd a bit, then up a flight of stairs to the lounge, which was actually in the Grand Central building. I was surprised to find just how much like a lounge it felt, and even more surprised that it wasn't mobbed. Mara got a small table and told me to stay and claim it while she went to the bar to order. This was a more assertive Mara than I knew at the office.

"Gin and tonic in the middle of winter!" she exclaimed when I told her what I wanted. She came back with two of them. "I was going to have a sherry, but if you want to pretend like it's summer, I'm happy to join in the delusion." We clinked glasses and wished each other a merry Christmas.

"On the way up," I said, "I was thinking that we've worked together for more than a year. Are you still able to balance your time as well as your uncle's books?"

"He doesn't care about my hours, just so long as I have the numbers when he needs them."

Mara lived in a doorman building on the Upper East Side, which told me she wasn't lacking for money. Considering what she earned working for me and her bookkeeper's salary at her uncle's plumbing business, I assumed her close-knit family helped out.

I sometimes wondered why she gave up another twelve hours of her week, plus commuting time, for her job with me. When I'd interviewed her, she said she wanted to do good with her time. Unwilling to have her talk about me as a charitable cause, I hadn't pursued it. Eventually it occurred to me that by "good," she might have meant the nature of my work. A year later, I sensed her view of my clients had become as jaundiced as Ray's.

What a contrast—Ray and Mara. At twenty-one, Ray brought out the twenty-one-year-old in twenty-eight-year-old me. Mara was a grown-up twenty-seven.

She told me about the thousands of relatives—that was the impression I got—who would surround her in the next couple of days.

"Me," I said, "I'll be playing cards with my parents."

"Just the three of you? You don't have any friends up there?"

"All my friends are spending Christmas somewhere else or their families moved away from Fairfield County after high school."

"What about—what's her name?—Caroline?"

"She's with her family."

"Interesting," Mara said to her glass. Then, her voice momentarily muffled, which I now knew meant she'd brushed back her hair, she said, "I liked your mother when I met her at the court building."

"You know what struck me then?" I said. "She was so much more herself than she is at home."

"Where she's under the shadow of your dad?"

"I think Mom decided early on that the best formula for peace was subservience."

"Or passive-aggression. That's my mother's way."

I considered over a taste of my drink before saying, "I don't think it's my mother's way. I doubt she gives any thought to being herself. I can hear her now—'Whatever that means.'"

35

On Christmas morning, Mom, Dad and I sat around and ate a leisurely breakfast, in no hurry to open gifts. Then we gathered around the same artificial tree Dad had put up ever since I was a boy. In the middle of the night, I'd crept down and placed my gifts next to the ones Mom and Dad had put at the foot of the tree. I mentally thanked Caroline for wrapping them and attaching the short messages I'd dictated.

When Dad surveyed the presents to decide which to distribute first, he said, "Hello, what's this? Look, dear. This one's for you. Oh, and this one's for me. Nick, here's something your mom and I have for you."

I opened a package that I guessed, rightly, contained a pair of pajamas. In my childhood, they'd known to buy me model plane kits and paint sets. After I lost my vision, I'd drop a hint about LPs I wanted that they'd act on. My college freshman year, they'd arranged for a book of poems to be brailled. My senior year, Mom had recorded Lawrence Durrell's *Clea* for me. I'd read the novel the summer after tenth grade on a talking book disc that had become obsolete with the advent of cassettes, and I'd mentioned how much I wished I could read it again. Seeing it as an opportunity to give me a gift that mattered, Mom couldn't possibly have realized how much eroticism was in the novel. I'd felt embarrassed the entire time I'd listened to her narration, though no such discomfort came through in the recording.

Otherwise, I was hard to find gifts for. Our occasional discussions about books and music showed our tastes had drifted too far apart for them to be comfortable choosing the right thing for me. So recent gifts had been socks, candy, checks, and now pajamas.

As Mom opened the present I'd gotten for her, I became anxious. Caroline had convinced me to buy a small collection of soaps and fragrances. Mom would know the idea hadn't been mine. I couldn't even remember the brand name. At least when Caroline and I had looked over sweaters for Dad, I'd been able to tell her his size and favorite color.

Mom began, "How—" Then she made noises of pleasure. "Did you try the scent?" Without waiting for an answer, she handed me the box and I dutifully sniffed.

"Do you like it, Mom?"

"It's very nice."

Dad added praise for his sweater. "Just the right shade of blue."

"My friend, Caroline, helped me choose."

"Caroline?" Mom said.

"I met her in the writing course."

"Does the class continue after the holidays?"

"It was just for a semester. I don't think I could take any more of the teacher."

Dad thought that was funny. "Well," he said, "I think I'll try on this sweater."

"Ooh, that looks good on you, dear," Mom said.

I'd been on the verge of saying Caroline and I were seeing each other. "Dating" was the word they'd have used. But, as usual, they changed the subject just when I was ready to tell them. Sometimes I thought it was out of unwillingness to pry. Sometimes I interpreted it as indifference, which it wasn't. I knew for sure only that our family had no clue how to respond to anything remotely personal.

36

EXPERIENCE TAUGHT ME THAT WHEN I returned from a few days with my parents, I would be tired, antsy and generally uncomfortable in my skin. So I suggested to Caroline that we not meet my first day back, and we agreed that she'd come over the next evening. I said that if she got there first, she should use the key I'd given her the morning we dispatched the vinyl couch.

I left the office looking forward to a happy reunion, and when I walked into my apartment, I was gratified to find her waiting for me. But Doreen was there, too.

"This is a surprise," I said, suppressing annoyance that Caroline had brought a guest to my apartment without asking. I hung up my coat in the closet.

"How was your day?" Caroline asked me.

I undid my tie. "It went well."

She touched a cold glass against my wrist. "Gin and tonic. When a man comes home from a long day at the office, he needs refreshing."

"Refresh that man," Doreen chimed in.

"I believe you two have had a head start," I said.

"We've been waiting patiently for the master to come home," Caroline said.

"Very patiently," Doreen echoed.

I gulped down some of my drink. "I'd better catch up." I gulped down some more.

Doreen urged me on. "Don't be a laggard."

Caroline called, "Music!" and put on the first side of the Four Tops' *Greatest Hits*.

"Hand me your glass, sir," Caroline commanded. I complied. "And off with your jacket." She took it from me and laid it on the couch arm. "Now, hold my hand. Doreen, take his other and mine."

I found myself dancing in a circle with them, Caroline calling encouragement, Doreen shouting back her enthusiasm, me laughing. We waved our joined arms and bumped thighs.

When the side ended, Caroline collapsed, bringing Doreen and me down with her to the floor. I landed on my back, still laughing, with Caroline on her knees at one side of me and Doreen at my other.

"That's one way to begin the night," I said.

We stayed there for who knew how long.

Then, "Look at this," Caroline said, her voice directed across me to Doreen. Her fingers were at my belt. She undid it. Then she undid the button of my pants, then my zipper, and my pants fell open. She pulled down my underwear.

She told Doreen, "Take off your shirt."

"Should I?"

Although Doreen had spoken to Caroline, I regained my voice and answered, "Yes."

I heard her breathing behind fabric. She was pulling her shirt over her head. I thought my own breathing had stopped.

"And your bra," Caroline said.

Doreen made that slight vocal sound women do when reaching back to unhook their bras.

"Come closer," I said.

She moved forward. I reached up from the floor and touched her hair, her face, her shoulders, her breasts.

I turned my head to Caroline. "Take off yours, too, so Doreen isn't on her own."

"Now take off your shoes and socks," Caroline told Doreen. The shoes landed somewhere across the room. "And your pants," Caroline said.

"You, too, Caroline," I said. Both women stood and shrugged them off.

"And your underwear," Caroline told Doreen. "I'm taking mine off."

I rested my hand on Doreen's calf and followed her body's movements as she tugged her underwear down.

Both women got down beside me again, and I ran my hands over them. Both were wet when I probed between their thighs.

"Lie on your back," I said to Doreen. I hurriedly undressed and kneeled in front of her, feeling her body all over again.

She sighed. "Fill me up."

It was only after I'd entered her that I thought of birth control.

I kept pumping, but nothing was happening. Maybe the birth control thought had inhibited me. Doreen's moans became less frequent, and my desire turned to embarrassment.

She pulled away, shrieking, "What's going on here?"

Unable to speak, I leaned forward on my elbows. Caroline stayed quiet.

Doreen jumped up and fled to the bedroom, where she yelled, "You two are weird."

Caroline shifted before me and lay on her back. I entered her. This felt like home.

"You're evil," Doreen shouted from the bedroom.

I came convulsively as Caroline tensed. Neither of us made a sound.

"What the fuck's wrong with you guys," came the voice from the bedroom.

I took one of Caroline's hands and kissed it. I mouthed, "Thank you."

"So good," she said, her voice low enough that I felt sure Doreen couldn't hear.

"Let's get dressed," I said, but not as quietly as I'd intended.

The voice in the bedroom sneered, "Yes, let's."

We all retrieved our clothes and put them on. Doreen announced she was going.

"I'll walk with you to the subway," Caroline said.

After they left, I put on weekend clothes and got the apartment in order. As I washed our glasses, I thought about the risks we'd all taken. Neither Caroline nor I had any venereal disease; we'd gone over that. But Doreen? Even worse, I could have gotten one or both women pregnant.

Just as I was finishing cleaning up, Caroline walked back into the apartment.

"I thought she wanted it, too," I said.

"She did. I don't know what changed. Let's not talk about her anymore. I'm telling you she wanted it."

We met in the middle of the living room and embraced. I said, "That was incredibly exciting."

"I thought you'd like it. Merry Christmas."

"You already gave me my Christmas present."

"Happy New Year, then—four days early."

PART 2

37

CAROLINE SAID, "I THINK I can see your building up there. Yes, over to the right of the Watchtower."

We were standing at the rail of a Staten Island ferry. I was enjoying the boat's momentum, its gentle, arhythmical motion, and the open space around us. It was a mild day for February, but still cold enough with the harbor wind for Caroline to have put up her hood. I never muffled my hearing by covering my ears.

We'd just set off from South Ferry Terminal, and Brooklyn was at our left. Soon we'd be passing Governors Island, followed by the Statue of Liberty and Ellis Island on our right. I'd asked Caroline to tell me when we were approaching them. Knowing they were close by would concentrate my imagination, and she might think to mention details that normally wouldn't occur to her.

That morning I'd told her I wished I could take a trip to get outside my head in order to think more clearly about my job and career. Where did I want to go, she'd asked. We'd named all kinds of fanciful possibilities, from the Aegean to coastal Northern

California. Then she suggested the ferry, just one stop away on the R train. It couldn't have felt more faraway.

Caroline was what for me? The woman I made love to. A friend. A fellow writer. A party person who was making me into some semblance of one myself. The dutiful daughter of that tightly wrapped couple in Riverdale. A good listener I talked to after a bad day at the office or during a sleepless night. Moments ago, she'd pointed out "your" building. I found myself wishing she'd called it ours.

When speaking of his impending marriage, Jack had used the word "gooey" to distance himself from sentimental love. What I feared was desiccated love—the dried-up prune of feeling. At Christmas I'd seen how my parents loved each other, but it seemed like an attachment filled with resignation. Would the joy I felt in having Caroline at my side one day degrade into such a love?

I squeezed her arm.

"Yes?" she said.

"Oh, nothing. Just checking you're real."

"I'm real."

Okay, so what about my job? I enjoyed the work, but hated having my ego pummeled. But didn't I frown on people who were all about themselves? Yes, but I was thinking more about self-confidence than ego.

Touching Caroline's arm again, I said, "Let's walk around."

It was a calm day, and I had little difficulty maintaining my balance on this large boat. We headed inside toward the bow and then back outside. I wanted the wind on my face.

I didn't believe all that inspirational talk about inner self-confidence. Yes, there had to be a core of belief in oneself, but we were social creatures. I couldn't help being affected by how the Alliance's supervisors thought of me. At least I wasn't bored, which was better than how many of my friends felt about their jobs.

"Do you mind the wind?" I asked Caroline.

"It's a little chilly."

I gestured at the closed deck, and we went back inside.

On land, in the St. George section of the backwater New York City borough of Staten Island, we traipsed up and down hilly, weathered-stone streets.

"You need a change as much as I do," I said. "What if it meant one of those places we talked about this morning, before you thought of the ferry?"

She turned the question back to me. "Which one would you choose?"

"Easy. The south of France. Not the Riviera—I assume it's too touristy. But towns like Avignon, where the bridge is, and Aix-en-Provence. Just saying those names . . ."

"Why don't we?"

"Oh, a small matter of money."

"Money," she echoed. "One thing I learned from Colombia is that anything's possible."

"Including paying too high a price. It could have gone really badly for you."

We returned to the ferry terminal. I find terminals at once mundane and threatening. This one felt like a barn where people got rounded up like animals. I fantasized that if I put the wrong change in the turnstile, a guard would appear out of nowhere and haul me off to an underground dungeon. But all that mental disturbance fell behind once I was back at the ferry's rail and we'd gained speed. It was displaced by the worry that had motivated this excursion.

"College and law school raised my expectations too high," I said. "Most people don't have the hopes I do for a job. A job is a job. It's a paycheck."

"I guess I'm lucky I don't carry around such a burden," she said. "But who knows? Maybe one day I'll get a college degree, and then I can be miserable, too. Does it bother you I don't already have one?"

"Of course not. But we have to get your catering business off the ground. What if we buy an answering machine so people can leave messages for you?"

"It would help."

We bought the answering machine a few days later for when she stayed at my place. It did nothing to advance her catering career, but it did save me from racing to the phone for fear of missing a call.

38

ACROSS MY DESK AS WE had lunch, Jack told me he'd been interviewing with law firms.

"Are you telling me you've been offered a position?"

"And I've accepted." He named one of New York's best-known firms.

When I didn't respond, he said, "You disapprove."

"What right do I have to disapprove?"

"I'm selling out."

"If I've learned nothing else working here, a career in the law is no different from any other. It's about looking after yourself."

"Looking after Number One," he acknowledged ruefully.

"You don't think you're Number Two, do you? Jack, look, I'm sad about your leaving, but my reasons are selfish. I'll miss you. Do you see the firm as your future or as a stepping stone?"

"Right now stepping stone, but once you enter the law firm gulag, there's no knowing."

"The weight of responsibility comes to the best of us," I said. "I take it this move has something to do with your decision to marry Elaine?"

"Elaine isn't sure it's best."

"My question stands, counselor."

"I suppose it is related."

"And, of course, you want to prove you can make money."

"Yet again the male ego struts its insecure stuff."

After Jack left, I found myself swinging back and forth in my desk chair. I'd been disingenuous with him. Although I knew better, I did feel that moving to a large law firm violated our tacit oath to do good and our commitment to the loose-knit community of public service lawyers. But we weren't a cell of Stalinists demanding orthodoxy or death. The mid-century internecine fights among New York's leftists were all but forgotten. The real cause of my distress was feeling abandoned.

On the Staten Island Ferry, I'd tried to convince myself that it was enough not to be bored at work. Now that my best friend at the Alliance was jumping ship, being less than bored no longer cut it. I was unhappy, and that mattered.

39

Caroline called from the Sullivan Street bar to say she wanted to come over. I'd resigned myself to an evening of brooding, for which the month of March can be ideally suited, but she sounded troubled, too. So we went through the rigmarole with a cab. It proved to be one of the times when she buzzed through from the lobby to have me bring out cash. Mike, the doorman that evening, chatted with her as I paid off the driver. He'd been formal with me since the party, all of four months ago, but he attached no blame to her.

She poured herself a glass of wine. I declined.

"I'll need to stay here a while," she said when we'd settled into the couch. "Doreen moved into my apartment."

"When?"

"Oh, a few days ago. I thought it was for the night, maybe a couple. I didn't see a whole week coming."

"Have you asked her to leave?"

"Kind of."

"Meaning no. Even though she's overstayed her welcome."

"Sure has."

"Then throw her out."

"She has nowhere else to go. She'll leave as soon as she finds a place of her own."

"We know from her obsession with her uncle's will that she has no money. Where's she going to find a landlord who doesn't charge rent?"

"She manages."

I sank back against the sofa's arm. I felt trapped. The way I saw it, Doreen had moved into her place, and Caroline was moving into mine. We hadn't worked out this arrangement in advance. I hadn't been so much as asked. Another time, I might have been touched. Tonight, I'd already been feeling gloomy, which always left me wanting to be on my own.

To deflect my annoyance, I sat up and asked, "How's she doing?"

"Pretty well. She's become a hit on Sullivan Street."

"You're the hit," I said. "She's your coattails."

"You underestimate her."

Apparently, Caroline had forgotten Doreen had proclaimed we were evil. I wondered if she'd let her stay in her apartment out of guilt. I had no way of knowing, and Caroline's careful answers to my questions told me she wasn't about to let on.

Neither woman had become pregnant, as she'd reassured me some weeks earlier, and neither Caroline nor I had contracted venereal disease. But now I knew birth of a baby and infection hadn't been the only possible consequences.

That night she had me spank her. I went through the motions with none of the sinister pleasure I'd felt the first time, believing that tonight her desire came from a perverse need for punishment. Yet once we made more conventional love, she was as affectionate as ever.

40

FOR THEIR WEDDING CEREMONY, JACK and Elaine had invited their immediate families and only a few friends. Taking in Judge Nathan's chambers, I realized they'd been wise. The room, while not stifling, was crowded.

In few words, the judge conveyed the depth of the moment. Elaine's father almost choked when he spoke, and Caroline told me afterwards that there were tears in Jack's eyes as the judge pronounced them man and wife. Even I felt a tug at my chest. Then the judge made a light remark, and relaxation flowed through the room as soft laughter.

Most family members and friends were waiting at the upstairs room of a restaurant in the West Village that Jack and Elaine had rented for the reception. Caroline and I planned on getting there by subway, but Jack maneuvered us into a cab with his favorite uncle and aunt.

As Jack and Elaine headed the informal procession into the reception room, the assembled multitudes burst out into applause and loud cheers. For two modest and quiet people, Jack and Elaine were gloriously popular. I hadn't realized.

Caroline directed us to the bar, where she asked for a vodka sour and I my gin and tonic. A band struck up. Now I'd have a hard time hearing people talk. And . . . yes, here it was.

"Come dance with me," she said.

"I can't dance to save my life."

"If Doreen were here, you could."

I shook my head at her bringing up the memory.

Putting our glasses on the bar, she drew me into the dance space, took my hand and gyrated. I tried to let go into the music, a sickening—others would say eclectic—rhythmic mix of disco and Motown. I kept my left hand near her body, initially to ensure I didn't drift away from her, but soon to feel her kinetic female energy. I loosened up, my performance less than graceful but short of spastic.

Then I stepped on her foot. Her fault for being as tall as me. The second time I did it, she got annoyed. Apparently, it was my fault.

We headed back to the bar, where Jack came up to us.

"Let me show you how a real man dances," he said to Caroline, loud enough for me to hear even over the music.

No doubt he thought he was being funny. And also egalitarian. After all, if I insisted on being treated equally, I should get the condemnation wretched dancers deserved. But I wasn't amused.

Caroline handed me her glass. "Mind?" She didn't wait for an answer before stepping away with Jack.

Okay, I was amused. But it didn't stop me from entertaining revenge fantasies.

"Hi, Nick, it's Wendy." She stood before me.

I hadn't spoken to her since the lunch when she'd shown me her knitting. I became aware of my preoccupied expression transforming into a social smile.

She said, "Jack's leaving is going to make it even harder to stay, isn't it? I just don't know where to go. This was the job I'd set my heart on."

"Me, too."

"He told you about the trick Frank and I played on the supervisors, didn't he?"

"I can't tell you how much it helped me."

"Helped?" she said.

"I find it comforting to know their judgments are full of holes. Maybe I'm not totally incompetent after all."

"I haven't gotten there yet. I feel too frustrated."

I asked how Frank was feeling in light of Jack's departure.

"He's the supervisors' favorite. And he never wants to go back to a law firm. Eleven years of that world was enough."

"Maybe Jack will come back after eleven years," I said.

"And maybe pigs will fly."

A chemistry instructor introduced himself to us as a friend of Jack's. From what I could tell over the music, he was yet another likable and interesting person in Jack's orbit. But in a three-way conversation at an occasion where talk relied on gestures and lip-reading, I was unable to hear everything Wendy and he said. I couldn't keep up, and they drifted off.

Caroline returned on her own saying, "He's almost as good as you."

"I bet he didn't stamp on your foot."

"That was a plus."

I made another adjustment as Elaine approached us. "Thank you for being there to witness our wedding, Nick. Is this the famous Caroline?"

"I'm Caroline. Not so famous. That was a lovely ceremony." Caroline knew to direct her voice so I could hear.

Elaine thanked her, then asked me, "So, how much longer will you last at the Alliance?"

Shrugging, I said, "You must be happy you won't have to listen to Jack agonize about Alliance politics anymore."

"He'll find something else to agonize about. He's good at that. I am a little worried, though. Oh, he'll do fine, but I'm not sure he'll be happy doing a law firm's bidding."

"Whatever happens," I said, "it will be valuable experience. He's making a good move."

"I'm glad to hear you say so. Caroline, what do you do in life?"

"Oh, this and that. Right now I'm trying out catering."

"If I'd known, I would have asked you to handle our reception."

"This would have been too big for me. I'd have felt terrible if I'd ruined it. And you? I think Nick told me you're in publishing."

"Underpaid and underappreciated, just like Nick and Jack at the Alliance."

I was about to work in that Caroline was a great story writer when another guest got Elaine's attention.

I put it to Caroline, "Do you think they'd think us rude if we left?"

We found Jack opining to some relatives on the ethereal sonority of a certain soprano. We stood by until he broke off.

"Going already, Nick?" he said, before I'd told him.

"I can't hear myself think, never mind what people are saying."

"I worried about that. I wish the band weren't so loud, but it's obligatory."

"We were both honored to be at your wedding. I can't believe how many people are here. You have so many different worlds I didn't know about."

"The many faces of Jack. Well, Caroline, I'm glad I've finally met the person who has occupied many a lunchtime conversation."

I asked him to give Elaine our best, and then we escaped to the respite of a frenetic Manhattan sidewalk.

41

THE WAY CAROLINE SAID SHE hadn't seen a dentist in five years told me it was an understatement. In a moment of weakness she'd said her teeth and gums were rotting. "Cocaine," she explained.

I liked the dentist I'd found right in Brooklyn Heights. I called to make an appointment on her behalf, but the receptionist told me Dr. Fussbaum was no longer seeing new patients. Well, I was also overdue for a visit, so I set up an appointment for myself. After biting down on X-ray film holders, the interminable tooth-buffing by the dental assistant, the prodding of my gums and the good news that I needed no fillings, I told Fussbaum I had a friend who was looking for a dentist.

"Any friend of yours I'll see," he said.

"She's terrified of dentists," I warned him, now that he was on the hook.

"I promise we'll put her at ease."

"She'll be paying in cash."

"Fewer forms to fill out."

The night before her appointment, I said, "Want me to go with you? I'd be happy to."

"I don't want you to see me if I get into a state."

"A state of terror?"

"You think you're kidding."

I called my apartment from the office half an hour before the appointment and she picked up. Outside it was a cold, damp March day. It had been bad enough in the morning, but it had turned even colder and damper by the time I went out for lunch.

"Are you doing okay?" I said.

"Just getting my stuff together."

"Sure you don't want company? I can get there in time."

"Don't be silly," she said.

At 3:40, Fussbaum's receptionist called. "Your friend got extremely upset and ran out. I tried to persuade her to stay, but she wouldn't listen. Do you think you can talk to her and see if she'll come back? Dr. Fussbaum said he'll make sure he's available."

"That's incredibly kind of you. I'll try to track her down."

I dialed my home number. She didn't pick up. I suspected she'd fled to her parents in Riverdale. I tried to reach her several more times over the next half hour, surely causing Mara to wonder about my sanity. Eventually I called Fussbaum's office and told the receptionist I hadn't been successful but that I'd call again if I heard from her.

"I leave at 5:30," she said, "and that's when Dr. Fussbaum sees his last patient. If she doesn't make it today, try to get her to make a new appointment. She seems really nice. I think she must have had a very bad experience."

42

As I walked into my apartment that evening, the phone was ringing. It was my college friend, Toby. When he'd flown up from Atlanta the week before, we'd had lunch at the restaurant in his midtown hotel. We hadn't been in touch for a long while.

At the restaurant, menu reading out of the way, he'd said, "Guess what. I'm going to business school."

"You? The man who worried that selling shoes was selling out?"

"The very same. They've yanked me out of sales and put me into management. And now the company's paying my way through b-school."

"You, an entrepreneur."

I shouldn't have been surprised, considering his outgoing

personality and drive, apparent even in freshman year.

It also made sense that he had friends who were up-and-coming lawyers in the private sector. At our lunch, he'd offered to ask them about the willingness of law firms to hire blind lawyers.

Now, after waiting for me to shed my coat and settle into the armchair, he said into the phone's earpiece, "The news is not all good, my friend."

"So there is some good."

"Start over. The news is all bad."

"At least I know this conversation can't go downhill."

Toby sighed. "When I asked one of my New York friends about his firm hiring a blind lawyer, he said, 'I don't think so.'"

"Meaning I shouldn't bother."

"The words were different, but the meaning the same. The other gave me a bit of a lecture. He said a lawyer who can't see couldn't do all the reading, research and other stuff the lawyers in a firm are expected to."

"But I could—"

"I told him. I said, 'How could this guy get through law school if that was true?' He said I had a point. Then I said, 'And now he's handling appeals for the Defenders Alliance.' He said that wasn't the same thing as a law firm but that I still had a point."

"A sharp one that you cover over with your fine head of hair," I suggested.

"That did seem to be the gist. Not very kind. Anyway, so then he went on to what the clients would think. I said, 'They'd think it's amazing how much this guy gets done considering the things in his way.'

"He's a nice guy," Toby continued. "He means well—I know, the road to hell. He said clients would be filled with admiration, but that doesn't make you the world's best attorney. I told him I think you are, but I'm just a shoe shuffler, so what do I know?"

Rah-rah talk about the feats of the blind normally bothered me, but Toby knew that, and I understood why he'd resorted to it.

He said, "I hear you ruminating, Nick."

Realizing I'd gone quiet, I said, "Weighing my options."

"I hope you'll still send out your résumé. I'm sure there are rational people even in the legal field." Then he said, "I just had an idea. It's a long shot."

"I'm a long shot, too. We'd be a perfect match."

"Let me get back to you," he said.

•

An hour later Caroline turned up. Under the circumstances, I thought her brave.

"I'm sorry, Nick," she said, mugs of Postum before us on the coffee table.

"Sounds like you've been traumatized by dentists," I ventured.

"I guess so."

"Fussbaum's receptionist said he'd like to set up a new appointment."

"That's nice of him. Let me think about it. I've heard about someone in the Village, too."

I knew what that meant. From now on, the subject was off-limits.

43

TWO EVENINGS LATER AT THE Sullivan Street bar, I was reminded that more had been going on in Caroline's mind than terror of dentists. Gavin pulled me aside. Well, there was no aside in that packed room, but he found a spot where we might not be overheard.

Giving my arm one of his quick jabs, he said, "You're a lawyer, right?"

I nodded.

"You know about this situation with Doreen?"

The noise around me fell away. Gavin had my attention.

"Which situation?" I wasn't playing dumb. Two possibilities came to mind.

"She's taken over Caroline's apartment."

"What has Caroline been saying about it?"

"She's upset."

First I'd heard.

"She doesn't want to bother you, you know. I told her to change the locks, but she said it would be illegal."

"It's her apartment."

"That's what I said, but she didn't believe me. She's a big one for legality. I figured with you being a lawyer and all, you could put her straight."

It didn't escape me that Gavin had made no reference to Caroline's having more or less moved in with me. Was he being discreet, a quality I wouldn't have expected of him?

"I really wasn't aware it was upsetting her," I said.

"That's Caroline for you. She acts like she takes life's punches and bounces right back up. A little like you, I suspect. Anyway, you have to know that about her."

I felt justly reproached, as well as naïve. From now on, I'd inquire behind that pretty, nothing-bothers-me façade.

"Let's go back to the crowd," Gavin said. "We don't want anyone speculating."

But Caroline had noticed. "What have you two been plotting, huh?"

Gavin said, "Just a little chat between guys."

I waited until we were in my apartment before asking how Doreen's search was going. Trying to make the question sound offhand, I took a sip of Postum.

She wasn't fooled. "So that's what Gavin was talking to you about."

"He's worried for you."

"I didn't want to burden you with my problems."

"You know I'd want to help if I could."

"I know."

"So talk to me."

"I haven't seen her in a while."

"If it were me, I'd be really angry."

"I have to tell you you've made me into a convert. I've been telling people to keep Postum around for every time they go off the caffeine wagon. You'd get the headache anyway, but it's still a help."

"Caroline?"

"Yes?"

"Do you want to do something about Doreen, or just let it go?"

"Of course I want to do something. What do you suggest? Should I sue her?"

"What for? Money? How about changing the locks?"

"How can I with her there?"

"Wait for her to leave and call the locksmith."

"It could be a long wait."

"So? I'll wait with you."

"And what if she returns before the locksmith finishes? There'd be a fight—literally."

"How about asking the landlord to intervene?"

"You haven't met my landlord. So long as he gets the rent and isn't being hounded by housing inspectors, he doesn't care. If he did, he'd be just as likely to turn around and evict me for letting someone live there who isn't on the lease."

"You've tried to reason with her?"

"Sure. Well, I mean, I do feel for her."

"So much that you let her deprive you of your home."

"She doesn't have you in her life."

I stayed on topic. "What about her parents?"

"We're talking broken marriage and trailer parks in faraway places. She's had a rough deal."

"What would you say if we go over there and talk to her together?"

"If you think so."

As I returned to my Postum, I wondered why she couldn't just say, "Yes."

44

TOBY'S LONG SHOT WAS A small civil rights law firm in that confusing borderland between Chinatown and Little Italy that has since become unambiguously Chinatown. None of the names on the firm's masthead suggested either Chinese or Italian, so I figured rent had dictated location.

The commute would be annoying. In those days the MTA ran an R train and, during rush-hour, also an RR train. At my local station they came to the same platform before splitting off along different routes. I had to depend on strangers to tell me which one was pulling in. I'd been misinformed just once, but it had made me anxious ever after about getting where I needed on the R train on time.

Toby's friend at the firm had been a gay rights advocate in college, a courageous rarity those days. Toby hadn't told me he himself was gay until I'd known him for a year.

"Walter says his firm does some gay rights work, much of it around AIDS. You do know about AIDS, right?"

It wasn't an idle question. Word hadn't spread around the country in the early eighties, and Toby encountered near-total ignorance in Georgia. But in New York, you had to be willful not to know.

"Walter said to send your résumé to him," he continued, "and he'll pass it along."

The day of the interview, I asked Caroline to go with me to the firm's address to save me from getting confused on the R and RR subway platform or lost in the illogical streets up there. When we arrived at the building, I thanked her and said I'd make it back on my own. She squeezed my hand and kissed my cheek. I felt loved and, with it, confident.

Someone in the lobby directed me to the elevators, and someone else pressed the button for the floor I needed. I found the law office with the help of yet someone else passing through the corridor. The receptionist told me to take a seat. It was a humid day, and I'd worked up a sweat. I hoped that sitting quietly as I waited would cool me down.

Toby's friend, Walter, appeared and sat next to me. "Sorry I couldn't come out sooner. You probably heard me yelling over the phone at that school principal. I love how the tables turn when you grow up."

I only now realized I had heard. The noises of the office had been at the fringe of my awareness.

"Phil will interview you with his first partner, Donna. I recused myself. You and I didn't know each other well during college, but I'm biased toward any friend of Toby's. I think you'll like Phil, but chances are he's told Donna to play the bad cop."

"She doesn't need telling," the receptionist interjected.

At that moment a door opened and a woman called, "Nick Coleman?"

Walter said a quick, "See you later," as I got to my feet. I started in her direction. Coming toward me, she said, "I'm Donna Scherer." I stuck out my hand and we shook.

"This way," she said.

Distracted by the need to follow with tentative taps of my cane, I tried to listen as she kept talking. At the entrance to Phil's office, I bumped against the doorjamb. I imagined Donna and him glancing at each other. The problem with blindness was that it was so many things, small and large, like banging into doors in unfamiliar places. I had to fight down a treacherous sense of futility if I was to get anywhere in this interview.

Phil told me, "There's a chair maybe ten feet straight ahead of you."

I reached it without further incident and sat down to find I was sweating again. I brushed the back of my hand across my forehead.

"So," Phil said, "what brings you to a civil rights firm?"

"You can see from my résumé that civil rights has been the theme of my legal career. Besides what I'm doing now, during law school I worked for a couple of legal services offices, as well as a public defender."

Donna said, "Your work is at the appellate level, right? Any client contact?"

She had to have known something about the Alliance's appeals office to ask that question.

"Other than correspondence, none. The office frowns on it. But I did have lots of client contact in my internships."

"What do you think about that policy?" she persisted.

I chose my words carefully to avoid appearing disloyal to my employer. "It isn't ideal. Our budget forces it on us."

"Here you'd be besieged by clients. Some will be angry, some will get in your face."

When she stopped speaking, I figured I was supposed to treat her statement as a question.

"I'd make sure I didn't get angry back."

"And that you get your work done."

"Of course."

I was glad Walter and the receptionist had warned me about Donna.

Phil said, "It's really important the quiet ones don't fall between the cracks."

I nodded.

"Mind if we talk logistics?" Donna said.

I held my palm up. "Go ahead."

"Like we said, we're a small firm. Lawyers do just about everything themselves, often including the typing."

Again, she let the statement hang.

"I can type, if that's what you're asking."

She had the good grace to chuckle. "I assume you rely on readers. How does the Alliance handle that? I mean, who does the hiring? How are they paid?"

Today, such questions would lead to all kinds of Americans with Disabilities Act mind-benders. Back then, employers might have worried about appearing discriminatory, but the rules for interviewing disabled candidates weren't as stringent. It made no difference to me. Any employer concerns I could allay would surely improve my odds.

"I hire my readers," I said. "When I started at the Alliance, I paid them. After six months, the Alliance agreed to reimburse my expenses."

Phil said, "They must like your work."

"Candidly," Donna said, "paying for your readers would be a hardship for us. Maybe one day we'll generate big-time fees, but right now we're a shoestring operation."

Fitting, I thought, considering Toby the shoe salesman had sent me here.

"I don't want that to be a make-or-break issue," I said.

"Of course not," Phil said.

Donna said, "We sometimes have to travel to the client's home or office."

Not a simple proposition, but I shrugged as if it were. I felt now that she was raising obstacles to put me off more than reflecting the job's requirements.

The interview over, Donna opened the door and grasped my arm, presumably to ensure I didn't try to exit through a window. Saying "Thanks," I gently removed her hand and shook it, as if that had been her intent. Then I passed into the short hallway. She wished my back a good day, and the door closed.

Only then did the receptionist say, "Can I show you to the elevator?"

"It would help if you press the right button for the lobby," I acknowledged.

Hurrying around her desk, she touched my elbow and said, "Do I take your arm?"

"Let me take yours," I said. I squeezed it in gratitude.

The elevator was so slow to reach the floor that I worried her bosses would emerge to find her missing from reception and give her a hard time. When it finally arrived, she reached inside and pressed the L button. "All set. I hope they choose wisely."

Caroline was standing at the building entrance. "Perfect timing," she said. "I was looking around at the stores and happened to look at my watch. I thought I'd see if you were done."

"Well," I said, undeniably pleased, "since you're here and it's lunchtime, how about we look for a place to eat?"

As we set off, she said, "How did it go?"

"Not well."

There must be hundreds of restaurants in Chinatown, but

unless someone has made a recommendation, it's impossible to find a good one. They're empty or filled with tourists; they're grungy or too upscale. Eventually Caroline settled on an upstairs Vietnamese place. It had tiny wooden tables with barely adequate wooden chairs that grated on the wood floor when you sat down.

Over large bowls of soup, I gave her the details of the interview. She spared me the phony optimism other friends would have inflicted on me.

That subject exhausted, I said, "Do you think Doreen could be at home?"

"At my home, you mean. Dunno."

"Shall we find out? We could walk from here."

"It's a hike. What are you going to say to her?"

"I was more thinking I'd like to give you support. What would you like me to say?"

"You're right, I'll do the talking. I'll tell her I want my home back."

In the moment, events can be too fraught with hopes and self-doubt to be experienced in full, while memory of distant events is sensual. Today, that afternoon's walk through Manhattan is layered with images of sun-reflecting display windows, suits darting among jeans, dresses sporting dashes of color. Cheerful conversations drift over the drone of the traffic, while even the city air is spring-fragrant. My wrist rests on the curve of Caroline's hip. At the time, though, I hardly noticed, still shaken by my interview and preoccupied by the confrontation to come. That I let anxiety override joy in Caroline's company is a painful regret.

We turned onto one of the West Village's less-traveled streets and walked maybe forty or fifty yards before she announced, "Here we are." She fished out her keys and we entered the stale interior of an old Manhattan building. We were hardly through the inner door when the steps to the second floor started. The wood banister was dusty and worn. Reaching her apartment opposite the stairway on the third floor, she pressed the doorbell.

"Why don't you just go in?" I said.

"She has a right to privacy, doesn't she? Besides, she'll have the door on the chain."

I saw I was being unreasonable.

The door opened a crack and Doreen said, "Oh, hi."

Caroline said, "You remember Nick, right?"

Doreen didn't answer.

Caroline must have realized her *faux pas*, but she kept her poise. "We'd like to come in."

"It's not ready for guests," Doreen said.

I said, "Caroline isn't a guest."

"But—"

I cut Doreen's protest short. "I'm Caroline's guest, and she's invited me."

"Okay then." Doreen slipped the chain from its lock.

Caroline stepped inside and I followed. A brief hallway opened to the right onto the studio apartment.

"Can we sit?" she said.

"Like the man said, it's your place."

Caroline took my hand and rested it on the back of an armchair. "I'll sit over here on the bed," she told me.

"How are things going?" she asked Doreen.

"Pretty well, all things considered." Doreen appeared to have taken a seat as far away from both of us as the room's dimensions allowed.

"How about the apartment search?"

"So-so. It's a hard market."

"Always is," Caroline agreed.

I checked out the armchair, a shaggy thing that I imagined had faded with time. Caroline had lived a spartan existence. Funny how determined she'd been that I spruce up my place.

"Doreen," Caroline said, "I'd like my apartment back."

"It's yours. You have the keys."

"So do you. I'd like you to give them back to me."

"Uh-uh."

"Do you think you have a choice?"

"Sure I do."

"Actually," I said, "you don't."

"Is that your legal opinion?" Doreen said. "Isn't possession ninety percent of the law? That gives me a pretty strong claim to the keys."

"Your logic is strained," I said.

Caroline stayed calm. "I'm the one who signed the lease."

"And your dad," Doreen sneered.

"But not you."

"I'm here. I have my ninety percent."

"Doreen," I said, "Caroline was kind enough to allow you to use her apartment while you looked around. Don't you think it's time to find another friend to help you out?"

"Um, no."

Caroline said, "I see you've put some of your photographs up and taken mine down."

"They're in a drawer. They won't get damaged."

I said, "I think Caroline's wondering how you could substitute your things for hers when it's her apartment."

"She's never here. I assume she's with you and your latest victim." She turned to Caroline. "The landlord and I have become good buddies. He knows you and I are pals, too. If you complain, he'll tell you it's between you and me. But since you gave me the keys, there isn't anything between us, so there's no problem, right?"

Caroline stood. Betraying no sign of anger, she said, "I'll come back another time."

"I'm sure you will. But without him. He brings back bad memories."

"Doreen, I'll bring who I like."

I led the way to the door, and we left without saying goodbye. The door closed and locks clicked into place.

On the journey home—my home—we stayed quiet, lost in our own thoughts. As soon as we walked into the apartment, Caroline said, "Got any gin left from that party last fall?"

In those days I drank to enhance a good mood, not for consolation, but that time I joined her. I sat on the couch with my drink before me, while she took her glass and prowled around the room. At last she sank into the Windsor chair at the desk.

"If I changed the locks," she said, "Doreen would get so mad that someone would get arrested—probably me."

"Just now you were the only one who stayed calm. How about asking your Sullivan Street guys to keep her occupied until you call the 'all clear'?"

"That would be sneaky."

"On a scale of evil, I'd put 'sneaky' way below stealing your apartment."

"I couldn't do it to her."

"Okay," I said, "how about withholding rent?"

"Dad co-signed, so the landlord would send demand for payment to him, as well as me. I can't let that happen. Anyway, I'd only end up being evicted."

"Looks to me like you're already evicted."

"She'll leave eventually."

"I wouldn't count on it."

"If I'm evicted, I lose rent control status. Anything I find after would be too expensive."

Rent control was a great deal for New Yorkers who had it. By the time I arrived in the city, the new regime, rent stabilization, was in effect for vacated apartments, including mine. It was still a great deal, but nowhere near as good as rent control.

"Caroline, how could you let her move in?"

Anger had risen to the surface before I'd caught myself. What I saw as Caroline's capitulation to Doreen's hateful attitude had been acting like a time bomb inside me ever since she'd announced she had to move in with me.

"I was trying to help," Caroline said.

"I wonder if you wanted what has happened to happen."

"That's ridiculous. Who wants to lose their home?"

"You're right, I've never known anyone who willingly gave up their home. You're the first."

"Well, they say—there's always a fucking first, right?"

Caroline had never before used obscenity in anger with me.

"Can't you see it's come between us?" Even the few feet separating us now felt like a no-man's land.

"My staying here has come between us? I didn't realize."

"It's something we never discussed."

"I thought we did."

"After the fact."

"Well, I can do something about that."

She jumped up, banged her glass on the desk, miraculously without shattering it, opened and slammed shut the dresser drawer where she kept her smaller belongings, gathered the clothes she left lying around and hanging in the closet, retrieved whatever she had from the bathroom's medicine cabinet and stuffed everything into a bag. Then she stomped to the front door.

"Is this what you wanted?" She crashed the door behind her.

It didn't take long for the significance of what I'd done to hit home. After she'd given me such support with my job interview and Doreen had refused to give back her apartment, I'd told her she wasn't welcome in mine.

45

I GOT A FULL NIGHT's sleep. Not exactly a good sleep, thanks to a hangover that started in the night.

I had no way of getting in touch with Caroline. I had her home number, but just now it wasn't her home. I had her parents' number, but I couldn't take the coldness in her mother's or father's voice. I should have asked her for the Sullivan Street bar's number. I didn't even know its name. Everyone said "the bar" or "the bar on Sullivan Street." I doubted the telephone operators at NYNEX Information would be able to figure it out, but I'd have to try.

My thoughts were so much with her as I got ready for work and then as I commuted into the office that I expected the day to be a waste. But then I realized that the bar wouldn't be in full swing until evening, so I'd be unable to reach her during the day. Instead of making me feel even worse, the knowledge that I could do nothing for several hours freed me to worry, instead, about work and my clients.

The morning proved productive. Still, when my reading session with Ray ended, sadness came over me again. I went down to my usual tiny corner takeout place and got on line.

"What will it be today, my friend? Turkey? Ham and cheese? Hamburger?"

The Hispanic order-taker didn't know my name, as I didn't know his, but he'd figured out that by listing what I most often ordered, I'd know he was speaking to me. I chose turkey, then squeezed aside to make room for the customers behind me. A few minutes later, he got my attention with, "Okay, my friend, one turkey sandwich," and he told me the price.

Lunch bag in hand, I walked over to J&R and up its numerous, irregular short flights of steps to the record department. I ventured a few paces onto the floor and waited.

A salesman named Alan always noticed me. "Hi, what can I do you for?"

"Do you have Manfred Mann's *Somewhere in Africa* in stock?"

"Wait here."

In no time he returned, told me the price, gave me his arm and jumped the line of people waiting to pay. "Geraldine, look after this guy for me." He handed her the album.

•

Mara arrived before I'd finished my sandwich. She said, "Shall I sit in reception?"

"Unless my eating offends you, stick around."

She slung what I assumed was a light jacket this lovely spring day on the back of her chair and sat down. "How are things going?" she said.

"Could be better. I had a fight with Caroline last night—our first."

"If it's your first, don't worry."

Her tone was definitive, and I didn't feel like disagreeing. I said, "How about you?"

"Wondering why I caved into family pressure to become, of all things, a bookkeeper. Who cares?"

"Your uncle does."

"He could hire anyone. They think they're doing me a favor by giving me something to do in the family business until I meet Mr. Right."

"What do you wish you'd done instead?"

"Don't talk shrink-talk at me."

"Sorry."

"I should have gone into business for myself."

"You have lots of time."

I could have said the same thing to myself. I was young enough to change careers. On top of that, a law degree gave me lots of options. So they said.

"Should I go for an MBA?" she said. "Could I stand another two years of school? Would my family be upset?"

"Law school was three years. If I could survive three, you could put up with two. And even if your family is upset at first, they'll be proud when you emerge with the degree."

"You don't know my family."

"I know you. You got your independent streak from somewhere."

"Aliens."

"What's wrong with aliens?"

"Compared to my family?"

"Oh, come on, Mara."

I'd done so much talking that I hadn't finished my sandwich. I wolfed it down, then wheeled my chair to the trash can and slam-dunked the bag into it. Marv Albert would have waxed ecstatic.

"And now to Mr. Ishmael Gains," I said. "I started the file with Ray this morning. He's nineteen and looking at twenty-five years in prison. So much for our problems."

46

"CAN I COME OVER?"

I made out Caroline's words over the crowd noise through my phone's earpiece. After vainly calling a NYNEX operator for the bar's name and number, I'd tried just as vainly to lose myself in a novel. I kept thinking I ought to drag myself to Sullivan Street, but for all I knew, she was in Riverdale. I'd convinced myself to wait at home, the only place she could call me. Now, hearing her voice, my heart, or something in my chest cavity, settled back where it belonged.

This time the cab brought her straight to my building without her needing to call on the way. Inside the apartment, we hugged each other tight. Relieving her of the bag she'd brought with her, I noted it wasn't big enough to carry even half the things she'd taken away the day before.

I reached across the desk for the LP I'd bought that lunchtime, still in its cellophane wrap, and handed it to her. "You open it," I said. "I got it for both of us."

As the first side played, I said, "How about we take that trip to Provence?"

She didn't skip a beat. "I'll go look around travel agencies tomorrow."

"And I'll order a talking book I noticed on places to stay and eat in France. I've also been thinking I should get a TV. You need something to look at and think about other than me when you're here. I wouldn't mind TV myself, once in a great while."

"You can't do Provence and a TV both."

"Let's find out how much we'd have to lay out for a vacation. Then we'll look into TVs. Maybe not the top-line model."

Two nights later, the big bag and clothes returned. That weekend we bought a 23-inch television and put it next to the turntable on the stereo cabinet. Caroline said she could contribute to the cost of our vacation, and somehow or other she scraped together a couple hundred dollars.

47

ONCE AGAIN LOUISE WAS IN full reading stride when she was interrupted. This time it was the office's executive secretary calling.

"Michael wants to see you."

"Now?"

"Now." She hung up.

I hadn't been in Michael Flurry's office since the day I'd come down from Connecticut for my final interview, three years earlier.

He told me to close the door and take a seat. "I got a call from Donna Scherer. We know each other from bar association committees. She told me you're interested in working at her firm and wanted to know what I thought."

"I didn't know she'd be calling you."

"Public interest law is a small world," he said, as if it excused her. "I admire the work Phil and she do. They're good lawyers."

He seemed to hesitate. I didn't know what to say to help out, nor if I wanted to.

"But," he went on at last, "I have to say my experience is that people who leave here for offices like theirs end up a lot less happy than they expect."

Was he trying to keep me at the Alliance? Didn't he know my work was viewed so dimly that the supervisors demanded to see the case files with my draft briefs? He'd supposedly signed my annual evaluations. Someone must have signed for him.

"If they offer you a position and you accept," he said, "I wish you well. But give it careful thought. Now I've got to get back to writing this brief."

•

At lunch, Jack said, "Donna did what?"

"You heard right."

"They must be planning to give you an offer. They wouldn't call Flurry otherwise."

"I'm pretty sure they aren't."

"Unbelievable. She could have put your job in jeopardy."

"I suppose that's the good news out of this. Flurry wants me to stay. God knows why. He's probably right that I'd be no happier over there than here. Donna's cut out of the same mold as the Alliance's supervisors."

"And from what you say about Phil, he's probably like Flurry—good man, first-rate lawyer, atrocious administrator."

I never heard from Donna or Phil again.

Two days later we had a farewell lunch for Jack. It was a subdued affair. And as if his loss weren't hard enough to take, Mara gave notice the week after. It turned out she'd been serious about business school, and she said she'd better prepare for the GMATs.

"So, are you going to take me out to thank me for all the great reading I've done for you?"

48

"Caroline and I are going to France at the end of May," I told my parents over the phone.

"Caroline?" Dad said.

Mom said, "They took the writing course together. Remember?"

"Vaguely."

"How are you getting there? Where are you staying?" Mom said.

"We'll fly Air France. We'll start and end in Paris, but we've bought unlimited rail passes so we can go to Provence, stopping off wherever and whenever we feel like. We'll be gone two weeks."

"Long enough to get acquainted," Dad said, "short enough that you won't be pining for home."

Mom said, "Does Caroline know France?"

"She's never been, and she doesn't speak French. We'll be reliant on me for that."

"Are you sure . . . ?"

Poor Mom. She wanted to ask if I was sure this was wise, or something like that.

"Yes, Mom. Don't forget I've already been to Paris—your law school graduation present." I'd joined one of my old college room-mates there.

"We'll come down and see you before you leave," Dad said.

While I'd been on the phone in the living room, Caroline had been snuggled in bed reading a novel.

When I pushed open the bedroom door, she said, "You look happy. You love your parents very much."

I lay down on the covers next to her and stroked her auburn hair, splayed on what I knew were sky-blue pillows. Though the Venetian blinds were drawn, aromatic air came through the open windows.

Turning on my back, I told the ceiling, "I declare this Irresponsibility Day—no work, no obligations."

Caroline leapt out of the covers and swooped down on me. Then, as suddenly as she'd pounced, she nuzzled her cheek against mine, and her hair fell around me.

49

MARA'S LAST DAY ARRIVED. SHE'D all but demanded that I take her out, and Caroline, sounding amused, had said she'd spend the evening with her parents.

As we finished work for the day—in Mara's case for good—I asked her to introduce me to her nook of the Upper East Side.

"Seen it once, seen it all," she said. "I've never been to the Heights. Any good restaurants?"

I handed her my checkbook and had her make out her final paycheck to herself, which I then signed. I trusted her.

As we set off down the hall, I noticed she was wearing heels, which she'd done before just for court appearances. The only other time I'd been aware of her footwear was the day Jack hinted at her ratty tennis shoes.

Leaving the Lex line's first station in Brooklyn, we walked along Joralemon Street to a Japanese restaurant called Tanpopo, just a block away from where Joralemon dips down under the Brooklyn-Queens Expressway. Tanpopo was so far off the beaten track that I wondered how it had survived, and done so with style. I'd been here with Caroline, too, but it hadn't become "our" restaurant the way the Old Hungary had. I think she suspected I'd taken previous girlfriends here, which I had.

Mara ordered teriyaki beef. "I hate people who pick at their food," she said. I hoped she didn't think less of me for choosing salmon. We both went with Kirin beer.

"You wouldn't stop payment on that check, right?" she said after taking her first sip of beer.

"What makes you even ask that?"

"The answer's no?"

"Of course I wouldn't."

"I have a question for you."

Apparently, I was about to hear something I didn't want to.

"Why do you keep Louise on as a reader?"

"How could I fire her? She reads well, and she does everything else expected of her. Not like you, but no one's like you."

"What about that spelling thing?"

Mara had also overlooked "wreckless," but when I'd pointed it out to her, her reaction had been very different from Louise's.

I said, "She thought the supervisor was being stupid. Jack thought so, too."

"It doesn't matter if the supervisors are stupid. You have to play along."

"Just as Louise has to play along with my stupidities. Besides, she's been conscientious about spelling ever since."

"Which leads to my real question," Mara said.

"You know, Mara, I'm recalling how much my bank charges for stopped checks."

"You wouldn't dare. So, why do you stay at the Alliance? You put up with so much bullshit."

"I need a paycheck as much as you do."

"Other places pay more, believe me."

"Not in this field they don't, and I love the work."

"That's your answer?"

I paused, torn between feeling annoyed and flattered by her insistence that I do better for myself. "I do love the work, but I am looking into my options." I gave her the potted version of my interview with Donna and Phil.

"Thank you," she said when I finished. "I feel better. I'm glad you don't plan on staying in a bad place."

"Let's drink to that," I said, raising my Kirin.

Despite that promising, or at least dramatic, start, we didn't get much of a conversation going the rest of dinner. As informal as we'd been with each other before, the occasion marked a transition. It unsettled me, and her, too.

While showing me where to sign the credit card receipt, she looked up, flipping her hair back in place. "So where's this vaunted Promenade?"

We walked up to Remsen Street and to the Promenade's lower

end. "We're too far south for you to see your neighborhood," I said.

She knew, of course. "I've seen it across the river from Long Island City. Great view, crummy neighborhood. Show me your apartment."

Caroline had left after me that morning. My first thought was that I hoped she'd left the place in decent shape. The next was that I hoped she wouldn't mind my bringing another woman to our home. Were her clothes strewn around? In the bedroom, perhaps, so I'd have to cross the living room swiftly and close that door. And sometimes Caroline left stockings hanging in the bathroom, but she hadn't worn a dress or skirt in recent days, so I might be in luck.

Mike was the doorman that evening. He always seemed to be on when I wished someone else was.

When I ushered Mara into the apartment, she walked straight to the windows. "If I had a vantage point like this, I'd spend all day watching the people go by on the street."

"And they'd look right back at you," I said, reaching to my left and gently shutting the bedroom door. Turning on more lights and closing the living room's blinds, I asked what she was in the mood to drink. "Tea? Postum? Alcohol?"

"What alcohol do you have?"

I went into the kitchen and discovered unwashed dishes. I turned the water on to fill the dishpan, squirted out some detergent and threw in the dishes and silverware. After wiping off the counter, I took the bottles out of the cupboard below and set them up for Mara's inspection.

"Give me some of that scotch," she said, picking up the bottle and putting it in my hand. "And give it to me straight."

I located two small glasses in the cabinet. After washing my hands again, I poured. Then I placed my left index finger below the rim to check when the scotch had reached half an inch or so. I hoped Mara wasn't put off by my finger briefly touching her drink. I poured the same amount for myself. Then I handed over her glass and said, "Welcome."

She clinked. "Nice to finally see where you live."

"You can tell I wasn't expecting company."

We returned to the living room. I was mulling over which album to play for her. It couldn't be Manfred Mann. That was Caroline. I decided I felt like a Mozart quartet and put it on the turntable. Sitting down next to her on the couch, I asked, "Is this okay?"

"It's beautiful." When the first movement's first theme returned in the recapitulation, she said, "I love that tune. Who's playing? It has such a crystalline quality. Let me see the cover."

Getting up to retrieve it for her, I said, "The Quartetto Italiano."

We talked about her plans.

"And you?" she asked. "Any more interviews lined up?"

"The one I told you about was traumatic enough."

"You mustn't give up."

"You're right, of course, but for now my mind is on the trip to Provence. When I come back, I'll start over."

The record ended. "Play the other side," she said.

Her willingness to relax into the music took the pressure off me to make conversation. I eased into the back of the couch. Couch, not love seat, I said to myself.

She said, "I want more scotch. Give me your glass." She went into the kitchen and came back with a more generous glass for me and, she acknowledged, the same for her. Then, voice directed at my desk, she said, "Is that where you write your stories?"

"Story," I corrected. "And that first chapter."

"Have you written any more of the novel?"

"Nope, just those seven pages."

"What's it going to be about? A high school memoir, you said, but we never really talked about it."

"If we do, I might not write it."

"I get that. Who are you going to have read the rest back to you?"

"Good question. Not Louise. And Ray would find touchy-feely fiction excruciating."

"Bring the next section to me. If I'm going to read it, I may as well do so aloud. Then we'll go out for dinner."

"That's nice of you, Mara."

"Selfish. Mind if I smoke? Something you didn't know about me, right? Only two a day—no more than three. I'd never ask in your office."

"I don't have an ashtray. Hold on." I found a shallow dish in the kitchen. Placing it before her, I prattled away. "I never got into the habit. Probably why I don't mind the smell of tobacco—until it turns stale anyway."

"Well," she said. "I'm going to miss working for you. I can't say I'll miss your clients. You'll stay in touch?" She blew out smoke with a clipped puff sound.

"You're going to read my novel back to me, remember?" I checked my watch. "Wow. Already 11:45. I'll call a car service."

"The subway's fine."

"No. They don't run often this late and half the time they get re-routed without telling you in advance. And you're as drunk as me."

"I am drunk, it's true."

"I'll give you $30 to cover the cost. That should about do it."

"No need."

"I know," I said, handing her the cash.

The car service dispatcher told me ten minutes. When Mara

finished her cigarette, we went outside. It occurred to me I should have told the dispatcher twenty minutes because by then Mike would have left. Then again, this way he saw that the woman I'd brought home wasn't staying the night. Who knew what hint he might carelessly drop to Caroline.

A couple of cars drove by. When a third approached, Mara said, "This is it, I think."

I offered my hand, but found myself wrapped in her arms. Tobacco and whiskey mixed alluringly with a perfume I hadn't noticed until then, and her breasts pushed against me. Then, heels tapping, she hurried to the car, opened the door, spoke to the driver, turned to shout, "Don't forget," and slammed the door shut. I waved as the car accelerated away.

Returning through the lobby, I tossed off a nonchalant "Goodnight, Mike."

50

AT LAST CAROLINE WAS TO meet my parents. Dad made reservations at Top of the Sixes, a restaurant that had views all across Manhattan and beyond. Mom and he would take the train to Grand Central and walk up to 666 Fifth Avenue. Caroline came to my office and we set off together for the uptown Lex.

"How was your farewell to Mara last night?" she said. "Did she show you around her Upper East Side?"

"She insisted on seeing the Heights."

"So, you took her to Old Hungary?"

"Tanpopo."

"And then the Promenade?"

"Naturally."

As we entered the restaurant, she said, "Two people are waving at us. Think it's them?"

At the table, Dad boomed, "You must be Caroline." He introduced himself and Mom.

My "Hi, I'm Nick" got an indulgent laugh.

I sat across from Dad and Caroline across from Mom. Dad ordered drinks.

"Nick says you're a very good writer," Mom said.

"Nick is biased," Caroline demurred.

"He doesn't give compliments unless he means them."

What message lay beneath that morsel, I wondered.

Dad asked, "What do you write about?"

"Oh, my travels."

"Speaking of which—" Mom began.

Dad finished her question. "We hear you're taking a trip to France."

"Anything you recommend we should do there?" Caroline said.

"Never been," Dad said. "We always do America when we go on vacation."

"Nick speaks French," Mom said.

"Not well," I objected.

"He'll do the talking," Caroline said, "and I'll do the gesturing. I'm really good at that."

"I'm sure you'll get noticed," Dad said.

Okay, so he found her attractive.

Dad continued, "This reminds me of the trip we took to New Orleans last year." He launched into a story from his trusty trove of anecdotes, entertaining the first time, sometimes even the second. My mind wandered, but Caroline acted extremely interested.

After we placed our dinner orders, Dad proceeded to tell us the plot of the movie they'd watched on television the night before about the hijacking of a subway train. It sounded familiar. Hoping to head him off, I asked Caroline if she'd seen it. She hadn't.

When he finished, Caroline managed to get in, "My father is an engineer with PATH—you know, the subway between Manhattan and New Jersey."

Mom said, "Really? How interesting. Does he—what?—design the trains?"

"Oh, no. But one of his jobs is to help test them when they're delivered."

"It still amazes me that New York's subway cars were made by a firm in a city that has no subway," Dad said. "You probably know the manufacturer was the St. Louis Car Company."

Caroline said she didn't.

"Got bought out around 1960, and I don't believe its name survived past the seventies."

Dad had a lot to say on a subject I would have thought held no interest for him. Although he took occasional trips on the commuter train to the city, the nearest he came to a subway was stepping around a sidewalk grate. Perhaps he'd once had financial dealings with the company.

When he finished, Caroline asked, "How did you get involved in finance and railroads?"

"Well, there's the résumé explanation and the avocation part— you know, the things that interested me even when I was a boy."

I said, "Dad, tell Caroline about that time you felt too sick to work at the supermarket."

Here was one story I never tired of hearing because it explained why Dad credited his mother with being the dynamo that got him going. I believed her determination had been passed through to me. When Dad was sixteen, he'd been a jack-of-all-trades stock boy. The store's owner stopped by the house one evening to find out why he hadn't shown up that day.

"I told him I was feeling under the weather, but Mother would have none of it. 'You're going to Mr. Davis's tomorrow, I don't care how you feel, and that's that.'"

"And you did," Caroline prompted.

"There was no refusing her."

Mom said, "It will be her eightieth birthday in September. Have you made reservations yet, Nick, or are you coming with us?"

"I can't stay the whole week," I reminded her. "Don't worry, I'll be there."

Without any prompting from us, Dad went on to tell stories about incidents on his way up his firm's ladder. Eventually, even Caroline gave up trying to hold up our end of the conversation. Dad was happy to carry the load by himself, with some lifts from Mom.

Every so often, Dad, Mom or Caroline would mention the spectacular view out the windows. I like to know about my surroundings, but there came a point that evening when their admiring asides about Central Park to the north and the sweep of the West Side out to the Hudson depressed me. It was hard enough not being able to see what everyone so admired, but still harder being unable to share a communal moment. I told myself, as often before, that by now I should have adjusted to social moments like this. What if this feeling came over me in France? Was I going to react badly when Caroline looked outside a train window or reveled in the sight of a cathedral? I turned my attention to my plate, making food my external stimulus, and the moment passed without anyone seeming to notice.

The good news was that Caroline had made a favorable impression. After brandies, which Mom alone declined, we all walked to Grand Central, where we said goodnight on the platform, the Greenwich train hissing at our side. After they boarded, Caroline picked them out a few windows down toward the front. The train eased into motion, and I waved until the last car was rolling into the tunnel.

As we entered my apartment, Caroline said, "Cigarette with lipstick."

When drawing out the details of my evening with Mara, she hadn't asked what had happened after the Promenade, and I'd made the mistake of not volunteering. Now I detected another giveaway: a trace of tobacco smoke.

I said, "She wanted a nightcap."

"I'm going to throw it out." Caroline strode into the kitchen, from which I heard the cupboard door under the sink open and the rustle of a plastic garbage bag. Returning, she paused at the coffee table, then continued out of the apartment to the compacting room. When she came back in, she went to the bathroom and ran water. At last she sat down next to me on the couch.

I held out my hand. She took it, saying, "I didn't think it would bother me."

51

PREPARING FOR VACATIONS FROM A LAW office is stressful. Unable to anticipate every emergency, I had to familiarize a colleague with my cases in the event something happened in my absence. Beyond our first days in Paris, Caroline and I had no definite plan. Back then, without cell phones, the office thus had no way of reaching me, and no one suggested I make periodic international calls. Who would pay for them?

All that anxiety slid away when Caroline and I sat together on the plane at the start of a Kennedy Airport runway and the engines flared for takeoff. She pressed my arm, conveying both her fear of flying and our shared excitement.

Air France gave us bulkhead seats, and I luxuriated in stretching out my legs. When a cheerful flight attendant served our meals, he produced a full-size bottle of wine instead of the usual on-board single servings. In French-accented English, he said, "Your introduction to France." Was it my disability that courted such favor or Caroline's attractiveness? Or both? For once, I let myself enjoy special treatment. We got maybe an hour's sleep as we flew toward an eastern Atlantic morning, neither of us knowing this trip was to be our turning point.

Arriving at our Paris hotel, a narrow edifice in a block of attached buildings, we dragged our luggage into the cramped foyer and announced ourselves. The *réceptioniste* grunted with concern. The hotel had overbooked. A nearby place had agreed to take the overflow. The length of the journey and lack of sleep threatened to get the better of me. I was on the verge of demanding my rights. I'd call the Embassy.

Sensing I was about to make a scene, Caroline squeezed my arm. "It's just around the corner."

Well, it was two corners and two blocks. It was also a dump. The day was cold for May, and there was no heat. Our room was seedy—chipped furniture, rough-fabric bedcover, makeshift bathroom door—but Caroline said it was clean.

Although she'd never been to Paris, she bowed to my desire to leave it behind for the countryside and small towns. Two days later, recovered from jetlag, we took the TGV to Lyon, then started a leisurely train journey south alongside the Rhone River, planning to stay a night or two wherever our guidebooks and my talking book on France lured us.

Our second stop was Tournon, which attracted us because of a claim in a guidebook that the town's bridge was the prototype for the Brooklyn Bridge. It turned out to be merely a wooden pedestrian crossing. When Caroline found it on the map, she said it wasn't worth the walk.

That night in our hotel's dining room, she read the all-French menu as well as she could. It contained just two main dishes. I picked up *poisson* for fish and *agneau* for lamb. She ordered the fish and I the lamb.

When she saw what the waitress put before me, she gasped. "It's a brain. The whole hemisphere."

Belatedly, I heard what she'd read: *cerveau d'agneau.*

"You look like you're going to throw up," she said. "I'll eat it. It doesn't bother me."

I didn't protest as she switched dishes.

The only other guests in the room were an English family. Out of the blue, the man projected his voice across to our table. "I see you have a retinal condition."

I pretended not to hear, but Caroline whispered, "He's talking to you."

"Yes, I'm speaking to you, young man."

"Why do you ask?" I said, though he hadn't phrased his observation as a question.

"I'm an eye surgeon. I'm curious if I've diagnosed your condition correctly."

"I don't know." Pointedly, I turned back to my fish.

"Where are you traveling to?" the man said, as loudly as before.

"We haven't made up our minds," Caroline replied. "Wherever we feel like getting off the train."

"Yes, I imagine driving would be a problem."

When we arrived at our Avignon hotel, it was already late afternoon, and the Palais des Papes, the fourteenth-century home of the Popes, had closed. We thought we should do Avignon justice by staying a second day, but our hotel was fully booked and we wasted much of the next morning looking for one with an available room. We found a place a few blocks away. Saying the room was being cleaned, they wouldn't show it to us, but they required payment in advance. At least we were able to leave our luggage there.

All that day, we were hemmed in by other tourists. Even the foreign voices and languages didn't redeem the grimness of people determined to see the sights. We ate a discouraging dinner at a tourist-trap restaurant and returned to our new hotel to call ahead to Aix-en-Provence.

Entering our room, we discovered why the hotel owner hadn't shown it to us. It was unkempt and the bed covers threadbare. Caroline settled into a sagging armchair and I took the hard chair by the phone. She read through reviews of Aix's hotels.

"I vote for the third one," I said.

"Which one is that?"

"I don't remember the name, but the third you read about."

"I skipped over some."

"Why don't you make a note against the ones that interest us?"

"Did you mean this one?" She read it aloud.

"No, the one before."

It wasn't the one before or the one after. My frustration increased, and she felt badgered. I took a deep breath. Eventually we organized a list of three hotels in descending order.

Exercising my schoolboy French, I made the calls. The first two hotels were full, but the third had a room available. They required only my name. It should have been a satisfying moment. Instead, we were both annoyed.

"Why do you get so impatient with me?" she said.

It wasn't yet eleven, but we went to bed in order to get up early and arrive in Aix before lunch. That's when Caroline was bitten.

"Bedbugs," she shrieked. She jumped out. Then I was bitten, and I flew out just as fast.

We closed tight all our bags and dozed on and off through the night, she in the armchair, I in the chair by the phone.

At six, we crept downstairs with our luggage. No one was in the foyer. I unlocked the front door.

Stopping at the threshold, she said, "We haven't paid the phone bill."

"They tricked us into paying a king's ransom for an uninhabitable room. Go before they hear us."

Leaving behind a record of the hotels I'd called ruled out Aix. Besides, we wanted nothing more to do with tourist towns. Half an hour out of Avignon, we got off at Arles, which had Roman ruins, but which our guidebooks said was also a town where people worked for industries other than tourism. We figured we'd stay a night. We ended up spending four.

52

NEAR THE ARLES STATION WAS a post office, and we had postcards to mail. While waiting on line, an American man approached us and asked, "New to Arles?" He had a deep voice that made him seem older than I guessed he really was. I put him in his thirties. Forty at most.

"Just got here," Caroline said.

"I'll show you around, if you like. I'm Dave—Dave Broadhurst."

We introduced ourselves and shook hands.

Caroline said, "Know anything about this hotel?" She showed Dave the page in one of our guides. We'd picked the hotel out on the train.

"No, but I know the area. I'll walk over with you. It's outside the town center, but still close. Did you know this is the largest town in France?"

"But Paris—" Caroline began.

"A trick statistic. But being a physics guy, I like the unexpected. It's largest in area. That's because it encompasses the Camargue."

"Where wild horses roam free?" Caroline said.

"You know about that. But the real town is very walkable."

Caroline yielded her suitcase to him, and soon we were strolling along a quiet street. Dave told us he taught physics in the States. He would get an appointment at a college, teach for a few years and live frugally, then travel for as long as his savings allowed. Then back to teaching. He was in the process of seeking a new position, so I inferred money was running out.

Outside the hotel, he said, "Care to share a carafe of wine before dinner? By then the paper factory will have stopped production for the day."

Letting that mysterious aside go, we agreed on time and place, then said goodbye for now.

We checked in with a woman who turned out to be not just the *réceptioniste*, but also the owner. After we unloaded our stuff in our room, she directed us toward town and recommended an affordable café for lunch. We should have been tired after a night dozing in chairs, but the day was fresh and meeting friendly people had revived us.

As we looked over the café's menu, I said, "What's that smell? Did you just blow an egg fart?"

"No. You did."

The sulfur stench stuck around for most of lunch, occasionally drifting away but soon returning. We'd skipped breakfast and were hungry. However, I couldn't have said if it was a good or a bad meal. It was food eaten half the time with nose held between finger and thumb.

We sauntered over to the Roman arena, which happened to be free of other visitors. The awful smell went away.

"Here," she said, "climb this step. It's steep."

"This is the stairway?"

"The stairway and the seating, both. Each row is a continuous slab of stone circling the stage. Well, ovaling, if there's such a word."

I climbed one more level and sat down. She sat beside me.

"According to the guidebook," she said, "I could whisper from anywhere in here and you'd hear me."

She walked off, while I stayed seated, imagining how I might have felt as a spectator in a frenzied crowd at a gladiator fight two millennia ago.

"Can you hear me?" Caroline said, softly.

"Where are you?"

"Over here."

"I have no idea where 'over here' is. You sound like you're in my ear."

"Maybe I am."

She struck a stone step with the guidebook to signal her location, but I still couldn't tell where she was. She reappeared at my side, and we walked together to the spot. After that, we returned to ground level and traversed the arena's substantial perimeter. In a voice of wonder, she described its perfect arches crisscrossed at right angles by equally perfect arches.

As the midday heat eased up, more visitors appeared. I resented their intrusion into my thoughts, which felt on the verge of being profound.

Dave was waiting at the café he'd suggested. I apologized for being a quarter hour late. "We were bewitched by the arena."

"I figured I hadn't done anything to frighten you off," he replied.

"But I'm glad you're here now to share this local red. Red is okay?"

We began with the usual biographical outlines. I hadn't detected an accent, but when Dave said he was from Alabama, I noticed he had a soft-spoken way about him that could only be from America's south or mountain-time west.

I said, "I love how present and past are one here."

Pouring wine from the second carafe, Dave responded, "That's the connection America lacks. We're all descendants of immigrants and imports. Our ancestors were disinherited second sons, escapees from persecution or cargo shipped to New World slavery. Connections severed. There you go, Caroline. Now you, Nick."

I held the stem of my glass as he poured. "You equate disinheritance, persecution and slavery?"

Caroline was with me. "Big difference between starting over and losing all options."

"No question," Dave acknowledged. "But none of those predicaments was a happy one."

I said, "You'd think people who escaped oppression would have wanted nothing to do with slavery."

"That's like claiming children of abusive parents won't abuse their own children," Caroline said.

"But many do," Dave agreed. "All I'm saying is the majority in America feels no link to the people who settled there long before our descendants arrived."

"I feel a connection with Native Americans," Caroline said. "I don't need monuments to feel a shared heritage."

"Do you think a Cherokee or a Mohawk would reciprocate?" Dave said.

She didn't answer, which emboldened him. "Here, you walk by the arena every day and there's your continuity back to Caesar and Ovid, along with everyone in between."

She said, "If the arena were in America, they'd Disney-fy it."

"They haven't Disney-fied the Civil War memorials," I countered.

But once again Dave agreed with Caroline. "Give it time."

"America does have traditions," I declared. "Thanksgiving. Democracy. Apple pie."

"No one eats apple pie anymore," Caroline pointed out.

Her narrow objection made Dave and me laugh, and then Caroline.

Sitting back in the metal chair, I let the sun warm me through. An image formed in my mind of the earth's curvature with the three of us and this table balanced on top. The sense of profundity I'd felt in the arena returned. It seemed that for me, profundity was nothing more than contentment.

Dave pursued his theme. "All tradition in America is contrived. Your vaunted Thanksgiving, Nick, is based on a dubious premise about friendship between the Puritans and Indians. Our real traditions are Hollywood and the tag lines from old commercials. We quote from movies and ads all the time. Remember 'Winstons taste good like a cigarette should'?"

I did remember. The infuriating commercial had aired for years.

Dave continued, "It encapsulated everything you need to know about America. It promoted cigarettes, a nasty habit that causes cancer, and it corrupted grammar, the epitome of tradition. Here they have the *Academie Française* to keep grammar constant."

"They also have commercials," Caroline said. "I don't understand a word they say, but I can tell they're just as stupid as ours."

"They are pretty stupid," Dave conceded. "Even stupider. But they're grammatical. At least I assume they are."

"Dave," I said, "that's the lamest act of backtracking I've ever heard."

"Tell you what," he said. "Let's ask every French person we encounter tonight if their TV commercials are grammatical. We can send the survey results to the *Herald Tribune*."

"Front-page story for sure," Caroline said.

Despite the light-hearted tone of our conversation, I was troubled. "Dave, what you're saying doesn't put us in a flattering light."

He took a sip of wine. "You're wondering if I hate America. I don't. I could get teaching positions here, but I need a regular dose of home."

"Like you need 'Plop plop, fizz fizz' for a stomach upset?" I suggested.

"Talk about stupid commercials," Caroline pointed out.

Dave said, "Your glass is getting low, Nick. Here." He poured. Some of the wine splashed on the table. "You, too, Caroline."

He picked up with her aside. "True, America is a country of vulgarity. France is lots of things wrong—look at their elitist education system—but one thing it isn't is vulgar. Yet America is irrepressible. Push us down, we bounce back up. Tell us we have no culture, and we bring you jazz. Tell us we have no class, yet our movies are watched around the world.

"Here's my point," he said, the wine making him even more emphatic. "All of Europe's empires faded. I predict America's won't. That's because of constant renewal. I admire tradition. I admire renewal."

"Now you're saying the French tradition we've been drinking to will someday go away?" I said. "Surely you contradict yourself."

"I don't know what I'm saying," he conceded. "I thought it sounded good, though."

"Definitely," Caroline said.

"I'll drink to that," I said. There wasn't much left to drink.

Caroline summarized, "You're saying change is necessary and even good, but we lose a lot when we forget the past."

Dave waxed enthusiastic. "If you'd said that from the start,

Caroline, you could have spared us this whole tortured conversation. Another carafe, or shall we go for a walk?"

"I'd like to go to the hotel and get my jacket," Caroline said. "It got cold all of a sudden."

"It's the dry air," Dave said. "Hot during the day, cool in the evening. At least at this time of year. The summer can get brutal, though nothing like the humid East Coast back home."

"Speaking of the air," I said, "what was that stink during lunchtime?"

"Ah, yes. Remember I mentioned a paper mill? Sulfur is a nasty byproduct of the paper manufacturing process. The mill is up north a ways. In the middle of the day, we're downwind from it. After that, it's all clear. You're sitting in Eden. Perfect climate, beautiful landscape. Forget the Tigris and Euphrates and Fertile Crescent. But like the Bible tells us, God thought the locals enjoyed life a little too much, so he put a lid on it by planting that paper factory up there."

Of the three of us, Caroline appeared the least inebriated. She certainly thought so. "You guys stay here," she said. "I'll go get my jacket and come back."

"Oh, no, you don't," Dave protested. "You might get lost. We're coming with you."

"Absolutely," I said.

Seeing she was out-voted, she said, "Okay, but so long as you promise not to go inside."

"You think we'll embarrass you?" I said, finding even the question hilarious.

"Yes."

In the process of trying to stand, I fell back in my chair with laughter.

Dave calmed down long enough to say, "Where's that waiter?"

No sign of him. We piled franc notes in the middle of the table, stuck a glass on top, and wove off down the middle of the street.

When we arrived before the hotel, Caroline said, "Guys, you promised."

"So we did," Dave said.

That set us off again as Caroline walked inside. Dave told me he could see all the way to the end of the hallway. After Caroline disappeared upstairs, he said, "The owner's sitting in there laughing."

When Caroline at last emerged, we waved at the owner, who waved back.

"*A toute a l'heure*," she called.

I translated for Caroline. "She's saying she won't lock us out."

53

THE NEXT DAY CAROLINE AND I explored more of the town. I particularly remember the Roman theater. According to the write-ups, the Romans' remarkable architectural acoustics made up for their failure to invent the microphone. We'd witnessed their acoustics in the arena, but all that remained of the theater were the stone floor and some pillars, in a few cases with fragments of roof on top. I thought of Shelley's Ozymandias, with the statue's legs and head severed from its trunk, and its pedestal declaring:

'My name is Ozymandias, King of Kings:
Look on my works, ye mighty, and despair!'

Yet I felt the continuity that Dave had celebrated the evening before, in some way more than I had in the restored arena. Here, so much was left to the imagination, which a finished restoration might try to but could never fill in completely. We clambered over piles of broken stone scattered about the site and through grass that had grown wild. Probably the town had run out of money after the arena and before they could fix up the theater, but I chose to believe they'd been seduced by the elegiac nimbus of slow decline.

Our third day, when we took a tour bus through the Camargue, began badly. Caroline made an effort to describe the landscape, but it was dreary and unchanging. She kept scanning for wild horses, while I waited for the bus to reach some place named Saintes-Maries-de-la-Mer, about which even our guidebooks had hardly anything good to say.

Hating to be this bored and powerless to do anything about it, I gripped the seat's arm for something tangible and tried to fall in with the rhythm of the bus's momentum. The lawyer in our writing class had been right after all: I did live in a vacuum.

"The guidebook does say there's a halfway decent place for lunch in Saintes-Maries," Caroline said, apparently picking up on my dejection and hoping to give me something to look forward to.

"Good," I said to the back of the seat before me.

"What did I do wrong?" she asked.

Obviously she'd done nothing wrong.

We got back to Arles at the appointed time to meet Dave.

"You two look like you've had not such a great day," he said as we sat down.

"Have you ordered a carafe yet?" I said.

"I see I hit the mark. Yep, a carafe of the *vin rouge de la maison* is on the way. Here it comes."

As he poured the wine, he asked Caroline, "See any horses?"

"Not one."

"I can't say there's a lot to interest me if the horses aren't out there," he said. "And Saintes-Maries is just a destination. Nothing there either, except the Mediterranean."

Caroline had said nothing about the sea when we took a short walk around the town. Did she forget to mention it, or hadn't it been in view? For the first time in my life, I'd been at the Mediterranean, but without knowing it.

"What's wrong, Nick?" Dave said.

"Just a little off today."

Caroline said nothing. I imagined her looking vacantly at the table.

"Happens to me every trip," he said. "There'll be days when I feel disoriented and purposeless. What am I doing here? It will all become clear again before you know it. I have an idea. Ever heard of the *course de taureaux*?"

Caroline said, "Something to do with bulls?" She might not know French, but she made fast word associations.

"Bullfighting, right."

"Bullfighting?" she exclaimed. "In France?"

"We're not far from Spain, remember."

He'd noticed there was going to be a *course de taureaux* event the next day, Saturday, in nearby Nimes. "They have a Roman arena, too, and that's where it takes place."

My first reaction was repulsion. Then I remembered I aspired to be a writer. Writers needed experience, however and wherever it came at them. Hemingway had subjected himself to bullfights in Spain. In Nimes's arena, I'd get a sense of what Roman bloodlust had been like.

Similar logic dictated that I should have eaten the lamb's brains in Tournon. Hemingway would have. Okay, so I was a hypocrite. Welcome to the human race.

Caroline declined to join us in the arena, but she perked up at the idea of an afternoon's shopping in Nimes. To me, she said, "Our guidebook says 'denim' comes from Nimes—'*de Nimes*.' Get it?"

That night as she and I got ready for bed, I said, "Dave certainly cheers you up."

"What do you mean?" She was doing something at the dresser.

"I'm just saying."

"Just saying what?"

"You enjoy his company."

"He's fun."

I got into bed. "Maybe you should spend more time with him."

She turned to me. "Why would I do that?"

"If he's so much fun."

"I can't believe you're jealous," she said.

"I'm not jealous."

"Then why give me a hard time?"

Why indeed? I knew the answer, kind of. Since that morning I'd been feeling inadequate as a traveling companion. If someone sighted—Dave—had been on the bus with her, they could have pointed out this and that to each other. Even today, without the white horses, she could have gestured and complained, "Look out there. Nothing!" With me beside her, all she could do was describe and summarize. Definition of one-way street.

She got into bed, but stayed on her side. I sat up, turned away and rested my feet on the floor.

If I wanted to travel, and if I wanted to do so with Caroline, I had to accept an occasional sense of exclusion, as she accepted the limits of what we could share. This was all about just a few hours, a single day.

And why blame her for saying nothing about the sea? I should have known to ask. Saintes-Maries-de-la-Mer. De-la-Mer—on the sea. What sea was there around here other than the Mediterranean? Besides, how could it be I hadn't detected the sound of waves or the ozone in the air? I must have been so preoccupied that I'd shut out the world outside me.

Self-pity was morphing into remorse. She'd remember this day as the one she'd sought in vain for wild horses and I'd made her miserable.

"Sorry, Caroline," I mustered.

It took her a while, but at last she replied, "It's okay."

I reached back and stroked her hair. But she'd gone inside herself, the way I had much of the day.

I got back in bed and turned toward her, but I didn't hold her the way I usually did. If she'd wanted me to, she would have signaled.

I woke up to find I'd slept through the night. Yesterday's emotions must have exhausted me. Caroline was at the dresser. Seeing me stir, she hummed some tune I didn't recognize. It felt good to wake up to it. She sounded happy again.

We hooked up with Dave and took the bus into Nimes. It had the feel of a busy, commercial town, and the café where we had lunch lacked the charm of the ones we'd frequented in Arles. Caroline walked with us to the arena before setting off for the stores.

Dave and I pushed through the milling crowd at the entrance. As at Arles, the stone seats were also the steps. He held my arm as I hoisted myself up to the next level. Those Romans must have been agile.

Without fanfare, some men appeared in the ring, and then a bull. I got the impression from Dave that they just kept prancing around. The crowd showed enthusiasm, but nothing like the bloodthirsty arousal I'd anticipated.

Dave said, "There's some sort of tassel—a red ribbon?—on the bull's horn. One of the guys seems to be eyeing it." A little later, he said, "The guy has this pole thing that he keeps probing toward the bull's head. I wonder what he's doing . . . Remember that tassel I mentioned? He just speared it . . . Would you look at that? He's walking off with it."

The crowd's applause made me think of the reception when the home team took the field in baseball.

"This must be the warm-up," I said. "They aren't really into it yet."

"I'm sure you're right."

We were wrong. After an hour, the crowd quietly filed out.

"It's over," Dave said, as bewildered as I was.

Caroline was waiting at the exit. "How was it?"

Dave opened the newspaper where he'd seen the event being promoted. "They call this *Course Camarguese*. I guess in Provence they don't kill the bull."

"Good for them," she said. "So what do they do?"

"It appears the object is to snag a tassel hanging from the bull's horn."

She touched my arm. "You look funny, Nick."

"I'm okay," I said, dismayed to find I felt let down.

Next morning, Caroline and I walked to a field we'd discovered our second day where rosemary and thyme grew wild. I ran my fingers along the leaves, and they came away smelling fragrant. I speculated that Provence's aromas had inspired the Troubadours eight centuries before. Around the time I met Caroline, I'd rejected the whole notion of Troubadour-like romantic love. No longer.

"In another month," Caroline said, "there'll be lavender around here."

"Next trip," I said.

54

I DID EVENTUALLY STAND ON the Mediterranean shore that vacation, but briefly. From Marseilles, we took the train a few stations up the coast before hurrying back to Paris, as our rail passes were about to expire.

Caroline was enthralled by the city, and I fell once again under its spell. We crossed and re-crossed the Seine, took random walks through the Marais and the Quartier Latin, window-shopped the Champs-Élysées, laughed at our discomfiture on passing among the Rivoli Gardens' nude sculptures, stood before the Mona Lisa as Caroline tried to convey what it was like to see it in person, contemplated whether Notre Dame was magnificent or terrible, ambled over to Île St. Louis to eat passion fruit ice cream cones, and, all in all, let our inner tourists loose.

The morning of our last full day, I woke early, eager to set off for some new part of the city. Even after Caroline stirred, she got ready slowly, much too slowly, only to announce she felt like staying in.

I slammed my open palm on the room's table. "Our last day in Paris, and you don't want to go out? Well, I want to. Will you join me?"

"Later, maybe."

To spare ourselves another wasted half-day searching, we'd returned to the hotel where we'd stayed the first night, so I had some familiarity with the area. Stepping outside, I followed a street down to an open-air market. I didn't wander among the stalls, but stationed myself nearby and listened to the chattering and bargaining. I picked up little of what was said, but I recall the atmosphere the way I do a lot of music. The themes are gone, but something about the music changed me. Call it a shift in neural activity.

Did Caroline come down to find me? I have contradictory memories. In one, I return alone to the room and she's come out of her funk. In the other, she does, indeed, find me, though how, I couldn't say. I choose to believe this second scenario. It might even be true.

55

BACK FROM OUR TRIP, WE had so many stories to tell that we more than held our own in company for weeks to come. Our Avignon hotel turned from a depressing low point to an amusing adventure. Caroline grew radiant in the telling. Our stories even livened up a visit to her parents in Riverdale.

I could no longer imagine life without her. The recognition had germinated even before our vacation, on Caroline's dismay at discovering Mara's cigarette. Why hadn't I thought to get rid of it? I knew what a Freudian would say. On the other hand, anyone with sight would have seen it glaring from the coffee table. Yet I still held back from telling her I hadn't slept with Mara, afraid that bringing up that evening would make the wound raw again.

I'd also be admitting I thought of our relationship as monogamous, even though I felt no need of another woman. Such a declaration would be tantamount to saying I was committed. I was sure about today and even tomorrow, but next year? Next decade? Who would I be then? Who would she be? True for everyone in this world but especially for us. In her late twenties, she was still figuring things out, and so was I in mine.

I kept coming up against a mental escape clause that had taken root inside me the day she'd cut herself off from her apartment. If I hadn't agreed to let her stay in mine, she would have been all but homeless, reduced to flitting between her parents and friends. She'd gambled I wouldn't let any of those outcomes happen to her, but it had been just that: a gamble.

Until then, I'd chosen to disregard earlier signs of instability, even though her escapade in Colombia had foretold a self-destructive streak. How could she have assumed the trip would be innocuous? Cocaine-induced escapism? She'd admitted to using drugs, but having seen no evidence of it while we'd been together, I couldn't imagine her so far gone. Still, so much was unexplained, from where she got her money to the people who came in and out of her life. Maybe our threesome with Doreen was another bad sign. If so, her dismay on seeing Mara's cigarette was a good thing. That time she'd asserted herself with exquisite tenderness.

And what did it say about me that I'd allowed myself to get involved with a woman who had such problems? Mara saw something amiss in me for staying at the Alliance, and even though I felt my options were limited, making the job more a cause than a symptom, I couldn't rule it out.

Still, if Caroline and I were both damaged goods, we were doing pretty well, surely better than if we'd never met.

•

My client Ishmael Gains was waiting for me on my return to the office. Not in person, but in the sense of the responsibility I felt for his future. I'd left my brief in his case half-finished.

For the first few days, it felt like someone else's project. That's how far the vacation had taken my mind from work.

I had a new reader, Beth. Advertising for Mara's replacement and interviewing candidates had occupied a lot of time before the trip. Beth's being a graduate student in English had no doubt biased me toward her.

I also had a new friend at the Alliance, a lawyer named Rob Feldman who had started a year after Jack and me. I'd entrusted the care of my cases to him during my vacation. He lived with his girlfriend, Samantha, in walking distance of my apartment in the Cobble Hill section of Brooklyn. On our second Sunday back from France, Caroline put on a summer skirt she'd bought in Nimes and, both of us feeling the afterglow of our vacation, we walked down to Rob and Samantha's brownstone.

While Rob gave us a tour of their second-floor apartment, Samantha, an up-and-coming fashion designer, trailed behind, making disparaging comments about the carpets, the chairs, the faded white of the walls. Rob had either bought or inherited everything in the apartment before she moved in except for the artwork, which she'd brought with her.

"I have no taste," Rob admitted on the tour. "That's why I asked Samantha to move in."

"You had me move in for my body." She turned to us. "I can't even think about getting naked around him unless I'm ready for him to fuck me."

I did my mute grin routine. Caroline also said nothing. Intuition told me she looked away as if she hadn't heard.

In the living room, Rob offered us beer, soda or joints. Caroline and I went for beer.

"Mind if Samantha and I smoke?"

I'd alerted Caroline to Rob's habit ahead of time. She told them to go ahead.

After we'd settled in with our social crutches, Samantha said, "Caroline, that's a lovely skirt you're wearing. What a deep red. Where did you get it?"

Caroline told her about her shopping spree in Nimes. Samantha stepped forward from her chair and bent to take the skirt's hem between her fingers, as I recognized when she said, "So soft."

I looked in Rob's direction and shrugged. I imagined his eyes rolling.

"While Caroline was out buying clothes," I said to Samantha, "I went to a bullfight."

"A bullfight!" she exclaimed, returning to her chair. "How awful."

"I thought that would get a reaction," I said.

Rob assumed that supernatural calm that some people feel when marijuana takes hold. "I think we should have bullfighting in this country. Nick and I would have to find new jobs, but it would be a small price to pay for less crime."

"What does bullfighting have to do with crime?" Samantha said. Marijuana hadn't made her any less animated.

"A bullfight is a vicarious act of violence, wouldn't you say, Nick?"

I nodded, but Samantha said, "Not to the bull it isn't. Nothing vicarious to him about being killed."

"Someone has to die," Rob said, reasonably. "Better a bull than you or your neighbor, no?"

"That's absurd," Samantha said. "They still have murders in Spain."

"Not as many."

I doubted Rob had recently checked comparative crime statistics.

Samantha said, "And you believe bullfights are the reason? You're crazy."

"You've got Spanish blood in you. Are you excitable Spaniards any less prone to violence than the rest of us?"

"They don't kill the bull in France," Caroline pointed out.

"They don't?" Samantha said. "How interesting. Why don't they?"

"It's a control group in an experiment," I said. "Two years from now they'll compare violent crime rates in Spain and France to find out if there's any statistical correlation with killing or not killing bulls."

"See?" Rob said to Samantha.

"You're making it up, Nick," she said. "I can tell from your face you're making it up."

"My face?" I said, arching my eyebrows to feign puzzlement.

Rob said, "Do you trust his face, Caroline?"

"Sometimes."

Samantha said, "I don't trust Rob's. Ever."

"Shall we go for a walk?" Rob said. We agreed. "Sure you won't have a joint first?"

We gave in. "Just a puff," I said, holding two fingers upright for him to slot in the joint.

The first times I'd tried marijuana, back in college, I'd delighted in how my senses gained focus and warmth. But by junior year, my occasional marijuana indulgence took a bad turn. If someone was talking, I couldn't follow what they said. And when I started to speak, I'd lose track of my thought in mid-sentence. I'd been wary ever since. Still, as I took the first drag, I looked forward to the moment it hit me.

"So," Rob said, "Where are the two of you off to next?"

Caroline answered. "Illinois. We'll be going to Nick's grandmother's eightieth birthday celebration."

"Wow," Rob said to me. "The whole tribe?"

I nodded.

Samantha rendered her verdict. "Not exactly Provence."

"I'm looking forward to meeting Nick's family," Caroline said. "I hear so many great stories."

I nodded my appreciation at her.

Samantha said, "Hey, Caroline, I keep thinking I've seen you before. Have we met? I hate to think I've forgotten a face."

"I don't think so."

"I wonder why I have this nagging feeling."

Caroline paused to take a toke. "You may have seen me in ad posters."

"Oh, wow, you're the girl in those Stelstone's leotard ads. God, you're just as pretty. How old were you?"

"Fourteen. Fifteen. It went on for a couple of years." She exhaled and said, "Okay, shall we go for that walk now?"

The four of us clattered downstairs to the street. We walked over to Hicks, and eventually I realized we were drifting toward the Promenade. I had no idea how the decision was made, if anything as clear-cut as a decision had been made at all.

I have one last memory from that day. Caroline, Rob and Samantha were deep in conversation against the din of the BQE traffic below the Promenade. Unable to focus on what they were saying, I mentally floated into the vast June sky. I liked it up there, alone with the cirrus clouds.

The loss of innocence is a long, inevitable process that goes almost unnoticed until the day we suddenly discover it's gone. That afternoon stays in my memory as my last carefree moment before I ran up against the implacable truth that sometimes damage cannot be undone, that some consequences cannot be reversed.

PART 3

56

NEXT SUNDAY WAS ANOTHER EXQUISITE summer's day, but by early afternoon Caroline and I were still indoors. Saying she felt sluggish, she was reading in bed, while I puttered around in the living room. Her torpor reminded me of the morning in Paris when I'd gone out to the market on my own. It was hardly the first time I'd been concerned for her since we'd returned. Before our trip, she'd always been up before I left for work. These days she stayed in bed, either asleep or sounding fuzzy. Still, by the time I saw her in the evening, she'd be her former lively self.

She appeared at the bedroom door and proposed she make pancakes. Hugging her, I noted she was still wearing a night dress and robe, which made me feel overdressed in jeans and a T-shirt. I put up the table we used for meals, dominoes and cards and set out the silverware, while Caroline hummed in the kitchen. Two plates of nicely-crisped pancakes emerged.

When we'd finished, I returned the dishes to the kitchen. As the water was filling the dishpan, I scrubbed the counter, even though Caroline had more than once criticized my failure to get every spot. I'd thought of pointing out that if she was going to abandon her own apartment and live here rent-free, the least she could do was make up for what she deemed my inadequate house-keeping skills. But that voice in my head sounded mean, manipulative and, God forbid, sexist. At least I could tell myself she could be as difficult to live with as me. Our vacation had shown me I was no bargain.

Dishes done, I returned to the living room, where I folded and moved the table back against the wall. By now she was sprawled on the two-thirds couch with her legs dangling over one arm. I prodded her tummy. "Make room."

She pressed against the couch's back, and I sat in the small space she created.

"Thanks for brunch," I said.

"You're welcome."

She spoke in a beguiling way. I heard, anything else I can do for you?

"Shall we go out?" I said. "Even in here you can tell it's a beautiful day."

"Make love to me first."

"By all means." I stood and extended my hand. She took it and raised herself to a sitting position. Such an effort, I thought. She went into the bedroom.

"I'll get the diaphragm," I called through to her. "Is that okay?"

"You know where it is."

Without a night table in the tiny bedroom, she kept it in the living room dresser drawer I'd set aside for her. I rummaged through her things: a manila envelope stuffed with papers, what appeared to be a diary, an unopened pantyhose packet, a notebook, lipstick, underwear, a roll of mints, the velvet-lined box in which she kept her costume jewelry, some odds and ends I couldn't identify. So few possessions. And how spare the furnishings had been in her apartment.

Back in college and law school, I'd thought freedom hinged on frugality. In yielding to Caroline's urging to buy the new couch and coffee table, I'd conceded limits on that freedom. Yet she was as frugal today as I'd been then, if not more so. I'd been content to accept her the way she was, but sifting through her drawer, I had a sudden doubt. Was her being unmoored by possessions, an apartment and a career something that should worry me?

Ah, here was the diaphragm case. And the tube next to it must be Ortho. I closed the drawer and took both items into the bedroom. Holding up the tube and hoping she could see it in the room's dim light, I said, "Ortho?"

"You got it," she said, from the far side of the bed.

"It looks like you're about out."

She didn't respond.

I got undressed, leaving my clothes where they fell. On the bed I reached across to her. Night dress still, but no robe and no underwear.

I ran my hand along her body, down to her hips, along her bare legs. Going back along her legs, I pushed the hem of her night dress up to her waist. Now I drew slow circles around her tummy, hips and thighs. She loved to be teased that way, the circles revolving ever closer to their center. When at last they got there, her pelvis arched.

"It's been a while since I put this thing in."

My voice cut through a spell. I opened the case, then shifted position on the bed so that I could be sure to squeeze the right amount of Ortho and get it on the diaphragm's center. Nothing came out.

"It's empty," I said.

"I'll go to the pharmacy later."

"Did it just run out?"

She didn't answer.

"Caroline, did you use it the other night?"

"I don't think so."

"You've been using the diaphragm for a while now without the Ortho?"

"Yes."

"During our vacation?"

"Mm-hmm."

After making love in the protective way sanctioned by the Catholic Church in which she'd grown up, we held each other against a change we couldn't say aloud, never mind fathom.

57

"So, Nick . . ."

Whenever Ray uttered this phrase, I knew I was in for a big dose of scorn. The client was Dmitri Sanchez, whose appeal I'd been working on for a week.

Seeing he had my attention, Ray continued. "You're going to say the cops coerced his confession? But it's not like they beat him up."

"Lots of factors make for coercion. They made him wait a very long time, don't you think? Just imagine. You're unlucky enough to be walking by as a crime—"

"Oh, I like that," he interrupted. "The defendant just chanced to be there when the purse was snatched."

"It happens."

"Sure, Nick."

I plowed ahead. "The police detain you and make you wait for three hours. No one's saying anything to you."

"So get up and leave."

"You know your rights better than most," I said, "and you don't have the kind of record this guy does. He gets up and leaves, and the prosecution will claim it's just one more sign of guilt. Besides, a Latino in an Italian/Jewish neighborhood? It's a different story for us, Ray."

I said his name because I was irked by his use of mine whenever we got into a discussion like this.

"Don't take it so personally, Nick."

"I'm just saying I know how he must have felt."

"Oh, I know how he felt," Ray countered. "The whole time he was wondering, did I succeed in ditching that broad's purse where the cops won't find it?"

"Presumed guilty," I mocked.

"It would be more honest."

"Were the cops being honest when they waited until after they'd started interviewing him before declaring him a suspect and reading him his *Miranda* rights?"

"I guess that's going to be your argument, right, Nick? No matter what, cops have to play by the rules."

The telephone rang, making me jump. Caroline wasted no preliminaries. "I'm pregnant."

I tried to speak gently. "I know." It explained her morning inertia since our last days in Paris. She must have known, too.

"I needed to tell you," she said.

I now heard she was in the grip of emotion. "I'm glad you did."

She didn't respond. Conscious of Ray across the desk, I asked, "Can we talk tonight?"

"Sure. I just needed to tell you."

"What will you do now?"

"Wander."

"Wonder? Yes, it's a wondrous thing."

"Wander through Central Park, I think."

"Take good care of yourself, Caroline."

Hanging up, I silently cursed myself for revealing her identity.

"Is she okay?" Ray asked.

"Just a little upset."

Belying my words, I stayed quiet as I absorbed her news, her tone, glimmers of the implications for her, for me. I reached for the phone to tell her I was on my way and to stay home and wait. But I pulled my hand back.

I said to Ray, "You were asking if I'm going to hammer home on the delayed *Miranda* warnings. You bet I am."

After he left, I emerged into a deserted hallway to go stand at a sink in the men's room and run hot water over my hands. Had I been home, I would have taken a long, hot shower. I needed the reassurance of warmth. Her pregnancy was no accident; she'd allowed it to happen, and yet I was touched that she'd want a child by me. I was glad I'd held her after discovering the empty Ortho tube.

Girl or boy? I liked the idea of a girl. But I was thinking in terms of "he." I must be imagining the baby as an extension of me, improved by Caroline's sweet nature. But no, the child would be equal parts Caroline and me. I was just used to "he."

There'd be those packed first years when the baby governed our lives. Then the years of filial loyalty and parental awe. I'd once been that loyal child. My teenage years had been skewed because I'd been more dependent than most on my parents. But later, in my own way, I'd rebelled, and my parents, in their way, had rebelled against the new, frustrated, assertive me.

Caroline and I would remind each other what we'd been like as adolescents and what we'd learned since. We'd accept his need to distance himself and impose ourselves only when his future required it. When he became an adult, we wouldn't interfere at all, but wait to be asked. We'd take pleasure in our young grownup's first attempts to cope with the world on his own terms. Or hers.

Yet all that was in the future. Today, I was still trying to establish my career. Practicing law was time-consuming and exhausting. And I aspired to write. I'd hardly shown the discipline it required, but it had been a dream for so long that it had become part of me. How could I do it all and raise a child with Caroline? I couldn't sacrifice my career, the source of our income. I'd have to give up the dream—perhaps a mere fantasy—of writing.

I turned off the hot water, pulled a paper towel from the dispenser, dried my hands, tossed the towel into the trash and set off back down the empty hall to my room. But though I had no appetite, I felt a despondency that I suspected was exaggerated by hunger. I switched direction for the elevators and went to buy lunch from the corner sandwich shop.

Back at my desk, I turned to my deepest misgiving about taking on fatherhood. What if our child inherited my disability? How would his losing—or even never having—vision influence the way I raised him? Would I yield to empathy and become overly indulgent? Or would I treat him harshly to ensure I didn't?

In all this mental ferment, I hadn't given any thought to Caroline. Here I was, eating without tasting at my desk, and there she was, wandering aimlessly. This was what I'd long feared. I was all about me. I should have raced home the moment she told me.

A knock on the door. A cheerful "Hi."

I pushed my public self to the surface. "How are you, Beth?"

58

I HAVE NO CLEAR MEMORY of how things went that evening. I don't think we talked about her pregnancy. I'm certain we didn't talk about what we hoped for in a baby and the joy it would bring us. I'm also sure I held her, but equally sure that it wasn't enough.

The week continued. Summer's early fitful stops and starts gave way to uninterrupted heat outside and air-conditioning indoors. Caroline spent at least one evening with her parents, but mostly stayed at my place. I have no memory of our times together; only my attempts to sort through my feelings.

A new objection to fatherhood came to me. Even if I didn't pass along my genetic defect, how could I do the job of father? How could I help with homework if a textbook had no audio or other accessible version? With my braille reading speed too slow for anything but notes, would listening with our child to a recorded bedtime story be good enough? I wouldn't be able to play ball or even watch a Little League game. And how could I credibly tell our child, "You're looking good, kid," and have it received as anything more than butchered Bogart?

Then there was the sheer physicality of caring for a baby. I thought about it over another lunch at my desk. There'd be cleaning up vomit, his mouth spraying milk, the grim business of toilet training. There'd be that cute baby paraphernalia, from simple toys to tiny clothes. I hated cuteness, especially in miniature and with bodily fluids all over it. I'd heard fatherhood changed attitudes toward such things, but that lunchtime I couldn't finish my sandwich.

Commuting home, I thought about Caroline's unhappiness over the leotard ads. Her girlhood had left marks that were bound to influence how she raised her child, just as my past would influence mine. I'd predict her gentle nature would lean her toward indulgence, but there was no way of knowing about either of us.

The decision to have a child required temporary insanity. No sane person took on risk that couldn't be quantified. Who knew what sort of being would emerge from the birth canal? Who could say how that little person would develop? Besides, hard enough as it was to live through the vagaries of an indifferent, dangerous world, to have a child could be to set yourself up to endure the suffering of someone you loved and felt responsible for.

Analysis paralysis. Talk about disability. No decision could withstand so much inspection.

Except Jack's had. After all his waffling, he'd gone ahead with marriage and planned to start a family. I'd felt happy for him and hadn't been able to understand his doubts.

But our circumstances were different. Elaine and he had agreed on his moving in before he went ahead, and they got married before Elaine became pregnant. Caroline and I were forever doing things backwards.

By week's end I knew what my decision would be if it were mine alone to make. Still, I kept it to myself. Let Caroline figure out what was right, or best, for her in her own time. Maybe we'd arrive at the same place. If not? Well . . .

After dinner Saturday evening, Caroline turned the television on, but nothing was worth watching and she told me to turn it off. After a week of mental turmoil, I felt at peace. Things needed to be said, but I wasn't impatient to say them. Just the opposite. The longer I lived in this state, where nothing on the surface had changed and I had Caroline at my side, the happier I was.

In the quiet, she said, "I think I should have an abortion. What do you think?"

59

NEXT SATURDAY MORNING WE WENT to a Planned Parenthood clinic in the Village. To my relief, we weren't subjected to a gauntlet of picketers. At the time, anti-abortion activism hadn't yet degraded to the murder of abortion providers, but noisy protests were in the news.

In the waiting room, Caroline appeared calm. From time to time we held hands, partly for comfort, partly to communicate in ways others would with glances. A woman appeared and asked us to accompany her. The three of us sat in a small office as she guided Caroline through her options and discussed physiological consequences I'd never experience.

The subjects, like the setting, were lopsidedly feminine. How could they not be? Everything we needed to accomplish from here on could be done without me. With backlogged sperm banks, men could be cut out of the propagation process completely, exactly the irrelevance that men in the so-called pro-life movement were said to fear.

It was a resentment I could understand. Two years earlier a girlfriend had said that if she became pregnant, she would have an abortion without telling me. I'd been indignant. How could she exclude me from such a momentous decision, even though we both said we weren't ready to raise a child? I was glad there was no such divide between Caroline and me.

Just when I'd accepted that my role here was to listen, the counselor asked me about my feelings. I said I thought abortion best, but that the ultimate decision was Caroline's. Later, I'd wonder if my endorsement of her autonomy had really been abdication of responsibility.

The counselor showed us into another tiny room with a hospital table, alongside which was a space that seemed hardly wide enough for anyone to stand and perform the operation, if this was where the procedure was done. Saying I could stay until staff was ready, the counselor left and closed the door. I helped Caroline arrange her clothes on the back of the room's only chair, and she put her underwear in her purse. Wearing one of those demeaning, flimsy hospital gowns, she lay down. I squeezed her hand, then sat in the chair at the foot of the table.

I couldn't think of anything to talk about. The news we'd heard that morning? Our plans for the coming week? Everything outside this room felt unreal.

She sat up. "I can't do this. I can't do this." She leapt down from the table, retrieved her purse, grabbed the clothes from behind me and dressed.

"Let's go," she said. "I need to go."

I tried to hug her, but she was already in motion and we collided in the tiny space. She made a halfhearted effort to reciprocate before distress propelled her forward again.

She all but dragged me through the clinic's short corridors to the street. No one tried to stop us.

In my living room, her sobs came in violent bursts. All the phrases of comfort that came to me felt hollow. Holding her while she was in such distress, powerless to help, brimming tears I'd trained myself not to shed, I thought I'd break in two.

At last exhausted, she squeezed my hand. "I need to sleep."

I went with her to the bedroom, where we lay together on top of the covers. She turned to face the windows, and I molded to her back with my arm around her.

60

I'D GOTTEN WHERE I HAD in life by being decisive, and so for me, Caroline's flight from the clinic only prolonged the agony. But I'd never had to confront a decision that carried so much moral weight, on top of the emotional and physical toll all surgery exacts.

I had to leave the next step to her. Whatever it was, however long it took, I knew I must neither judge nor try to influence her.

To make sure I didn't, I threw myself into work with even greater zeal. For two whole days, we didn't call or see each other. Was she at her parents'? Probably. But she could also have been staying with one of her friends.

Then once again we were in my living room. I find myself wondering how she got there. Had she come by cab? The idea that she'd called for help or that I'd gone out to pay the driver doesn't fit. There'd always been an implicit joke behind her playing damsel in distress, when in truth she was self-reliant. This time the joke wouldn't have been funny.

We sat with mugs of Postum before us on the coffee table. She'd sworn off alcohol in deference to her pregnancy, and in support, I'd done the same. She told me a friend of hers had recommended a gynecologist on Park Avenue who performed abortions. Would I come with her next Wednesday?

"I'm sorry," she added, "it will mean taking a day off work."

"Work doesn't matter," I muttered.

Just after lunch hour on Wednesday, we emerged from the subway a block over from Park. Venturing through the city when the rest of the world was on the job usually made me feel like a happy truant, but today recollection of that *schadenfreude* grated against my anguish. West to Park and south two blocks. Curious how clear the route is in my head, and yet I don't recall what the cross-streets were or which station we got off at. I do remember the humidity had broken. It was a warm, pleasant day, reminiscent of Provence.

The doctor's ground-floor office was spacious and the furniture several levels removed from Planned Parenthood's plain fare. The receptionist was soft-spoken, as you'd expect at places that serve the well-to-do. I signed a check. Caroline said we were the only two people waiting.

When the doctor was ready, Caroline asked the receptionist if I could go with her. "No," the receptionist said, "that won't be necessary." I squeezed Caroline's arm. She didn't respond. In that instant, she made the transition. She was on her own.

After she'd gone through an inner door, I had a terrible thought. Hadn't I as much as told her I'd want nothing to do with the child if she carried it to term?

I imagined rushing past the receptionist and calling out, "Marry me. Let's have the child."

But I stayed seated. I didn't even feel free to get up and pace, not with the receptionist there. Walking back and forth, up and down, might have taken me to the door behind which Caroline was talking through her decision with the doctor.

Or maybe she was right now being anesthetized. Maybe he'd already begun the procedure. The wait was interminable. All I heard was the hum that stretches out time in every office.

The door to the interior rooms opened. Reaching my chair, Caroline said, "We're leaving."

I followed her to the exit. I imagined the receptionist staring at us and Caroline staring ahead without seeing. When we stepped outside, she gave me her arm and we set off along Park Avenue.

I said, "You couldn't go through with it?"

"I'm sorry, Nick."

"What happens now?"

She didn't answer.

My bottled-up frustration burst out. "You can't keep putting off the inevitable. We've agreed we can't have a child, not now."

"It's that simple, isn't it?"

"Basically, it is. I feel for you, Caroline, but—"

"Oh, thank you for your sympathy."

"I don't mean it like that."

"I should be an adult and get it over with, right?"

"I mean . . ." I trailed off.

We'd reached the cross-street where we'd turn for Lexington and the subway. I became aware again of how pleasant the day was, and midtown was eerily quiet. Despite a steady stream of traffic, there were no sirens, no planes or helicopters overhead, no shouts from delivery guys, doormen or bicycle messengers.

"You mean," she snapped, "I shouldn't make such a fucking stupid fuss over a little fetus who doesn't have a chance in this world anyway. Right?"

I let go of her arm and stood still. "I know we're not talking about something trivial. But I am talking about a decision you've made and the two times you gave in to your fear."

"My fear? My fear or my conscience? My fear or my humanity?"

"Why bring humanity into this?"

"Because it's about a human being, isn't it? It's about a little person who can't look after itself, who can't stand up for itself."

"Emphasis on 'itself.' It isn't human yet. It's closer to being a figment of our imagination than a fully-realized human being."

"'Emphasis on,'" she derided. "Maybe I'm too stupid for you."

I yelled at the top of my lungs. "I can't keep doing this."

She yelled the words back at me. "*I* can't keep doing this."

I lowered my voice. "Then go back and get it over with."

"Too late. I was the last appointment."

"What a great excuse."

"You call it an excuse?"

"That's exactly what I call it."

She howled like a tortured animal.

"I can't deal with this," I said.

"I can't deal with this," she wailed.

Long since trained to note traffic patterns, I'd taken in that vehicles had just started moving on the cross-street. I turned my back on her and dashed across the three downtown lanes of Park Avenue. When I reached the median strip, cars were still going along the cross-street, so I stepped into Park Avenue's uptown side. Unless one of the waiting drivers was a psycho, they'd wait until I reached the curb even if the light changed.

I propelled onward to the subway station, down the steps, through the turnstiles, onto the platform, all the while hoping Caroline wouldn't catch up and hoping she would. The train came right away, and I got on for the forty-minute trek back to Brooklyn.

61

WHY DIDN'T I BACK DOWN on Park Avenue? I know now that withheld feelings demand expression. But when it comes to self-justification, ordinary logic breaks down. Explanation doesn't equal vindication. One plus one doesn't add up to two. One plus one can add up to a mere fraction, even a negative.

When contrition inevitably crashed over me that night, I realized I still hadn't obtained the number for the Sullivan Street bar. The only other place I knew she might be was Riverdale. I called and, putting on a relaxed voice, asked for her, but her mother told me she wasn't there. I'm pretty sure she was telling the truth. If not, she was as good a dissembler as I fancied I was being.

What did Caroline go through that evening and night? Even thirty years later, the pain of imagining is still raw. I have no idea whom she saw, what she did or where she stayed.

She didn't call for three whole days. When she finally did, I was at the office.

"Hold on." I covered the phone and asked Ray to leave. He hurried out and closed the door.

I said, "I'm so sorry, Caroline."

"I know."

"This is a terrible time for you."

"And for you."

"I made that clear, I know, but what I'm going through is nothing compared to you."

She didn't disagree. She said simply, "Are you willing to see me tonight?"

"Of course. Caroline, you've got to give me phone numbers where I can reach you when you aren't with your parents."

"I don't always know where that will be."

"So give them all to me. Tonight."

"Okay," she said, but in a way that said she wouldn't, or couldn't, but that she didn't want to argue about that or anything else anymore.

"I'll be there around seven," she said. "Is that okay?"

"Of course it's okay."

"Bye." She hung up.

I willed myself not to burst out crying. It would have been from overwhelming guilt for having deserted her on Park Avenue, from relief that she'd come back, from distress at the changes I sensed in her, for what she was suffering and for what I was. When I stood up, my heart was hammering. I punched my chest, then rested a hand on the desk to steady myself.

At last I went around to reception, where Ray was waiting, and told him we could get back to work. Belying his attack-dog personality, he acted as if nothing unusual had happened.

That night Caroline told me she'd rescheduled with the Park Avenue doctor for the next day. "I don't need you to take the whole day off, but can you meet me there at three?"

The doctor's office would be easy to find. It was close to a convenient subway line, it wasn't on the upper floor of some complicated building, and the office door was the first I would encounter as I walked from the southwest corner of that Park Avenue intersection. Caroline knew my methods well enough to have taken it all into account.

62

A MINUTE BEFORE THREE THE next afternoon, I pushed open the door to the gynecologist's office. The receptionist said, "Ms. Sedlak is in with the doctor. You can wait on the couch over there."

"Over there" are meaningless words if you can't see, but I had the room's layout in my head and I easily found a chair.

So, Caroline had told me to come after her appointment time. I found myself smiling at her cunning. My role today would be to help her get home. But she wasn't just looking after herself. She could have had one of her women friends accompany her, but she'd known I'd have been devastated if she'd gone through with the abortion without me, so devastated that our relationship might not survive. It didn't mean she'd eventually want it to, but for now, she'd keep me involved, if in the least disruptive way possible.

The receptionist surprised me by wishing me "Goodnight." The next thing I knew, she'd gone out to the street. Once again, Caroline must have been the last patient.

I tried to stop myself from checking my watch after the third time I became convinced the minute hand was stuck. Was the operation happening now? Surely the doctor wasn't talking Caroline through the decision again.

The inner door opened. "Mr. Coleman?" A man's voice. "You can see Ms. Sedlak now."

I assumed this was the doctor. Caroline had told me he'd had no female assistant the last time. It was unethical, I said, but she said he didn't worry her—not in that way. Still, I felt hostile toward him.

I rose and started in his direction, then negotiated my way around a chair and the receptionist's desk until my cane touched the open door.

"This way," he said.

Down a short corridor, he opened another door, and I went in.

"I'll be in reception," he called inside.

Caroline replied, "I won't be long."

The door closed behind me. I stepped toward her and bumped up against another of those hospital tables. I held out my hand. She gave it a light squeeze.

Easing down from the table, she commented, "A little dizzy. Where did I put my purse?"

I happened to have brushed against it on a shelf by the door. It had brought on a wave of sadness. More than one woman had told me that no matter how messy a purse might be inside, it was her mess, part of her identity. Handing Caroline's purse to her, I silently made a wish that she recover soon and return to the Caroline of before.

Finished dressing, she opened the door and I took her arm down the hallway to reception.

"Feeling okay?" the doctor asked.

"Yes. Any more papers to sign?"

"All done. You can go home now."

We headed for the exit. Although it was I holding her arm, I was using the contact to support her and to sense for weakness. I kept my cane extended before me.

On the sidewalk, she said, "A woman was with him in reception.

I don't think she's a staff person or patient."

We speculated the woman was a date. Weird that she would meet a gynecologist at his office for an evening out. It could only remind her that he must know hundreds of women literally inside-out. Not an especially helpful thought as I asked myself how to get Caroline home.

"Look for a cab," I said.

"I'll be okay on the subway."

New York's notorious four o'clock shift change makes late afternoon a bad time to find a cab, but she promised to look out for one as we walked to the station. Maybe she did. Either way, we ended up taking the subway.

63

OTHER EVENTS FROM THOSE WEEKS are blotted out from memory, but when I page through my mental calendar, I realize that in the midst of it all I applied to the Environmental Protection Agency. A law school classmate with contacts there had urged me to.

Before the Alliance, I hadn't been one to describe someone as "normal" or "neurotic," but I'd come around to agreeing with Jack that the Alliance's supervisors were neurotic. By contrast, the EPA's interviewers were normal. My interactions with them were open and amicable. In time I might like or not like them, and vice versa, but I'd see the reasons why in terms of personality rather than weirdness.

"Why environmental law?" an EPA lawyer named Joanna Leavitt asked at my first interview.

"For me," I replied, "the law provides two satisfactions. One is puzzle-solving. How do I organize a slew of facts into a coherent case? I'd be doing that in any law office. The other is helping people. I hope that doesn't sound too soft. Right now I'm trying to help people most of the world wants nothing to do with. Each of those people has a name. The EPA's work benefits whole communities, but I imagine I could give them names, too."

"Sure you could," Joanna responded. "The whole world has heard of Love Canal."

I still had reservations. Human behavior intrigued me, and I doubted it had any bearing in environmental law. In the eighties, courts applied a strict liability standard to polluters. All the feds had to do was prove a connection, what the law called a nexus, between the company and the environmental damage. No doubt I'd mull over the motives of the people who ran the companies that polluted the area around them with disregard for the people who lived there, but intent would be irrelevant to my work. By contrast, in most criminal cases, intent was fundamental.

This difference between the Alliance's and the EPA's work may have explained the contrast in their managerial personalities. Preoccupation with human behavior pretty much guaranteed neurosis.

Of course, this implies that I, too, was neurotic—nutty, crazy, whacked. I hadn't allowed for the possibility before moving to New York. I'd grown up in Illinois and Connecticut. It was New Yorkers who so relentlessly examined their feelings and motivations that they made themselves mad. Woody Allen proclaimed it. However, if it hadn't already been obvious, the way I'd responded to Caroline's pregnancy made my own neurosis inescapable.

Meanwhile, an Alliance supervisor approved a brief of mine with hardly a revision. The timing was fortuitous because the EPA had asked to see a writing sample. I'd decided beforehand to give them a copy of one of my Alliance briefs and admit that it had been heavily edited. Now I could give them one I could legitimately claim as my own.

Even so, when I called Joanna Leavitt to alert her it was in the mail, I told her, "It's almost all my own product, but you should know our work is reviewed here."

"We assume every writing sample we see has been edited. Hardly anyone admits it, though. I appreciate your honesty."

How refreshing. How not neurotic.

Being government, especially the federal government, the hiring process would take months, so any job offer was far off in the future, if it was to come at all. But the prospect alone made me feel a window had been opened.

64

WITH ALL THE TATTERS OF disappointment blowing at us, I saw less of Caroline, whom I assumed was staying mostly at her parents'. I say "disappointment" because I believed she was disappointed in me. Nothing is more demoralizing than sensing the woman in your life has come to think less of you. Unless it's being disappointed in yourself, which I was.

My feelings for her became an undercurrent of pain that merged with the muffled roar of the BQE through my windows. Sublimating worries that I could do little to resolve, I lapsed back into habits I'd developed before she moved in. My neighbor Jenny, who complained I'd neglected her, nevertheless resumed accompanying me to the store. She still held forth on the healthiness of the food items I considered, but she was flexible about time, going on a Saturday instead of a Sunday morning if I expected Caroline to stay over Saturday night. These days Caroline rarely stayed two nights in a row.

I went out on my own to dinner with Jack and Elaine. Rob came over to listen to my more obscure records and interspersed music with his ideas for how to use the law to help the environment. My plans to switch to the EPA intrigued him, even though his distrust of government dissuaded him from making a similar move.

On my way to work one morning when Caroline had stayed over, I stopped in the bedroom to whisper, "Bye." She was awake.

"I think I'll stay here today," she said.

That evening, when I got home dripping perspiration from the sweltering streets and the packed subway, Caroline called, "Hi," from the couch.

I mussed her hair as I passed her. "It's nice to come home to find the air-conditioner on. But I still need a shower. It'll only take a minute."

"Be my guest," she said, her head in what I assumed was a book.

I changed into a bathrobe and passed by her again on my way to the bathroom. "What are you reading?"

"Some women's magazine. Just turning pages basically." She turned a page.

After my shower, I toweled myself off as much as I could in the bathroom, but the air was even soggier in there. I put the robe back on and passed Caroline yet again as she continued turning pages. I finished drying in the bedroom and put on a T-shirt and chinos. At last I felt civilized enough to sit next to her.

"What are we doing about dinner?" I said.

"Oh, I don't know. I'm not really hungry."

"I am."

This wasn't the first time I'd been ready to eat at the normal time and she wasn't, but usually she came around to joining me. This time she stayed quiet.

"You're really not hungry? Not even a little?" I said.

"Uh-uh." She turned more pages.

I thought about my options. There might be leftovers to heat up.

I could have a frozen meal that I'd bought with Jenny last Saturday morning. Or I could order in, which I didn't like to, or go out.

"If I go to the corner Greek place on Clark, will you come and keep me company?"

"I'm not sure I feel up to going out."

"Is something wrong?"

"I took some pills before you got home."

"Pills?" I kept my voice calm. "What kind? How many?"

"Aspirin. Maybe a couple of other things."

"A couple of other things?"

"I'm sorry, Nick, but I finished off the aspirin."

"It was nearly full. I just bought it."

She didn't reply.

"You didn't have any alcohol, did you?"

"A little, I think." Her words were becoming slurred.

"Caroline, how long before I got home?"

"I don't know. A few minutes."

The magazine slipped onto the coffee table, then the floor. She tilted away from me. I held her arm to save her from falling. No protest.

I arranged her on her back and placed a cushion under her head. Then I dialed Jenny's number.

"Jenny, it looks like Caroline's taken an overdose. I'm not sure I can get her to the emergency room on my own."

"Call a car service. I'll be right down."

"The door will be unlocked."

The dispatcher told me ten minutes. The hospital was only a few blocks away and the car service was reliable, so I didn't explain the urgency. He might have told me to get an ambulance, which would create all kinds of complications.

I grabbed all the cash I kept in a box for emergencies and

hurried to unlock the front door before returning to Caroline. I spoke her name. She responded with a drowsy mumble. I kneeled down to be close to her ear. "Caroline, don't fall asleep."

I just made out her reply. "But I want to."

I repeated her name, threaded my arm under her shoulders and lifted her partway.

"You're hurting me," she complained, but in a way that told me I was making her uncomfortable, not causing real pain.

I rocked her shoulders side to side, not roughly but also not gently, to keep her from dozing off. That's how Jenny found us when she rushed into the apartment.

"Is the car on the way?" she said.

"Ten minutes. By now more like five. We have to get her to the sidewalk."

"Here." She pulled the coffee table away from the couch. "Let's get her standing. At least she's dressed to go out."

Noting that last point for later, I lifted Caroline from the back, while Jenny eased her legs off the couch and her feet onto the floor.

"Why are you doing this to me?" Caroline muttered.

Jenny said, "We're going to take you for a short ride."

"Oh, hi, Jenny." Caroline's head rose, as if she were focusing.

"Try to stand," I said to her.

To my relief, she made the effort. I tried to rise with her while supporting her back and middle. Jenny got her hands in there, too. One way or the other, Caroline became vertical.

"My purse," Caroline said.

Jenny said, "I see it, Nick." She crossed the room to retrieve it.

"Would you also get all the drug containers you can find in the bathroom?" I said. "There are shopping bags under the kitchen sink."

I guided Caroline toward the front door. Jenny jumped ahead

and opened it, and Caroline and I crossed the threshold.

Jenny closed the door. "Got your keys?"

I handed them to her and told her just to do the top lock. The second key she tried was the one. She handed them back.

There'd be no hiding Caroline's condition from the doorman and anyone else who happened to be in the lobby. At least Mike wasn't on duty this evening.

I supported Caroline by one arm and Jenny did by the other. Caroline cooperated by putting one foot in front of the next. Her head was bowed and she muttered incomprehensibly.

As we turned the corner from the hallway, the doorman called, "Hi."

I said, "Caroline isn't feeling well, so we're taking her to the emergency room. Is there a car waiting?"

"Yeah, I think there is." The direction of his voice told me he'd looked outside. Then he said, "Can I help there?"

We were at the two steps descending from the hallway to the lobby.

Jenny replied, "We're okay. Right, Caroline?"

Caroline took the steps without tripping. I guessed it helped that she was looking down.

We escorted her to the car. I maneuvered her onto the back seat, and then Jenny kept her there as I raced around to the other side. I climbed in and reached across to pull Caroline toward me as Jenny pushed.

"She's in all the way now," Jenny said, and closed the door. She got in next to the driver. As the car shot off, I held Caroline to save her from jarring her head.

"I'm okay, really," she muttered.

"We're just going to make sure."

Long Island College Hospital's emergency room was

morgue-quiet when we entered. We stood in front of a glassed-in reception desk as Jenny explained the gravity of the problem.

"Fill out the forms," the woman said. "Is there insurance?"

"I'll pay in cash," I said.

Soon after Jenny took the completed forms to the receptionist, we were admitted inside. The doctor asked me what Caroline had ingested. Jenny handed her the drug containers. Did Caroline have a history of suicide attempts? Not to my knowledge.

Jenny and I were told to return to the waiting area. I considered urging her to go home, though she showed no signs of impatience. But the emergency room was a bad situation for me. I was unfamiliar with the layout, and I didn't know the people. I couldn't afford to miss my name being called or any other signs of what was happening.

Somewhere between ten and eleven, we were summoned back inside. Caroline was talking coherently and even cheerfully.

"Hey," I called out, by way of greeting.

"They've got me all fixed up," she called back.

"You look great," Jenny said.

The doctor told us, "We pumped her stomach and got everything out."

"So, what's next?" I asked.

Jenny said, "I expect they'll be keeping her overnight."

But the doctor surprised us. "That won't be necessary. She told us she has a therapist and promised to see him tomorrow. I'd like to keep her here for observation for another hour, just in case." She turned to me. "You're sure this is her first attempt?"

This time I was firm. "Positive."

Caroline's great capacity to communicate well-being must have won the doctor over even in these dire circumstances. Her lack of insurance no doubt contributed. I was happy to do my part to spare her a night or more in a hospital.

Fifteen minutes before Caroline was due to be discharged, Jenny called the car service from a public phone. When the car drew up, the three of us were waiting on the sidewalk. I cradled Caroline's arm, but she was able to stand without help.

As we entered our building's lobby, the doorman said, "Is she okay?"

Caroline said a clear, "Haven't felt better in weeks."

Jenny said, "Looks like you'll both be okay from here." She took the elevator to her floor.

In bed that night, Caroline talked a mile a minute. I have no recollection of what she said, except that she sounded glad to be alive. Eventually, she slowed down and fell asleep.

65

I SET THE ALARM FOR the usual time, but when it went off, I called the office to say I wouldn't be in until the afternoon. Then I called Ray to save him a wasted trip and went back to bed. Caroline had stirred when the alarm went off but shifted to her other side. I could tell she was aware of me returning, but once again she fell asleep. I lay there in thought, dozing off and on. Eventually I got up and made coffee.

Passing me on her way to the bathroom, Caroline said, "Make some of that awful stuff for me, too."

We sat together as the coffee dispersed the cobwebs in my brain and, I hoped, hers.

"So," I said, "you have a therapist. I'm surprised you haven't mentioned it before."

"Bart Goodweather, in the West 90s. He makes time for me whenever I need him."

No wonder he's a therapist, I thought, with a name like that. I said, "Is he a psychiatrist, psychologist, M.S.W.?"

"A Ph.D. psychologist."

"Are you going to see him today?"

"Soon as I've finished this coffee, I'll call his office."

"Has this happened before, Caroline?"

"Have I had a drug overdose before? No, thank God. After having my stomach pumped, I wouldn't do it to myself again."

"You got really unhappy yesterday."

"I've been in and out."

"Since you had the abortion?"

"I guess."

"Were you ever in and out like this before?"

"I get unhappy, sure. Everyone does."

"Not everyone gets so unhappy that they swallow a container of aspirin."

"Oh, I don't know, Nick."

"You sound great this morning. I want to be able to help when you aren't feeling so well. Can you tell me if you've tried to end your life before? I told the doctor last night you hadn't."

"Sure I've thought about killing myself. Haven't you?"

"Thought about it. Never acted on it."

"Me, too, basically. I'm too terrified of what lies beyond—you know, hell—that sort of thing."

"I've never really thought about you and religion, except I know you're Catholic. I'm not even sure how I know that."

"We've never talked about religion. Did you know the Catholic Church won't bury people who kill themselves in sacred ground? They didn't used to, anyway. Sure sign they want them to go to hell."

We'd strayed from the subject, which I assumed was her

intention. I decided to be blunt.

"Forgive me, Caroline, but you've never made an attempt on your life before?"

"The answer's no, never. Okay, can I call Goodweather now?"

"No one's stopping you."

Thankfully, she didn't pick up on my reflexive sarcasm.

Goodweather agreed to see her at four. She announced she would go shopping beforehand. I asked her to let me go with her, but she refused, saying she needed time to herself.

"But you'll come back here after Goodweather, right?"

"Let's see how I feel."

We left together to take the subway into Manhattan. My stop was first. Stepping off the train, I said, *"A toute a l'heure."* How I hated to leave her.

As soon as I reached my desk, I called Rob's extension. "Can we have lunch together?"

Rob and I had a different lunch place from the one Jack and I used to frequent. Up on Nassau Street, it lacked the personal touch of the waitress Jack and I had befriended, and it had a jukebox. But the food tasted better and most of the time we could hear each other.

"Rob," I said, after we'd placed our orders, "I want to tell you something involving Caroline. Do you think you can listen without getting judgmental? I don't mean don't say anything. I just don't want you to think less of her. Of me, that's fine. I'll take my chances."

It was an impossible request. Without knowing what I was going to tell him, he could hardly guarantee how he'd react.

"I'm my own worst judge," he said. "Everyone else gets a free pass."

Sandwiches and cups of coffee arrived. Should I start at the beginning, wherever that was? But unless he knew about the culmination, the rest wouldn't mean anything.

"Last night Caroline took a drug overdose."

He didn't respond right away, which communicated his shock more than words could have. Finally, he said, "Where's she now?"

"They didn't keep her, if that's what you're asking. They released her after pumping her stomach and making sure she was physically okay."

"I'm surprised."

"Me, too, but I'm glad. In high school, I worked for a suicide intervention program. The lessons I learned there helped last night, but I don't know what to do now."

I outlined what had led up to it: her discovery that she was pregnant when we returned from France, her twice running off from abortion centers, her finally going through with it. Telling even the abbreviated version was draining. My chin was resting on my templed fingers by the time I finished.

He said, "I had no idea. I can't believe you didn't say anything."

"I guess it didn't feel real. Must be my way of handling guilt."

"Guilt?"

"If not for me, I don't know if she'd have gone ahead with the abortion."

"Does she have a shrink?"

"She made an appointment with him for this afternoon. I'm not sure how much good he is. Wouldn't she have called him in a crisis if she thought well enough of him? She didn't yesterday."

"Nick, how about finding your own therapist for advice on how to help her?"

"And spend the first six months sorting through my childhood? I would if I thought it would help, but they don't like giving advice about other people. Something else I learned from the suicide intervention program."

66

SHE CALLED THAT EVENING FROM Sullivan Street. I'd been unable to do anything to distract myself. I'd start reading, but discover I hadn't taken anything in. Music irritated me. Worry mingled with guilt, and both mingled with a sense of powerlessness.

At least I'd convinced myself the overdose was more a cry for help than a real suicide attempt. It surely explained why she'd been dressed to go out.

When the phone rang, I leapt at it. In the earpiece I heard the background noise of dozens of loud conversations.

"How are you doing?" I said before the caller had spoken.

"I'm fine." Yes, it was Caroline.

"Are you on your way?"

"I'm going to be here late, so I'll crash here in the Village."

I told myself not to argue. "Did you see your therapist?"

"Yeah."

"How did it go?"

"He was supportive, like always. Listen, I can barely hear over this noise. I just didn't want you worrying."

"I appreciate it, Caroline."

I heard the formality of my words.

"Talk to you tomorrow." She hung up, cutting off the cheerful background noise.

67

DURING THE TEN OR SO days following Caroline's overdose, we may have seen each other once—no more than twice. For the most part she stayed aloof. Then, on a Saturday, she called.

"I'm going to be hospitalized for a while. My parents contacted a doctor they know, and he wants me to go in for observation for ten days."

"A psychiatric hospital?"

"Some exclusive place on the Upper East Side."

"When are you being admitted?"

"This afternoon. It was arranged in a hurry."

"You don't sound worried."

"I'm not."

"Will you be allowed to see visitors?"

"They're discouraging it."

"Even me?"

I saw my question betrayed that, once again, I was hurt, and so did she.

In a sympathetic tone, she said, "For now, Nick."

I kept my voice under control. "Will you let me know what's going on?"

"I'll call as soon as I can."

I phoned my parents.

"Caroline's going into the hospital. A psychiatric hospital."

"Really?" Mom said. "She sounded so—I don't know—happy when we met her."

"She's a cheerful person."

"I don't get it," Mom said.

"She took a drug overdose the week before last."

Mom gasped.

"Wasn't she hospitalized then?" Dad said.

"Jenny and I took her to the E.R., but they released her that night."

"What brought this all on?" Mom said. "Does anyone know?"

"She had an abortion."

Silence. Then Dad said, "There weren't any complications, were there?"

"No."

"She must be in anguish," Mom said.

How little I knew Mom. Without thinking, I'd expected her to take a hard line. I felt something like gratitude to her for not judging Caroline or, for that matter, me.

"Is there anything we can do?" Dad said.

"I don't think so. Her parents have taken charge. I'm supposed to lie low. I don't know how long this will go on or how different things will be."

"Are you still, you know, together?" Mom said.

"I hope so. I want to be."

Dad said, "Come up for the weekend. Next weekend, I mean."

"Or today," Mom said.

"Not today. I'm exhausted. Maybe next weekend."

I came around to being thankful that at least I didn't have to worry about Caroline's safety.

PART 4

68

RAY WAS AS CAUGHT UP as I was in the transcript we were reading when the phone rang. I waited for him to finish a sentence before picking up the receiver, at which he dropped the file on the desk with a decisive thud. He knew the routine by now.

"Hi," Caroline said.

I turned my chair toward the window. I couldn't ask Ray to leave every time she called, but at least he didn't have to see my expressions.

"How's it going?" I said.

"I made the bed, had some cereal and read an Alice Munro story."

As long as she wasn't reading Anne Sexton or Sylvia Plath, I thought. She would be sitting at the telephone next to my stereo. I pictured her sprawled in the armchair, one piece of inherited furniture she'd approved, with her shapely calves extending from a knee-length robe.

I said, "Tell me about Munro's story."

She gave me a brief synopsis and talked about what she'd gotten out of it. I enjoyed her thought process. I wished we could have these discussions in the evening, when I wasn't feeling pressured by work, but by then her mental energy was low.

"Tell me about your morning," she said.

"We started a new case. Our client allegedly robbed a pharmacy—"

Ray, not one to pretend he couldn't overhear, said behind me, "No allegedly about it. He was tried and convicted by a jury."

"Is that Ray?"

"Of course it's Ray. Do you know anyone else who makes such simplistic assumptions?"

"Tell him hi."

I turned half around and said, "Caroline says hi."

"Hi there, Caroline," he called.

I turned back to the window, hoping my face wasn't reflected in it.

"Anyway, it's the middle of winter—January—two years ago. The client is seen getting in his car three doors down from the pharmacy. The police spot his vehicle right away and follow him. He heads for the Long Island Expressway and crosses to the BQE. But get this: Because of an overnight snowstorm, even the major roads have barely been plowed. The fastest he can go is thirty miles an hour, and the police can't catch him because they can't go any faster. They chase him like that all the way from Queens down to Sunset Park, where they finally stop him."

Behind me, Ray said, "He's lucky they weren't shooting. Couldn't miss at that speed."

Caroline heard him and laughed. "How's Ray?" she said.

I turned again, "She wants to know how you're doing."

"Tell her I'm really happy to have more confirmation that the justice system works."

"Did you hear?" I said into the mouthpiece.

"I did."

"So, you're staying in the apartment?" I said, facing the window again.

"Until after lunch. Then I think I'll go to the used bookstore on Montague."

This was good. A plan meant she'd make it through the next few hours.

After we said goodbye, I heard her sigh as she took the receiver away from her ear and reached for the cradle.

I turned around and said to Ray, "Okay, remember where you left off?"

"No, but I put a mark here to tell me. Ready?"

Since Caroline's release from the hospital, I'd been getting as many calls as Howie, the supervisor whose embittered wife kept trying to harass him at the office. Unlike Howie, I did nothing to discourage Caroline's calls, least of all have them intercepted. I had enough of a rapport with our receptionist to trust she wouldn't rat me out to the supervisors, despite the telltale light for my line on her console.

I couldn't afford to draw attention to the calls by sending my readers to the waiting area every day for long periods of time, but it was excruciating to hold such conversations in front of them. It was bad enough comforting Caroline with Ray watching on, but even worse during Louise's sessions. At least Caroline didn't try to talk to her. Fortunately, Louise maintained her air of see no evil, hear no evil; or rather, hear no melodrama, see only how much time is left on the clock. For whatever reason, Caroline called only in the morning, so Beth, who worked just afternoons, was spared.

69

ONE EVENING AS WE WALKED along Montague, Caroline said, "A psychic has opened up a storefront. We're passing it right now. I went to see her. She listens well. What she says kind of fits what I think."

Until now, Caroline had shown no interest in the paranormal. Refraining from my usual denunciation of fortune-tellers, astrologers, seers and the other witches' crew, I said, "It's good to have someone reflect back to you what you're thinking. What did she tell you?"

"Oh, nothing really."

I smiled at her evasion, but I wouldn't intrude on the little privacy she had these days. I said, "I'm surprised fortune-tellers can afford Montague Street's rent."

"She isn't cheap."

I guessed, or more like hoped, that the psychic had hinted at a future beyond Caroline's cramped present. Since leaving the hospital, she was spending every night at my apartment, tethered to amateur caregivers—me, and by phone, her parents. She regularly saw a psychiatrist, as well as Goodweather. Everywhere she turned, she was monitored.

These days, when her parents wanted to speak to her, they had to call my number, which helped thaw the ice between her mother and me. Hardly a full-fledged melt, but at least a ray of sunshine on an Arctic landscape. One evening, when Caroline was out, we actually talked for half an hour.

For all my fears, and despite the care I took to be available for her at all times, I didn't truly accept that Caroline would follow through on her suicidal urges. Characters in novels killed themselves, and sometimes real people in the news did, but no one I knew would do something so drastic, so irreversible.

I'm not sure skepticism was a bad thing. I could have been immobilized with dread. But it might explain why there was so much I didn't think to ask. I didn't inquire, for example, what medication she'd been prescribed. Also, we'd ended our abstinence from alcohol when her pregnancy was terminated, but I didn't find out about how it interacted with her medications.

I reckon this stage lasted two months. I made no plans for the future beyond keeping on top of my application to the EPA. But our situation was more ephemeral than ever.

Nor was it all peace and light, the way I'd like to remember. Caroline would complain I'd left a coffee mug ring on my desk or forgotten to put groceries in the refrigerator. I'd hold back from countering by complaining about her leaving dirty dishes in the kitchen sink for me to wash after a day at the office, but I quietly resented it. The risk in suppressing resentments is that they can metastasize into angry outbursts when they have nothing to do with the moment. That's the only way I can explain one terrible Sunday morning.

"Couldn't you do the dishes once in a while?" I said.

"I didn't have the energy."

"The least you could do is keep the apartment in shape."

She slunk into the bathroom, and I went to my desk to work at some task. When she emerged, she stopped at my chair and announced, "I've cut off my hair." She grabbed my hand. "See? Check it out." The sides and back had been crudely lopped off.

"How could you?"

"I felt like it. Time I had short hair. Easier to wash."

She went into the bedroom, then came out and headed for the front door. I followed, not knowing what to say. She slapped my face. As I stood there, stunned, she ripped open the door and went out.

I was angry, but also sad, knowing her own anger came from depression. For once, I sat in the narrow rocking chair, easing backwards and forwards. I was still angry when she returned. She must not have taken the key with her because she pounded on the door. I stayed put in the rocking chair.

Then I heard Mike the doorman's voice and a different knock. I walked over to my side of the door.

"Why won't you let her in?" came the muffled voice.

I opened the door and stood aside as Caroline walked in. Then, ignoring Mike, I shut it.

The rest of the day was a standoff. We both went from angry to sad and withdrawn. On Monday I persuaded her to see my hair-dresser, who made time for her that afternoon and styled her hair as though it was meant to be short all along.

A couple of weeks later I came home to find her sounding up-beat. We nibbled at cheese, ham and crackers that she'd bought at the deli.

She said, "My parents have arranged for me to stay at a psychiatric hospital upstate. They say it's in a picturesque town on the Hudson."

"What's so special about it?"

"The head psychiatrist—guy named Muir."

"Some kind of miracle doctor?" She didn't take the bait. I softened my tone. "How long this time? Do you know?"

"Longer, I think."

I took her hand. "I'll miss you."

"I'll miss you, too. Will you make copies of the two Manfred Mann albums for me?"

"Of course. When are you going in?"

"Tomorrow."

Her parents must have communicated these arrangements to

her over the past several days while I was at the office. I held back from saying they should have informed me. The fight had gone out of me. All that mattered was that she get well. I coaxed her face toward me and kissed her. I missed her long hair, but now her lovely face was out in the open.

"No visits, no phone calls again?"

"No visits. But no one has said anything about phone calls."

I never thought to ask if she was formally committed at either or both hospitals. If yes, which seems likely, I'm guessing she spared her parents from signing the papers by doing so herself. After all, she treated the loss of her apartment and the abortion as her own decisions and never blamed Doreen or me. She'd run away from the dentist and was evasive about so much else in her life, and yet through it all, she held on to a sense of accountability for her actions.

70

A WEEK LATER, CRAVING CONNECTION with Caroline, I went to Sullivan Street. None of my friends knew her the way these guys did. And though these guys knew me only as Caroline's appendage, they'd always been considerate.

Reggie, the long-haul train engineer, was in town. He and Gavin, the contractor, directed me to a corner table.

"How's she doing?" Gavin asked me.

"She was in good shape when she left."

He sighed. "You'd never know there was anything wrong, would you?"

Then Reggie said, "You know what happened at Borough Hall?"

"What?"

"You know, the subway station on the Lex line."

"I use it when I go to the East Side."

Gavin said, "Caroline's always making friends."

I sipped my beer and nodded.

"There's a girl who sometimes comes here. She isn't here tonight."

Reggie picked up the thread. "About ten days ago, Caroline went down onto the tracks."

"At Borough Hall?"

"Some track workers saw her and got her back on the platform. She told that girl, Linda."

Gavin said, "And Linda told Reggie."

Tears sprang to my eyes. I swiped them away, hoping Gavin and Reggie saw only a nervous tic.

Reggie said, "Knowing Caroline, she gave them a song and dance about how she'd dropped something down there or got curious about something—you know, acted like a ditz."

"It must have been late at night," Gavin added. "It's a busy station."

"Maybe it's a good thing Caroline's in a place where they can get her through this," Reggie said.

I noted his "maybe." I, too, had my doubts.

Gavin changed the subject, although the new direction hardly made me happier. "Any word on Doreen?"

"I was going to ask you the same thing," I said.

"She's still in Caroline's apartment, you know. She doesn't come here often, but once in a while beer and the crowd lure her out. Want me to call you the next time she shows up?"

"Sure. Just so you know, she's openly hostile to me."

"We'll do a good cop-bad cop routine. You can be bad cop."

Reggie said, "I'll be chief of police. Don't do anything unethical. Can't have that on my watch."

71

THE NIGHT BEFORE CAROLINE LEFT, while I was recording the albums onto cassette for her, I'd asked what her longtime therapist, Goodweather, thought about her being hospitalized.

"He thinks it could be a positive."

"Does he have any suggestions for what I can do to, I guess, help?"

"Why don't you ask him?"

I grinned. "He's not my therapist, Caroline. He won't want anything to do with me."

"One reason I stay with him is that he isn't like all therapists."

"You really wouldn't mind if I spoke to him?"

"Of course not."

I called Dr. Goodweather the next Wednesday afternoon and left a message that I was a friend of Caroline's. When he called back, not wanting him to think I was trying to pry information out of him, I stated the facts.

"Caroline and I have been together for the better part of a year. Now that she's hospitalized again, I'm wondering if I could be doing anything better to help her get through this. She said to call you."

"You realize I can't discuss any conversations I've had with her. But feel free to make an appointment."

The consummate professional. He could have said he'd like to help. Instead, he'd made it clear that whatever happened was on my head.

Goodweather's dusty waiting room was uninviting. The chairs were mismatched, judging by the steel one I sat in juxtaposed against the battered wooden one next to me, and the secretary seemed so insecure in herself that I could hardly hear the few words she addressed to me, even when she told me the fee.

A door opened just three or four yards away and Goodweather said, "You're Nick?"

In the thick of an emotional jungle, I was tempted to say, "Dr. Goodweather, I presume."

His office was small, and I promptly found the back of the chair in which he indicated I was to sit, across his desk from him. I took his age as anywhere from the forties to the sixties. Later, detecting tenor tones in his voice, I'd settle on mid or late forties.

He went quiet. Okay, I'd heard about this shrink trick. The initiative had to come from me, even though I wasn't having my head examined. At least, I didn't think I was.

"Why am I here?" I began. "I've watched Caroline suffer ever since she learned she was pregnant. I believe I'm telling you nothing new."

Naturally, Goodweather didn't respond.

"I feel like I'm floundering around in a place where there are no rules. School has rules. Jobs have rules. Friendships have rules. Even relationships between parents and their adult children do. But what do I do when my girlfriend has attempted suicide and has been in psychiatric care ever since?"

I sat back as if to say, your turn.

He asked, "Do you want this relationship to continue?"

"Yes."

"Do you have any reservations?"

"Yes."

"And they are?"

"Right now, I worry I'm inseparable in her mind from the abortion."

"I can't address that. You say 'right now,' as if you've had other reservations."

"They have to do with where she is in her life and where I am in mine."

I guessed he wouldn't delve deeper because doing so would put him at risk of violating patient confidentiality. I guessed right.

"Have you discussed any of these compatibility issues with her?"

"We've gone through so much since she became pregnant that I haven't been able to."

"For the time being," he said, switching from the voice of caution to the voice of authority, "Caroline is in a protective, therapeutic environment. I would suggest you bring up these issues with her while she's there."

"I'm not allowed to visit. When I call, she's in a ward with other people around her. She has no privacy."

"I'm suggesting you write a letter."

"Really?" The idea made me uneasy. "How honest and direct should I be?"

"Totally."

"Even if I know it will upset her?"

"If your letter upsets her, the doctors are there to talk it through with her."

Assuming this visit was a one-shot deal, I tried to anticipate what difficulties and permutations would come to mind after I left.

"Any other advice for when she's discharged and we're back together?"

"Unfortunately, there are no rules, as you said."

I stood up and extended my hand. "Thank you for seeing me."

He gave me a dead-fish handshake and asked if I'd be able to find my way out.

72

GAVIN CALLED ME FROM THE bar to say Doreen had shown up.

"I'll be there in forty-five minutes," I said. "I hope she sticks around."

"Reggie and I will detain her."

"Be careful. She's liable to sue you for false imprisonment."

"Not to worry. Reggie's working his charm on her."

When I got there, I stood just inside the entrance and waited for Gavin or Reggie to notice me.

"She's still here," Gavin said, by way of hi. "Reggie is chatting her up at a table in the back." He gave me his arm and we plunged into the crowd.

"Oh, you," Doreen said on seeing me.

Reggie said to me, "Here, take this chair." He rose, grabbed my arm and pulled me to where I inferred he'd been sitting. "See you later," he said.

"So, this is a setup," Doreen said, her voice shifting between Gavin and me.

"We thought we'd have a talk," Gavin said, still standing.

"I'm talked out."

"Just a few words," I said.

"A single word from you is one too many." But she didn't get out of her chair.

"We just want to ask what your plans are concerning Caroline's apartment," I said.

"My plans? I haven't really come up with anything like a plan."

"So you don't intend to leave?"

"Not any time soon, so far as I can see."

"You're aware it's one of the things weighing on her right now?"

"The way I hear it, one of the lesser things weighing on her."

"So you know she's having a hard time."

"If being locked up in a nuthatch means a hard time, sure I have. But you aren't going to lay that one on me. First place I'd look is in a mirror. Oh, but that's something you can't do, isn't it?"

"I do worry about my part in Caroline's situation," I admitted. "How about admitting yours?"

"Oh, I don't believe I have any. If you're thinking about the apartment, it's not like she's in any position to use it now, is she?"

"It would help her to know she has a place to come back to."

"She has your place. Or are you saying you're such a big part of her problem that it's no good anymore?"

"Doreen, I won't get into an exchange of barbs with you. I'll deal with my share of the blame. What saddens me is you won't deal with yours."

"Saddens you? Drives you crazy, more like."

Gavin, who had kept himself out of it until now, said, "It isn't about Nick. It's about Caroline getting well. I'm sure you can understand that."

"Has he told you what he did to me?"

"I don't know and I don't want to."

"Just as well. I don't feel like talking about it."

"Then, can you think about Caroline's needs?"

"She's the one who set me up for him. I don't see why I should think about her needs. She isn't exactly thinking of mine."

"Actually, she thought about your needs all along. She introduced you to folks here, she tried to help you find a job, she lent you her apartment. That's one hell of a lot of thinking about you." Gavin didn't raise or sharpen his voice.

"One man's opinion," Doreen said, which even she had to know was lame.

"Think about it, will you, Doreen?" Gavin said. "I know life's hard on you, too."

She said, "Gotta go. See you, Gavin." She heaved a big sigh as she lifted herself up. The next I knew, glass shattered on the floor by her chair, a barely audible crash against the bar's din.

"So sorry," she said, sarcastic as before.

My chair was between her and her direct route to the exit. That was no doubt why she walked all the way around the table.

I assumed she'd made it to the door when Gavin took her place and emitted a bewildered, "Well."

It turned out the table had a third chair because Reggie pulled it out when he rejoined us. "Who's going to pay for that glass?" he inquired, deadpan.

Neither Gavin nor I answered.

Then Reggie said, "Any progress, gentlemen?"

I said, "Gavin seemed to get through to her."

"You laid the groundwork," Gavin said to me.

"So she's moving out?" Reggie looked from one to the other of us.

Gavin mused, "There might yet be a trace of conscience there."

73

I WAS ASTONISHED TO REALIZE my grandmother's eightieth birthday party was a month away. Caroline and I planned to go for a long weekend, and it was time I bought the tickets.

When I phoned, she was for once able to speak without being heard. She still lowered her voice.

"The three other people I share a room with are all away for a while. One's in a group therapy session, one's out seeing her husband. I don't know where the third is."

I hadn't known even this much about her setup. I said, "I'd find it hard having no place to go when I need to be by myself."

"You don't know the half of it. In the bathroom there are no doors on the stalls, and they have one-way mirrors so they can look in."

"To make sure you don't drown yourself in the toilet bowl?"

"And that we don't jerk off."

"What?"

"We're supposed to have no thoughts about sex."

I almost said, "That's crazy." I was on the verge of indignation, but I didn't hear annoyance in Caroline's voice. She seemed to view her situation as interesting, which was just as well, given that she couldn't do anything about it.

"Listen, would you still like to go out with me to Illinois for Grandma's birthday?"

"Of course. I'm looking forward to meeting your family and seeing a part of the country I don't know."

"I need to buy tickets now so we're not stuck with last-minute high fares. Have they given you any idea when you'll be discharged?"

"Uh-uh. You can always call my psychiatrist here, Dr. Muir."

Funny how she kept encouraging me to speak to her doctors. Why not ask him herself? I took it as one more instance of the weird wonderland we'd entered. I speculated she was simply preserving time and energy for the more consuming questions she must be confronting in therapy. But there was another possibility. Maybe she hoped Muir would say no for her.

I didn't call him that night. I needed to formulate my question to make sure I didn't sound as though the trip was more important to me than Caroline's health. The next evening, I reached his answering machine. It was disconcerting to hear the matter-of-fact-sounding voice of the man right now in charge of Caroline's life.

I left a message: "Hi, I'm Nick Coleman, a friend of Caroline Sedlak's. We're planning on going to my grandmother's eightieth birthday celebration in Illinois next month. I'm wondering if you can say if she'll be discharged by then so that I can buy airline tickets. She told me to ask you directly." I recited my home and office numbers.

He didn't return my call. I left a similar message a week later, but he still didn't call back. Caroline told me he hadn't brought up the subject with her. Resigned, I didn't ask why she hadn't brought it up, either.

I turned to the letter Goodweather had suggested I write. Sitting at my desk in that old apartment of mine, I'd type a paragraph, pause, type another. All in all, I wrote three pages. I didn't keep a copy. I'd never succeeded in making a carbon copy as I typed, and I couldn't ask any of my readers or friends to photocopy it because it was meant only for Caroline.

What did I write? I remember reiterating that I didn't feel ready to settle down; that we still weren't in a committed relationship. Today this insistence strikes me as so thoughtless, juvenile and outright false that I want to reach back in time and rip up the letter.

I'm pretty sure I suggested that on her side, she needed direction before she could be sure about the rightness of our relationship for her. Direction? Again in retrospect, this feels like exploitation of her revelation the morning we greeted the dawn on my old vinyl couch. Had I been talking to her rather than engaging a written monologue, the self-serving nature of my statements would surely have become clear to me, either because she would have pointed it out or because I would have heard my words as if with her ears.

One thing I know I couldn't bring myself to admit, despite the Goodweather-induced hallucinatory honesty that guided my words, was that her psychological state made me apprehensive not only for her well-being, but also for mine.

I typed an envelope, folded the three pages inside, put on two stamps just in case, walked to the corner mailbox, and dropped it in before I could have second thoughts.

74

THE EPA CAME THROUGH AND offered me the job. When Joanna Leavitt called to tell me, she sounded genuinely pleased, and I was grinning as I hung up the phone.

"Yes?" Beth said.

"Will you come work with me at the EPA?"

"You got the job? Cool."

"Keep it to yourself until I give notice. I'll draft it at home tonight and we'll go over it tomorrow."

Later that afternoon, I found myself on the elevator alone with the Alliance's president. An affable, well-connected man, he stood aloof from the organization's day-to-day operations. I rarely encountered him, but he was unfailingly gracious when I did.

"Congratulations," he said in his executive baritone.

I was shocked. Joanna Leavitt hadn't asked my permission to contact the Alliance even for a reference. It hadn't occurred to me she was the kind of person to repeat Donna Scherer's lapse by calling my employer without authorization.

I had to ensure I wasn't making a false assumption. "Thanks, but for what?"

"You know, the highest case production rate in the appeals unit. A great achievement."

The doors opened at my floor, two below his. I thanked him again and stepped out.

Michael Flurry and the supervisors hadn't told me about this "great achievement," even though the city auditors' criticism of our productivity drove them berserk. They indulged other lawyers' special situations: men with divorce problems, pregnancy, lawyers who refused on principle to handle rape cases. These were concerns the supervisors had also wrestled with or could viscerally understand. But my omission of the prosecutor's summation in an early case had ever after tarnished me as unreliable. And a spelling error that with another attorney would have been an occasion for good-humored mockery was seen in my case as further proof of incompetence. They viewed me as a burden, and then they exaggerated it. Couldn't they at least have admitted I did more than my share?

The next day it was with satisfaction that I handed the envelope containing my resignation letter to the executive secretary. In two sentences I stated I was resigning in a month and thanked Flurry for the opportunity.

75

I SET ABOUT WORKING ON the novel I'd begun with the chapter about the suicide prevention program and the blind walk. The novel would work forward from some point further in the past to show how the narrator gradually acquired the confidence to guide the girl and eventually make it through high school. But what should that point be? When my character was born? Before he moved to the school that I based on mine in Connecticut? I settled on the phase when his vision was fading in and out, slight for part of one day and none at all the next, returning for part of the day after. It would mean more going back-and-forth in time, and I wasn't sure I could pull it off. As I sat at the typewriter to begin writing, I hoped I'd anticipated enough plot development to maintain a continuous narrative.

I never got that thinly disguised memoir to work. It's more a series of anecdotes than a novel. Still, packrat that I am, I transcribed it to my computer around the same time I did "The Portrait." Without it, many memories of my adolescence would have faded away.

Reading it over, I find this passage, set after my character's loss of sight and at least two years before the blind walk.

I had no activity I could do with others, whether basketball or driving cars, mocking a poster or laughing at someone's weird clothes. In math class, the teacher was drawing geometric diagrams on the board that I couldn't reconstruct, leading the other students into conclusions whose premises I hadn't shared. What the others apparently understood, I might spend hours in the evening trying to apprehend with the aid of raised line drawings.

Each Friday as Mom drove me home from school, I'd think to myself that another week had gone by with no relief from grinding alienation. I decided to give myself until eighteen for a big change to happen. If it didn't, I'd end my life. Setting a deadline (a *'dead* line') was comforting.

There it was. Like my first-person narrator, and as I'd admitted to Caroline, there'd been a time when I'd contemplated suicide.

Except for the first chapter that Albert Stern ridiculed in class, Caroline never saw the manuscript. Curious that I was writing about suicidal feelings as she was suffering from hers. I somehow didn't connect the two. My mind apparently allocated distress to one compartment and detached analysis to another, a separation that may well have kept me going. But if my emotions and intellect had merged into a single compartment, would I have responded better to Caroline's crisis? Would I have made less ambiguous demonstrations of affection?

Or would I have walked out of her life? "Cruel to be Kind" was a hit song in the eighties. If I had ended our relationship, would it have been kind to Caroline?

76

REACHING A POINT IN THE novel where I needed to have what I'd written so far read back to me, I called Mara to take her up on her offer.

At first her reaction was muted. "After all this time, I was wondering if you'd call."

"It's thirty-one pages. Then you can help me celebrate my new job."

She told me that since leaving the office, she'd passed the GMATs and started classes at Fordham's Lincoln Center campus.

In her apartment, she had me sit on some beanbag thing. "I'm not big on chairs," she said. But when I reminded her she'd need to make handwritten revisions, she raised herself to the chair at her small desk and pulled another over for me to sit beside her.

I'd forgotten she read in a monotone, with just occasional modulations. Someone else narrating my work like that might have put me off, but with Mara I found it endearing.

She read without comment all the way through to the end, when, brushing back her hair, she asked, "That's the last page?"

"You're done."

"Okay. There's a Viennese place two blocks from here. It isn't cheap. Are you game?"

"Isn't game something you eat?"

Once we were seated at a table, Mara announced we were ordering a Riesling she liked. Then she told me not to get too cute by ordering some entree out of the ordinary. "Wiener schnitzel. That's what Viennese restaurants are for." I complied.

When the wine was brought to us, she told me to taste it. I hated this ritual. I was slow to decide what I thought about a wine, and my judgment was uninformed. But I went through the charade, flicked the wine around my mouth and swallowed. Assuming a look of judiciousness, I said, "Good." I imagined the sommelier, or whatever the wine guy called himself, was wishing he hadn't been reduced to suffering such a fool.

"So, what do you think about your novel?" Mara asked when he'd gone.

"I'd like to rewrite it."

"Don't."

"Why not?"

"Keep going forward. Don't pause to edit. You'll never get to the end."

I fished. "You like it?"

"I do. It makes me nervous—anxious."

"Why, and why do you like it in that case?"

"Losing one's vision is everyone's fear. Finding out how you coped made me anxious. I was afraid to find out and I was eager to. The blind walk is a great place to start. When we read that chapter in the office, I put myself in Hillary's place. With this new material and with you as the focus, I put myself in yours."

Mara's reaction sparked my fear about perpetuating morbid curiosity. But I took encouragement from her identification with my main character. I wanted readers to experience him as a human being, or, to use today's circumlocution, a person who happened to be blind.

To explain Caroline's absence, I told Mara she was in a psychiatric institution, but I held back from saying she'd attempted suicide. Mara voiced conventional expressions of sympathy before changing the subject.

We finished the bottle about the same time we finished our entrees. I wasn't up for a heavy Viennese dessert, and neither was she. However, we were both up for more alcohol. She suggested we leave for a bar she liked where the drinks were cheaper.

We set out on an outright bender. Memory of the places we went and what we talked about are long since gone, if they ever reached my brain. When we settled in somewhere, our wine- and whisky-breaths mingled as we angled close to each other to hear over the crowd's noise. In my mind's eye, I see glints on polished bar railings, strangers in pools of light among the night shadows, rectangles of paving stone in the sidewalk under my feet as we strayed from one Upper East Side bar to the next. What a scene we must have made, propping each other up and howling with laughter. Her talk, her directness, her scent of smoky perfume, her leg pressed against mine each time we sat together were intoxicating. But for alcohol, I would have been overcome.

I pulled myself together around midnight, when I told her I had to get home. "How are you going to function in class tomorrow?" I asked.

"I'll deal with it. How about you? Who's your morning reader?"

"Fortunately it's Ray. If I'm hung over—"

"You will be."

"He'll think, what do you expect from a guy who defends human trash?"

"He'd have a point."

She flagged down a cab for me. Before climbing in, I turned to her and we hugged, her body again imprinting itself on mine.

My pulse was racing all the way down the FDR, but by the time we'd negotiated the tight curves onto the Brooklyn Bridge, it was under control. Nostalgically recalling Caroline's cab adventures, I directed the driver to Henry Street and on to my building.

Our building staff was gone for the day. I unlocked the entrance door and stumbled through the lobby. From euphoric, I became dejected. The single life, I thought, as I entered an apartment that tonight felt uninviting. Leaving Mara in the street, a block away from her home, hadn't been the evening's natural conclusion. But then, I wasn't single. I was in limbo.

77

DURING ONE OF OUR ABBREVIATED, almost impersonal calls, Caroline told me she'd been given permission for me to visit her. A burden lifted that I hadn't known was weighing on me. She did want to see me.

I contemplated the logistics of getting there. The town was near the end of the Hudson Line that Mara had used on Christmas Eve. I'd neither taken that train nor visited the town, which was far enough north to be semi-rural. After going all that way, would I be able to get from the station to the hospital and back? Would there be cabs? Today, Google might have the answer. But even if there were cabs waiting nearby, would I succeed in getting a driver's attention? Caroline didn't know enough about the town to help.

But so what? One way or the other, I'd reach the hospital and I'd see her.

The next day, I had lunch with Rob. He asked how I was getting to such a remote place.

"By train."

"Wouldn't it be easier if we rented a car and drove there together?"

We settled on what turned out to be a warm, dry, fall day. Reaching the town early, we stopped at some open land, perhaps a park, by the Hudson, where we inspired the curiosity of a flock of geese. I'd heard about "goosing," but hadn't known what it meant beyond some prank that high school kids played on each other, causing merriment in the gooser and distress in the goosee. That morning I found out. When a goose goosed me, I turned to frighten it off, only to have it respond by poking at my crotch while one behind me took its turn at my backside.

Annoyed, I told Rob, "I thought I liked geese."

"They look nice in the sky," he said.

I pictured a V formation of geese in flight, from afar so beautiful. Close-up, jabbing at you, they were nightmarish. It made me think how sight can transcend the jabs of the moment and to wonder whether my flashes of anger with Caroline might have been tempered had I been able to see the hurt in her face.

Almost as soon as we got back on the road, Rob announced a sign for the hospital, and we turned onto a long driveway. In the lobby, a staff member greeted us. I explained why we were here. When Caroline appeared, I wanted to fold her into an embrace that said, "I'll never let you go." But her reserved demeanor and our surroundings discouraged even holding hands.

"I have permission to go out for lunch," she announced. She'd been told about a place a short drive away.

I yielded the front passenger seat to her and got in the back. Rob proposed to leave us at the restaurant while he went for a spin.

Caroline said, "But I haven't seen you in ages, and you've come all this way."

She was being polite, no doubt, but I heard flirtation. Rob didn't put up any resistance.

At one of the restaurant's outdoor tables, he demonstrated a gift for small talk that carried us through the first awkward minutes. He offered ample evidence that the Alliance needed Caroline's psychiatrist more than she did. Caroline told us about life in the hospital. Relaxing, I talked about my hopes for my new job.

I felt a weight on my lap. Caroline had rested her leg there. Her skirt might have been knee-length, but elevation hiked it up, and I ran my hand from foot to thigh.

"What are you doing?" Rob said. He stood up and looked over to my side of the table. "Ah, I see." Then he ventured, "You have great legs, Caroline."

"Thank you," she said.

The rest of lunch, I stroked her leg.

She told us, "There's a guy in his sixties here. The nicest man in the world, but alcohol fried his brain and he can't function outside."

"He's there permanently—forever?" I said.

"Looks like it. Don't worry, Nick. I won't be here forever."

"Any indications how much longer?"

"Not really."

"How about making outgoing calls? Still banned?"

"Still banned. What time is it? If I violate my parole, they'll cut back my privileges."

"Parole?" Rob said. I was glad he was the one to ask.

"Lots of rules," she said. The way she spoke, apparently at one with the program, stopped us both from pursuing it.

Getting up from the table and holding out my arms, I said, "I won't be able to do this at the hospital." We hugged, though as a man and a woman who knew each other well more than as lovers after an absence.

78

My last day at the Alliance, my colleagues gave me a fare-well lunch. At the long table in the restaurant we used for such occasions, I developed a sudden cold. As my eyes watered, Rob gave a short speech, which was met by a round of polite applause. Punctuating my remarks with nose blows into my handkerchief, I told them I'd miss them. What a fitting end to my Alliance career. I just hoped they didn't think I was crying.

Back at the office, Beth shrugged off my apologies for sneezing and spluttering. We worked until eight, gathering all my person-al items, including the research files I'd created, braille notes at-tached. They would have been thrown out if we hadn't.

Standing on the sidewalk outside the Alliance's building, I blew my nose into one tissue after the next as Beth tried to hail a cab for me and the boxed remnants of my Alliance career. I wasn't thinking about a fresh start. I was depressed about the years spent at the Alliance: the dozens of cases, the innumerable hours of re-search and writing, the time and effort that my readers—even Louise—had given me. The supervisors might have treated me unfairly, but couldn't I have made it work anyway? For them I'd soon be a faint memory, but this had been my first full-time job, and they'd be on my mind for a very long time.

At last a cab responded to Beth's signal, and we threw my files into the back seat. As I followed them inside, she said, "See you in Federal Plaza in two weeks." Adding, "Feel better," she slammed the door.

Within minutes of my arriving home, Mara phoned to say, "Now you can really get drunk. Tomorrow night. My turn to see you in Brooklyn."

79

MY COLD WAS GONE THE next morning, as suddenly as it had started. With it went last night's depression. The idea of starting over energized me. It helped that Beth and Ray were staying with me, that Louise wasn't, and that I'd found Louise's replacement for her.

That evening, after a meal at one of the restaurants that have come and gone on Montague, Mara and I walked down to a bar on Atlantic, near where Rob lived. He was on his own for the week because Samantha had gone on a business trip to Dallas. I reached him from the bar's payphone, and he showed up while we were still on our first beers. He took the stool on Mara's other side.

She told us about business school. "You two should get MBAs. I didn't realize business could be so creative."

"Law can be creative, too," Rob said.

I nodded. "Those judges' opinions often are."

"When they bother to write one at all," he agreed.

To me, Mara said, "Seriously, I thought your briefs were often very creative, though nothing like your fiction."

That piqued Rob's curiosity. "You've read his stories?"

"One story and the first chapters of his novel."

"Should I ask to read them, or will I be too embarrassed for him?"

"You won't be embarrassed. Even I wasn't."

"What's the novel about?"

"It's based on my experiences in high school. That could embarrass you all right."

"You don't know the meaning of embarrassment if you didn't know me in high school," he retorted. "My parents were weird, which took me way too long to figure out. When I was a sophomore, Dad left."

"I never knew," I said.

"Ancient history."

"Ancient history has a way of biting the present," Mara said.

I raised my glass to her. Today, it disturbs me to realize I didn't think how, at that very moment, Caroline's past had come to haunt her present.

To Rob, I said, "Are you in touch with your dad?"

"No. But I see my mom a lot. She's still weird."

"All moms are weird," Mara said.

"Does yours answer the phone, 'House of Pain. Who's this?'"

"Are you serious?" Mara's horror was a more fitting reaction than my laughter.

"It depends on her mood. Sometimes it's 'House of Anxiety' or "House of Fried Brains.'"

"Is it ever anything positive?" I asked.

"How about 'Home of the Survivor'? Does that count?"

"I don't think so," I said.

He thudded his glass on the bar. "Well, one of us has to work tomorrow. And don't you have classes, Mara?"

Mara and I walked with him to Henry, where he turned south, away from the Heights. She said, "Show me the Promenade again."

I had us walk a few blocks the other direction, up Henry, so if Rob looked back he'd assume I was escorting her to her train. We strolled the Promenade's six or seven blocks as she detailed an ongoing family quarrel. I listened with one part of my mind while conjuring up the image of Manhattan across from us, this time as a big blob of light against the night. Beyond, as Saul Steinberg had depicted it on a *New Yorker* cover I'd reconstructed from visual memories, I imagined the continent falling away in irrelevance.

I thought again about how sight opens up distances. But the image of geese in flight, which had started me on that symbolic path, could represent any number of things: longing for the unattainable, the elusiveness of beauty, the beauty of aspiration. Inability to see geese in the sky didn't render me incapable of bridging distances. Through voice and other cues, I did apprehend the moods and reactions that facial expressions also signaled. If anything, I was too susceptible to them.

As we reached the Promenade's far end, Mara said, "Nightcap?"

If Mike, on duty in the lobby, recognized her, he kept it to himself.

I poured us each a glass of whisky and carried them to the couch. Although while wandering the Upper East Side we'd practically merged like reunited halves of an Aristophanes' soul, I settled against the couch's arm.

I checked my watch and was surprised to find it was after midnight. "Mara, you're going to be a wreck tomorrow. I'm a bad influence."

"Did you make me stay?"

"I said 'bad influence,' not kidnapper. I'll call for a car."

"How about if I sleep on your couch? It opens out, right? I can take the 2/3 train to school. It will be easier getting there from here than from my place."

"But you don't have your books and stuff."

"I have my notebook and a pen. That's all I'll need."

"Well, of course, you're more than welcome to stay."

I took the empty whisky glasses into the kitchen. She went into the bathroom as I pulled the coffee table aside and opened up the couch. When she reappeared, she took the other edge of the bottom sheet I'd started arranging and we stretched it out over the mattress. Then she walked around the foot of the bed and put her arms around me. At first I thought she was naked, but she still had on her panties.

With her hands on my sides, she made a gap between us. Knowing she wasn't wearing a bra and sensing invitation, I touched her chest. She had small, shapely breasts. Then I touched her face. Her expression was serious, her nose and chin prominent. Her hair had fallen over her eyes.

"My turn to do this," I said, as I lifted her hair to the side.

She buried her face in my shoulder. "You noticed."

"All right," I said, "let's go to bed together. But we can't have sex. You understand."

Could she? Could she understand my loyalty to Caroline? That I couldn't be unfaithful while she was hospitalized and there was hope for our relationship? Yet my desire was hard against Mara's thigh.

At my shoulder, she nodded.

She went into the bedroom. I folded the couch back up, returned the sheets to the linen closet and finished up in the bathroom. When I rejoined her, she was in bed. I wondered if she'd taken off her underwear. If she had, she'd feel bad if I kept mine on. I took everything off.

We rolled into each other's arms, hugged, groped and writhed. She still had on her panties. Was she honoring my condition? Or waiting for me to take them off?

I lay back, and she went still.

I said, "We should go to sleep." I put my arm around her middle and hoped the gesture of affection would at least serve to apologize. Last I remember, she was still on her back.

Awake at six, I got up as quietly as I could and closed the bedroom door. Half an hour later, Mara appeared. Retrieving her clothes from where she'd left them on the desk, she took them with her to the bathroom. When she returned and sat down beside me on the couch, I had a mug of coffee waiting for her.

I asked how she'd slept. She answered with a monosyllable. Maybe she took a while to get going in the morning. But even as she drank her coffee, she spoke only when I put questions to her. As soon as she finished, she left.

80

I GAVE UP ON THE hospital discharging Caroline and bought my roundtrip airfare to Chicago just a week before Grandma's birthday bash. Stuck in a small town for four days with relatives I rarely saw, I felt disconnected from the ones I liked and bored with the rest. No, that's wrong, as well as unkind. I was the bore. My mind kept straying to a small town on the Hudson. But some events are designed to be remembered more than enjoyed, and I am glad to have those memories of my grandmother.

Back home, I was tossing clothes from the suitcase into the hamper and returning books to their shelves when the phone rang. Caroline said, "Oh, hi. You're back."

"So are you."

"So I am."

She had to be out of the hospital to be making a call.

"For good?" I said.

"For good, yes, but not necessarily forever. They want to see how I do. They've partnered me with another patient, a friend of mine named Kim."

"Partnered you?"

"She was released at the same time, and she has no home to go to. She's staying with me and my parents. They told her to look out for me."

"She'll be chaperoning you everywhere you go?"

"Not if I'm with someone else."

"Does that include me?"

"Yes."

"When can I see you?"

"How about in an hour? Kim and I are in the Village."

"I can meet you at the West 4th station," I offered.

"No need. She'll put me in a cab."

I scoured the apartment for any trace of Mara from the night before I'd flown to Illinois. I'd already thrown out the cigarettes and returned the dish I had her use as an ashtray. Now I got down on my knees and combed the floor for several feet around to make sure none had fallen on the carpet. Sniffing, I could detect no trace of smoke in the air, but I opened all the windows anyway. Mara had drunk scotch and coffee when she'd stayed over. To make sure no lipstick stains remained, even though I'd done the dishes after she left, I rewashed all the glasses and mugs. I'd already changed the sheets to have fresh ones on my return from the trip, so I was saved having to do laundry. There wouldn't have been time anyway.

As I raced through my chores, I told myself I should have been firm about meeting Caroline at the station. From what the doctors had told her, that twenty-minute gap between Kim and me put her at risk.

The phone rang. With fond resignation, I heard her voice muffled by the narrow enclosure of a public phone booth. I reminded her of the directions, and three minutes later Mike the doorman buzzed her through.

I opened my apartment's door as she turned into the hallway. After she'd stepped inside, we at last hugged like the long-lost lovers we were.

"Your hair's grown back," I said. She nodded.

After we settled in on the couch, she said, "Dr. Muir told me on

Friday I'd be discharged on Monday."

I sensed nervousness behind her words.

"The day after I left for Illinois, he told you. He really wanted me out of the loop, didn't he? But you're still under observation—with Kim, I mean."

"They gave Kim and my parents a list of instructions."

Not me, I thought. But this wasn't the time for resentment. I said, "Tell me what they are so I know what to do."

"Oh, basically someone's supposed to be with me all the time. No solitary walks on the beach." Her ironic tone told me she was well aware summer was over.

Obviously eager to change the subject, she said, "I've decided to go to college. Columbia General Studies. I'm waiting to hear back if they'll let me start in the spring semester. But next September at the latest."

"Are you excited?"

"Nervous. But yeah, I'm excited."

Her plan, and even more the way she talked about it, told me there'd be an end to her long ordeal.

"You'll do great," I said, holding out my mug of Postum to hers. She clinked.

"It will be hard."

"Not too hard," I said, "not for you."

Waking up early, I managed to leave the bedroom without disturbing her and settled on the couch to read at a volume level she wouldn't hear behind the closed door. I felt fulfilled. Last night's lovemaking had been simple and moving.

My mind drifted to the morning we'd sat on the old vinyl couch at the curbside, when I'd asserted we weren't in a committed relationship. Yet by then, she'd already become part of me. I can be so slow to recognize my feelings that by the time I express them, what I say isn't just old news; sometimes it's no longer true. No doubt it was due to the way I'd trained myself to delay reactions as my vision deteriorated. It had served me well then. But today?

A couple of hours later she was sitting beside me in her robe. I discovered I'd missed her first-thing-in-the-morning aura.

"Slept well?" I said.

"I feel rested. But then sleep isn't my problem."

In the early evening we took the subway to the Village, where Caroline introduced me to Kim by the basketball courts outside the West 4th Street station.

"I've heard so much about you," Kim said. Her voice conveyed no irony, but I still heard the mixed message that this line always sends.

She showed concern when she asked Caroline, "How are you doing?"

"I feel good. Come on, time for you to meet the guys at Sullivan Street." Caroline started us along West 3rd.

At the bar, she talked about her absence as though she'd spent a couple of months at an upstate spa. Everyone played along. Her gift for celebrating, regardless of all the reasons not to, was infectious.

Gavin got my attention with his customary opening tap on my forearm. "You know Doreen's gone, right?"

"Gone from the apartment? From New York?"

"Both. At least, I think she's left New York. No one's seen her around for a week."

"Has anyone been to the apartment?"

Despite all the noise and being at the center of it, Caroline overheard. "Kim and I checked it out yesterday. It needs a big clean, but she didn't trash it."

Gavin resumed as if we were all alone. "I had the locks changed.

I know the locksmith, so he didn't give me any trouble."

Caroline and Kim were returning to her parents' that evening. We walked to the 14th Street station where I'd take the Brooklyn express train home and they the local to Riverdale. After we passed through the turnstiles, they each kissed me on the cheek before striding to their platform, like two New York women en route to the next cool event.

81

WHY I CHOSE OUR OLD haunt, the Old Hungary, to ask Caroline about the letter I'd sent her in the hospital is beyond me now. Maybe I thought that we, or rather I, could talk about it rationally in a public place where we both felt comfortable. But the good humor with which I'd responded last time to the psychiatrist's stratagems this time failed me.

"A psychiatric nurse read it before giving it to me," Caroline said.

"They read your mail, too?"

"Sure. I told you we had no privacy."

On reflection, I'd known. How else could they have protected her, as Goodweather had assured me they would? I guessed I hadn't counted on them opening and reading her mail before she did.

Caroline took a sip of white wine. "Just one glass," she'd told the waiter, as if he might be worried. She was rationing alcohol because of the medications I still hadn't asked her about.

"She said you aren't the right man for me."

"She what?"

"Don't be upset, Nick."

"How could she know that from a letter?"

"They're pretty shrewd."

"You agree with her?"

By reporting this claim that I wasn't right for her and calling the staff "shrewd," I felt Caroline was having them speak for her, the way I worried she'd used Muir's silence to back out of our Illinois trip. I lay down my fork.

"Nick, this is no big deal."

"It is. I wrote that letter to you, not one of Muir's turnkeys so they could tell you what to think before you'd had a chance to make up your own mind. Your guy, Goodweather, told me I should lay out all my concerns while you were in a safe environment. I wish I'd never met that bastard."

It was so obvious that putting my tentative thoughts in writing had given them permanence. I should have waited until we could talk.

"Nick, please. You did the right thing."

I blundered on. "These past months, everything I've said and done has been filtered through people at the hospital who've never met me but who blithely put me in a negative light."

That her unsettling calm might have been due to her medications finally occurred to me as we were walking home. If either of us had a right to be unhappy with her doctors, she did. Right now they were her hope. I had to live with their mistakes, including their attitude toward me, if that was, indeed, a mistake.

Snuggled with her on the couch, I said, "I'd like to talk about what I was trying to say in that letter. It must have sounded much worse than I meant. I can only guess."

"I know what you meant. Don't worry about it, Nick."

"It doesn't mean—"

"One day . . . Right now I'm just glad to be here with you."

She had me play Manfred Mann. "Sounds a lot better on the

stereo than my Walkman."

When "For You" came on, I made out for the first time the line, "And your Chelsea suicide with no apparent motive . . ." It was as if Caroline's early enthusiasm for the song had foreshadowed the psychiatric episode waiting just around the corner for her. And what was I to make of ". . . you did not need my urgency"? Had I been that worst of all combinations, urgent when it was better to back off, and not urgent enough when intervention was called for?

I said, "This song makes me sad now."

"It's a sad song."

The next afternoon, she said she'd take a cab to the Village to join up with Kim for their trip to Riverdale, but I insisted on going with her and having Kim meet us in the West 4th Street station.

"I feel like one of those boxes I watched being transferred from the plane in Colombia," she said.

Kim was waiting on the platform. I stepped out of the train as she brushed by me to join Caroline just inside the subway car's doors.

"Good luck at the EPA tomorrow," Caroline called to me.

"Oh, yeah," Kim said, "you're starting a new job, aren't you?"

"Yep," I said, "we're all getting a fresh start."

"So true," Kim said, as the doors closed.

82

JUST AFTER I'D PUT STOUFFER'S macaroni and cheese in the toaster oven, Caroline called. I recognized the Sullivan Street bar's cheerful background as she talked over it.

"I know we said we'd get together tomorrow night, but how about tonight instead? Kim and I had to come into town today and now we're—"

"I know where you are."

"How? Oh, yeah. Mind if we stay over?"

Caroline directed the cab to my building without calling for directions. No way she'd let Kim think she couldn't get here without my help. Standing in the hallway by my door, I was laughing to myself when they turned the corner.

Caroline told Kim she had to try Postum. I boiled the water and drew up a chair for myself to the coffee table. When the kettle whistled, Caroline did the honors and joined Kim on the couch.

"I see why Caroline loves New York City," Kim said.

I asked her where she was from, and she named a town I'd never heard of near Albany.

"Don't go there," she said. "It's no wonder I went crazy, growing up there."

She'd been hard-done by, like Doreen, but unlike Doreen, she'd developed empathy. I surmised her tough past had a lot to do with her determination to protect Caroline.

As eleven approached, I announced I had to go to bed in order to get up for work in the morning. I returned the chair to its place, and Caroline and Kim moved the coffee table out of the way. Caroline and I opened up the convertible, and Kim helped her make it into a bed. Had it been only two weeks since I'd made it up for Mara?

Closing the bedroom door for the night, I half-whispered to Caroline, "She's nice. Are you looking after her, too?"

"We're kind of looking after each other. But she's allowed to be alone."

Big difference, I thought.

"Tell me more about her—what does she do, what she looks like."

"She does odd jobs—waitressing, cleaning. Brown hair, pretty face. She's heavy. I don't know if that's the way she is or the result of medication. Maybe both."

I sat down and reached out to Caroline. She was lying on her front with the covers turned back. I traced her back, as if I didn't remember its contours.

"Spank me," she said.

"Caroline!"

"Spank me."

"We can't do that with Kim in the next room. She'll hear."

"Please?"

"No, Caroline."

I did rest a hand on her rump, but I didn't want to do anything resembling violence in her fragile state, even if she would have found it cathartic. Kim's nearness provided whatever other inhibition I needed.

I lay down, and we held each other. At last she rolled onto her sleep side, and I molded to her. It was the alarm that jangled us awake.

I don't remember how we parted that morning. With Kim there, did we at least give each other a polite kiss? I just don't remember.

83

THAT EVENING, CAROLINE CALLED FROM her parents' as I was about to leave the office. "How did it go?" she asked.

"It's a hell of a lot of work. I'll need to hire a reader to work a night each week. I had Ray record part of a book on environmental law this morning while I was stuck in a meeting, so at least I made good use of the time today."

"You always make good use of your time, don't you, Nick?"

She spoke with the spookily detached-sounding voice I remembered from between hospitalizations.

"How about you?" I said. "How are you doing?"

"I want to go somewhere."

"Where?"

"You know, somewhere."

"Not really, Caroline. Tell me more."

Her end of the line went quiet.

"Caroline?"

"I'm here."

"Is Kim with you?"

"She's in the TV room. I'm in the living room."

"And your parents?"

"Out shopping."

"I was looking forward to seeing you tonight," I said. "You should have come tonight as well as last night."

"I should have. But it's good that Kim likes it here, and my parents like her."

"Caroline, I was just leaving. It will take me forty minutes to get home. Will you be okay until then, or do you want to keep talking? I'll call as soon as I get in."

"Go home. Offices get lonely at night. I'll be fine."

"So, I'll call you in forty minutes, right?"

"Okay."

"Talk to you, Caroline."

She'd hung up.

I didn't have my new commute down yet. I got home in more like fifty minutes.

Kim answered the phone. "They took Caroline to the hospital."

"Who? Why?"

"When her parents came home, they saw her medication bottles were empty. They got her in the car right away."

I thought Kim was calm, but now I heard the sobs she was holding back.

She burst out, "I feel awful. Awful. It was my job to watch over her, and this happens. I was just in the next room."

"I know how conscientious you've been, Kim. If Caroline was determined to try again, there was nothing you could do."

She said, "I have to go. I'll call you as soon as I get word."

"Promise? You have my number?"

I was too tense to eat, but I told myself this was another cry for help. Caroline had come too far and had too much going for her to give in now. She was going to get that education I'd believed all along she dearly wanted. I could help her with her coursework. We could make a shared voyage of it. At the end of it, she'd have a degree that would open doors. Knowing her, she'd make all kinds of contacts and hatch any number of schemes, some of which were bound to reach fruition.

I managed to read for a while, then I tuned into a Nets basketball radio broadcast for the announcers' familiar voices and the game's reassuring patterns. Every so often I went to sit by the phone, but I didn't want to tie up either of our lines, and I felt certain Kim would keep her promise. When Jenny and I had gone with Caroline to the E.R., we'd had to wait until around ten before the doctor told us she could come home.

The phone rang at 11:05, the only call that came through that evening.

"I have bad news," Mrs. Sedlak said. "Caroline took an overdose."

"Kim told me. She feels terrible."

"Caroline is dead."

84

I DIDN'T EVEN DROP THE phone. It must have been like the way adrenaline kicks in after someone sustains a serious bodily injury.

I heard myself saying, "I'm so sorry, Mrs. Sedlak."

"Hard on you, too."

"She . . ." But I couldn't ask my questions. "I'm grateful you called to tell me," I managed.

"We'll talk tomorrow," she said.

In the kitchen, I poured whisky without caring, except that the amount be large. Then I returned to the chair by the phone. In my head I lurched around for something about the call I could believe in. Her mother could never have lied about such a thing. But it was impossible to accept that someone so alive even at the worst of times, someone I'd spoken to just five hours ago, was now completely and utterly unreachable.

If she really had died, then what drove her to it? Okay, the abortion. All the doubts I'd had about my role in that terrible unfolding of events became self-accusations. I honed in on our first time at the Park Avenue doctor when I'd had an urge to rush into the interior rooms to tell her we should marry and have the baby. Instead, I'd just sat there. After we left, I'd deserted her in the street. Even then, I'd had a whole week to talk about having the baby after all.

There was so much more to regret. There'd been the times I'd moodily felt sorry for myself, especially on our vacation. There was that catering idea. I should have wheedled and goaded her into setting up a business so she could gain a sense of autonomy, even though from what she'd said, catering required you to work incredibly hard with no guarantees of success. There was my angry response to the hospital's handling of my letter. There was our last night together, when I'd asked about Kim's appearance. Why remind her of my roving blind eye?

"I want to go somewhere."

Her words from the afternoon. I saw now that she'd been

saying she wanted to leave this world. Why hadn't I seen it while I could have done something about it? I kicked back at a chair leg. Why hadn't I stayed on the line until her parents got home? Even if Caroline had already consumed the drugs, I might have persuaded her to bring Kim to the phone. Maybe then she would have reached the hospital in time.

Into my third glass, I checked my watch. Not quite two. I called Jack. He sounded bewildered, as anyone would who'd been woken up in the middle of the night.

"Jack, Caroline committed suicide."

He asked me to give him a moment. When he returned to the phone, he listened with care and talked with a kind of sympathy for me and sorrow over Caroline that I needed to hear.

After we spoke, I dozed off and on in the chair.

At 8:30 I called the office to say an emergency had come up and that I hoped to be in later. I called Ray and told him what had happened.

"Plan on coming in tomorrow," I said.

"Are you sure?"

"Yes."

A preoccupation on my nighttime roundabout of anxieties had been a memory of her saying the Catholic Church denied suicides burial in consecrated ground. Though she'd waffled, she seemed to think it still did. As childish as the notion had seemed to me until then, had terror of damnation afflicted her in her last moments? I couldn't bear the thought. I became single-minded in my resolve to get answers.

Back when she overdosed in my apartment, I'd looked into places in the neighborhood that might help. She hadn't taken up any of the suggestions, but I remembered someone had mentioned a Catholic psychiatrist, although I hadn't noted his name.

I now called one of the local Catholic churches. The woman who answered gave me his name and phone number. The doctor himself picked up when I called and agreed to see me in an hour.

Walking in the autumn air, I passed through an alien region where familiar landmarks had been transplanted from my neighborhood. A wall jutted out where my cane anticipated it, while getting around that tree required the same old fancy footwork. Every feature was a three-dimensional replica. Like a ghost, I passed people on the sidewalk without exchanging greetings.

In his cramped office, I told the doctor the basic details and asked about the church's attitude toward suicide. He never got around to answering. Instead, he asked how much alcohol I drank. Although I thought his question had nothing to do with mine, I told him about my insomnia. He asked more questions about alcohol use. I left feeling the tables had been turned on me. Years later I realized that after my all-night marathon, I must have bathed his tiny office in whiskey fumes.

Around noon, I put on a suit and mentally prepared myself for the office. Work had carried me through past crises. Maybe it would get me through this. But there was no hurry. Caroline's dying said there wasn't much point.

Kim called. Speaking through the membrane of mourning, I said, "How are you doing?"

"I have to leave. I can't stay here with her parents."

"Where will you go?"

"Worse comes to worst, back to the hospital. I'm sure they'll take me in, unless they blame me."

"They couldn't."

Surely Dr. Muir wouldn't hold Caroline's death against Kim. It wasn't as if she'd been a paid attendant.

"Her parents blame me. They don't say so, but they're different with me. How could they not be? I was here, and yet I wasn't here."

"They're grieving, Kim. Don't read anything more into it than that."

"Caroline went crazy on them on the way to the emergency room. When they got out of the car in the hospital's parking lot, she tried to fight them off and railed against them for making her do those leotard ads—you know about that, right? Her mother has scratches on her face."

I made it to the office during lunch hour. Joanna Leavitt, formerly my interviewer and now my boss, was in her room. At her doorway, I heard no one talking, so I took a chance that she was alone. "Can I close the door?"

"Is something wrong?" she said from her chair.

Familiar with the layout of her office, I took the seat before the desk. "Joanna, last night my girlfriend died."

I'd been anxious about the need to make this melodramatic statement, and then how to answer the predictable follow-up question: What happened?

All she said was, "Go home, Nick."

I stayed on message. "This is a bad way to begin my job. I've always worked through crises. I just wanted to alert you that I might be erratic for a while. I'll keep reading the training materials and getting acquainted with my cases."

She sat back. "Nick, not to minimize the importance of our work, but it can wait. I don't doubt your determination. Do what you need to. But whenever it gets to be too much, leave."

Hoisting myself out of the chair, I all but sleepwalked to the door.

Beth was waiting in my room. Knowing how haggard I must look, I explained.

Like me, she was a believer in getting on. Explanations over, she said, "Do you think you're up for reading the mail?"

I nodded, and she began. The information found a hole through the fog in my brain.

Eventually the hole closed as Caroline's voice, too substantial for mere memory, took over. I mustn't forget her voice. My answering machine had at least one message from her. I must save that tape.

And her hair. I should have kept some from when she cut it off, as horrible as that morning had been. I thought about her hands—how large they were, though by no means mannish. I hadn't consciously thought it before. How much else would go forever forgotten?

Kim had mentioned the leotard ads. Caroline had never explained why they'd upset her. But I realized now that I, too, had modeled. I thought back to the hour I'd sat self-consciously before the artist I called Len in "The Portrait." My experience could have been nowhere near as intense as fourteen-year-old Caroline's of fashion modeling, but even at eighteen, it had opened me up like a cadaver under a pathologist's knife and exposed the rawness of my feelings. Why had it taken me all this time to make the connection? Why now?

How had she gone from the seemingly tranquil "I want to go somewhere" to lashing out at her parents? Had she meant, this time, to die? When it was too late, had she changed her mind?

How was it that someone who left so many questions behind couldn't return to answer them?

My mind drifted to the chair by the phone in my apartment. I was sitting in it, as I'd done all last night. I dialed. The telephone at the other end rang and rang. Then it stopped. Not even the automated NYNEX message that there was no forwarding number, crushing as that would have been, penetrated the void.

"Nick? Are you listening?"

Beth walked with me as far as my subway station. Caroline must have felt something like this when I'd escorted her after she'd gone through with the abortion.

PART 5

85

THE SEDLAKS ARRANGED FOR CAROLINE's body to be put on view at a funeral home in the Bronx. Just as he'd joined me at Caroline's upstate hospital, Rob said he would meet me for the viewing. This time, however, he didn't need to drive me.

The day before, I took the train to Connecticut. Meeting me on the platform, Mom hugged me and said, "I'm so sorry." Dad said, "What a terrible thing to happen." I fought back the tears I still hadn't shed. During dinner I picked at the stew Mom made especially for me, and Mom and Dad talked through my silence.

The next morning, I discovered I hadn't thought to bring a suit or even a jacket to Connecticut. While getting ready in a daze for the train, I'd packed only a formal shirt. I went downstairs to find Mom and Dad in the kitchen.

"I don't have a suit or tie. Can we go down to my apartment and back up to the Bronx?"

"That's one hell of a drive, never mind parking," Dad said, by way of refusing. "You can borrow one of my suits."

"Dear," Mom said, "yours won't fit him."

"Well, my ties will." He helped me select something somber.

On the drive down to the funeral home, Dad said, "Barbaric Catholic custom, putting the body on display."

Neither Mom nor I responded. In the past, both of us would have agreed.

At the funeral home, Mom and Dad expressed their condolences to the Sedlaks, gave me a last hug, then returned to Connecticut. Just then, Rob arrived.

In shirtsleeves, I felt disrespectful. Without a jacket, the tie felt more stupid than appropriate, except when I thought about taking it off. Tieless seemed even less appropriate.

At my side, Rob said, "It isn't important. If Caroline were here, she'd be teasing you."

Besides Caroline's parents, he was the only person I knew. Poor Kim had returned to the hospital.

Caroline had a sister, Lucy. I remembered only when she introduced herself to us. After confirming I was Nick, she said, "Caroline spoke very fondly of you."

Lucy had flown in from northern Vermont, where she owned a florist business. Not as tall as Caroline and giving me an impression of muscular compactness, she had the take-charge demeanor of one who got things done. The rare times Caroline had mentioned her, she'd talked in a wistful voice, suggesting affection mixed with regret. It turned out Lucy reciprocated those feelings.

"We were never close after our grandfather's death," she said, taking a seat at my side. "She was two years younger than me, and until then we'd gotten along great. Then she withdrew into herself."

"What's this about your grandfather?" I asked.

"I guess she never told you. He shot himself. Caroline was the one who found him. She was only ten."

Caroline had told me. It was during one of our early pillow talks. How could I have forgotten?

Lucy stood up, saying she had to join her parents. It seemed everyone else did, too. The crowd dispersed, leaving Rob and me alone in the room.

"I'd like to go to her," I said.

He didn't reply right away. Then he said, "Okay, over here."

I stood up and walked maybe four paces.

At my side Rob said, "She's right in front of you. The coffin is low to the ground."

I kneeled and probed forward with the back of my hand. Wood.

My voice directed at the coffin, I asked Rob, "Do you think I can touch her?"

"I don't know."

I extended my fingers. They touched a cold surface.

"Her cheek," Rob whispered.

I moved my fingertips a fraction. Skin, yes. But I couldn't go farther. I couldn't take that one last tactile look at her face. It was too cold. It had no animation. It wasn't about to turn and kiss or nibble my fingertips.

86

LUCY TOLD US WHERE THE funeral mass was to be held the next day. That night I stayed in my own place, and in the morning I put on a suit.

"This is going to be weird," Rob said when we met at the subway station nearest the church. "I've never been to a Christian service. They aren't going to say I killed Jesus, are they?"

"It will be different for me, too," I said. "I've never been to a Catholic mass. They're more serious about the Eucharist than I'm used to."

"The what?"

"Where the priest gives you a sip of wine and a wafer. It means one thing in the Catholic Church and something a little different for Protestants."

I doubted either the Catholic or the Protestant version would make sense to him. It hardly made sense to Christians, regardless of denomination.

Rob found seats for us toward the back of the church. The organ was playing, but he couldn't see Caroline's parents or sister anywhere. Then the family arrived in a procession with the closed coffin and set it down before the assembly.

As the service continued, Rob kept me apprised of the mass's choreography—when to stand and when to kneel.

On the sidewalk after the service, Lucy invited us to join the cortege of mourners for the drive to the cemetery. Rob and I were shown to a limo whose other occupants I didn't know and didn't take in. On the way, I reflected that Caroline was to be buried in consecrated ground after all. Yet it didn't end my anxiety about the fear she might have felt in her last moments. Even if she'd known, would it have allayed her terror?

The day was summer-humid, but with a hint of autumnal smoke. As I stood in the crowd of mourners, a priest intoned words I couldn't hear. Only an occasional cough broke into the dread ritual. Rob whispered indications of what was happening. When the casket was lowered into the grave, I resisted the gravitational pull to collapse on top of it.

Then we were driven to the Sedlaks' home, where a buffet lunch waited. The guests chatted away as if it were an everyday social function, with Caroline's parents setting the tone, in glaring contrast to the awkward brunch when I'd first met them. They didn't speak to me. Nor did Lucy. Nor did any of the guests. The family had either kept quiet about my relationship with Caroline or communicated disapproval. None of her friends could have been invited, or else they would have said something. I might have been comforted by Gavin's preliminary touch on my arm or Reggie's calm demeanor. In their absence, and in the room's cheerful atmosphere, Caroline, who had touched the lives of so many people, felt more ephemeral than ever.

I declined Rob's offer to get me something to eat and met his attempt to draw me out with monosyllabic replies. Finding words was even harder than making room for food. It was just as well I was otherwise left alone. As soon as we decently could, we took the long subway ride back to Brooklyn. I left him at my stop, one short of his. The solace of scotch awaited.

87

ROB NEVER ASKED ME FOR an explanation of the Eucharist. Had I inflicted one on him, I would have said the Catholic Church believed it was literally real, while those Protestant churches that performed the rite treated it as metaphor. Right now the distinction between real and metaphorical was no trivial matter to me. I was haunted by an image of Caroline's back as she trudged along dimly lit, endlessly turning passageways, their walls, floors and ceilings hacked out of subterranean rock. I yearned to catch up to her as she walked wearily but steadily away to declare I loved her. I needed to tell her we must bind our lives together, whether in what was my world or what was now hers.

But in an age when myths were nothing more than stories, I couldn't bargain with the gods. I couldn't promise that if they let me bring my Eurydice back to this world, I'd refrain from turning around, even though my whole purpose would be to look forward.

So it was that I climbed a flight of steps on Montague. At the top was a makeshift entrance framed with sheetrock. Ahead of me, a woman asked, "Can I help you?"

"I'm looking for the psychic."

"I am she. Please, take a seat. There's a chair in front of you."

I sat down and said, "The woman I love died this week. I want to reach her."

"I can help."

"How?"

"I can light candles. I have a church in Newark. I can communicate prayers to her."

"How much will it cost?"

"The candles are $25. The prayers in church are $200."

I had $60. I handed over the bills and promised to return the next day with the rest.

"What was her name?" the psychic asked.

When I told her, I waited for a sign of recognition. None came. So I didn't volunteer that Caroline had been here herself.

I said, "I see her walking and walking through passageways. There's just enough light around to make out her shadow."

"And you're following her?"

"Chasing."

"Of course, chasing. But you never catch up."

"No. To catch up, I have to go down there myself."

She got my meaning. "There are other ways of reconnecting with her. After you leave, I will light two candles for her. Tomorrow I will say prayers for her. I will say your name to her. What is your name?"

"Nick."

"Nick, she will be consoled."

88

As Thanksgiving approached in all its irony, her parents drove down to collect her things, their first and only visit to my apartment. I expected them to rush in and out, but when I invited them to stay for tea, they accepted. I'd regained some of my composure and didn't present them with the silence that had transfixed me after the burial. They sat on the couch and I on a chair I placed to face them. Mrs. Sedlak did the talking, while Mr. Sedlak was quiet. I talked about my job; they talked about possibly moving to Vermont to be near their remaining daughter.

I'd thought of them as unemotional. Now I saw them as intensely private people who kept their emotions to themselves. Caroline had been just as private. Though we'd lived together off and on for a year, it seemed she'd kept her deepest fears to herself. It made her more her parents' daughter than I'd realized. While I'd been moving away from my parents, however gradually, she'd stayed close to hers, possibly even closer. Why else had she entrusted decisions about her care to them?

Sitting before them, I thought how Caroline's flailing away at them about childhood grievances even as she was dying must have made their loss still harder to bear. Yet I didn't think she targeted her suicide at them. Her anger? At that moment, yes. But not her suicide. She'd made her initial cry for help in my apartment. If that overdose had been a message to anyone, it was me. But when she wandered onto the subway tracks, she was alone. She must have seen death not as revenge, but as relief from an intolerable burden.

I wished I could have said this to them, but they wouldn't have heard it from me. Just as in their grief they blamed Kim, consciously or not, their distancing me at the funeral told me they also held me responsible.

We didn't speak about Caroline except with regard to the possessions I was returning: her clothes, most of the things in her drawer. There wasn't much else. I'd thought of holding back the dresses, which after all, I'd bought. But I'd bought them for her. I wouldn't be giving them to anyone else. Same with her jewelry box, though I'd bought some of its contents, too.

After they left, I brought out the objects of Caroline's that I'd spared from the purge. There was a pantyhose package on which she'd made notes during our vacation. I figured her parents wouldn't miss it. She must have kept her serious writing in Riverdale, or else thrown it out. I wished I had her Colombia story.

There was the recording of her voice, but I listened to the tape only once to confirm it was the right one. Those elongated seconds were so painful that I haven't listened to it since. There was the single photograph I had of her. I can't remember when or where it was taken. I'm told its quality is poor, but it's here if I ever want it described again. There was the small portfolio she'd made as my Christmas gift. It had traveled back and forth with me to the office. Now I put it in a drawer to reduce wear and tear. It is in that drawer today.

89

ON A WHIM ONE LATE afternoon when I happened to be in the Village, I went to the Sullivan Street bar. It was oddly quiet. Poised at the entrance, I realized I'd come too early for the regulars. I was about to leave when a man greeted me.

"Hi, I'm Reggie. What's your name again?"

"Nick. You're the railroad engineer."

I think he nodded as he said, "How are you doing, man?"

I heard in his voice that while my name had escaped him, my connection with Caroline hadn't. But as we meandered through a bland conversation, I got the impression he didn't know how close she and I had been. Perhaps in his mind she'd belonged to the bar rather than to any one person.

Had I come here to have my relationship with her in some way validated? The opposite was happening. Not Reggie's fault. He was a kind man. The fault—the absence—was in me.

Then I realized what I was really waiting for. As if I, too, believed she belonged to Sullivan Street, I'd expected Caroline to appear. I made an excuse and hurried out before he saw in my expression that Caroline had died all over again.

90

I WALKED OVER TO THE parish church I'd called to locate the Catholic psychiatrist. Every time I went out these days, I had to concentrate on each step as if it were the most difficult task I'd ever performed. I'd joked that Jack was so indecisive that he couldn't take a step without worrying. Worry wasn't my problem. It was my will.

Thanks to a tip from a passerby, I located the entrance to the church's administrative office and asked to see a priest. A Father Edward showed me to a room and sat in a chair angled at my side.

"You should know I'm not Catholic," I began.

"I've heard worse."

In spite of myself, I smiled.

"I'm here because my girlfriend died."

"I'm truly sorry."

I nodded. "She committed suicide."

This time the priest stayed silent.

I said, "She was what's called a lapsed Catholic."

"There are many who consider themselves lapsed."

"But as you suggest, there are many among those who think themselves lapsed who might be—I don't know—still susceptible?"

"You could put it that way."

"I worry if in her last moments, she was tormented with a fear that she wouldn't be buried in a Catholic cemetery."

"Those are old rules. Where was she buried?"

"That's the irony—in a Catholic cemetery. In the Bronx. It's her state of mind that troubles me."

"I seriously doubt a Catholic would be worried about the Church's old ways."

"She once told me she thought the Church would deny her a proper burial if she committed suicide. Only once, but it came back to me after she died."

"Of course, I never met her, but I'm guessing she was an intelligent woman."

He waited for confirmation, so I said, "She was."

"There are parts of the world, even parts of this country, where it's true, the old ways still prevail, but I can't seriously believe a Catholic in New York would really be anxious on that score, least of all one who has wandered for a time outside the fold."

"That could cut either way, couldn't it?"

"I suppose so. Let me ask you this. Did she sound like she was worried, or was she just complaining about the church's creaky ways?"

I felt the tension in me deflate. As Father Edward was saying, I couldn't know how deep her anxiety about an afterlife went, if it had existed at all. That one time she'd mentioned it, she was fending off my questions about her first suicide attempt. I'd never know what she was thinking in her last moments.

He apparently saw in my expression that his words had done their work. He said, "I want to say your name, but you haven't introduced yourself."

I offered my hand, which he shook firmly. "Nick Coleman. I live in the neighborhood. Hers was Caroline."

"Welcome, Nick. I'm sorry that such a terrible event is what has brought you to our church. How do you think I can help?"

"You already have. You're saying she had to know the rules were outdated."

"That was too easy. What else is on your mind?"

"At the funeral, I was excluded from the family when they gathered around the coffin."

"Caroline and you weren't married, I take it."

"Correct."

"Still, it would have been hard. How long were you and Caroline together?"

"A year. Only a year."

"Long enough," he said. "You feel you haven't said a proper goodbye to her."

"Yes."

"Would you like to go through the funeral mass for her again?"

"How?"

"You and me, tomorrow, after regular services are over."

The next afternoon, Father Edward showed me into the church proper. As we walked the few paces to the front pew, I sensed an empty room—echoes where parishioners might otherwise sit, no whispers, no clatter of hymn books being dropped or firmly closed. Sitting beside me, he said not to bother standing or kneeling; just to listen. He would do the same. He proceeded to speak and chant the entire funeral mass. I fixed my attention on him, nodded here and there, sometimes lowered my head.

Finished, he let silence surround us. Then he offered to show me to the sidewalk.

91

THEY SAY THE FIRST YEAR is the hardest. I counted the days to the anniversary. And after it came and went, some of the weight did lift. In other ways, my troubles had just begun.

The night of Caroline's suicide, Jack had been the one friend I'd disturbed from sleep. Two years or so later, I brought my then girlfriend along to a restaurant to dine with Elaine and him. She was lively, happily employed and thoroughly sane. When the two women went off to the bathroom, Jack said, "You've got to make this one work, Nick."

But I wasn't in love. I realized it soon after when I fell in love with someone else. I made the mistake of confiding in Jack about the second woman. His manner turned cold.

One evening, I came home to find a message from Jack announcing the birth of a son. By the time I called back, no one was picking up at his apartment. I left a message of congratulations marred, as I afterwards realized, by scotch-slurred self-pity. He didn't return the call, and I was too ashamed to call again.

Before Caroline, I'd been perplexed by self-destructive behavior. Jack still was.

Not so Rob, perhaps thanks to his mother's weirdness. After the birth of their first child, Samantha and he moved out to Long Island, and I stayed overnight there several times. But their tempestuous marriage was hard to take. For me, it came to a head one winter's weekend. Rob was on an obscenity kick, and Samantha wasn't in the mood.

Finally she yelled, "Stop talking about shit!"

"Okay," he said, his voice heavy with the scotch we'd been sharing. "No more talk about shit. Let's talk about flowers. Know where flowers come from?"

My laughter apparently dissuaded Samantha from making further protests. Maybe that was a good thing, at least that night. Still, Rob faded out of my life, as did so many other friends from that time.

I didn't consume alcohol twenty-four hours a day or even every day. My determination to function at the office saw to that. Even so, alcohol ruined not only friendships, but also a stream of affairs and relationships. Maybe they were also made possible by alcohol, but saying that would be unjust both to the women and my feelings. The time I told Jack I was in love, I meant it, and the end of that relationship was especially painful.

I'd wonder what might have happened had Mara come into my life, say, a year after Caroline's passing. A ludicrous question sticks in my brain: When she left my apartment the morning after our night together, did she go to class or back home? I didn't find out because we never spoke again.

I didn't lose everyone. Ray went on to practice law. Despite his taste for abstract vengeance, individual situations touched his heart, as if his worldview pulled him one way while his humanity tugged the other. He never joined a big firm, but stayed in the trenches with small outfits. Possibly he didn't fit the big-firm mold, but I think his brand of idealism dictated to him, just as mine has to me. He's married and has two children, but the two of us haven't exactly had a grown-up influence on each other. The last time we spoke, a few months ago, he snickered as he called me a "liberal pantywaist," which in his mind is redundant. I'll come up with an equally sophomoric name for him the next time.

Another friend who didn't give up on me was Toby. Sometime

after Caroline's death, he was caring for a man dying of AIDS.

"His parents still won't come to see him," Toby told me on the phone during one of the many calls I made, in search of comfort, to my remaining and new friends—to anyone who would listen.

"Because he's gay?" I said.

"Because he's gay." He added, "I can't help thinking something along those lines was going on with Caroline's parents and you."

He was suggesting my disability explained their attitude toward me. Maybe so, maybe not. I wouldn't be the first man in a daughter's life to distress her parents for no obvious reason.

92

THREE YEARS AFTER CAROLINE DIED, Dave showed up in New York. He and I had corresponded occasionally since Arles. I wrote to tell him of her suicide, and he sent a touching reply. Now he was back in the States to teach physics at a Southern university. When he called me from a Manhattan phone booth, he said he'd read about a bar on Court Street, right in my neighborhood. Trust Dave to find a congenial place I'd never heard of even though it was within walking distance of my home.

I met him there late on a spring afternoon, yet another of those beautiful days that are the backdrop for just about all my Caroline memories. In "The Portrait," I'd described my fear that if I ever found Eden, I'd destroy it. Dave had said we'd found it in Arles, but it had been temporary, a glimpse. The weather I associate with Caroline seemed to say, "Here is Eden, and you've lived down to expectations."

We sat at the bar with beers before us. He told me about the university, the last month of his European trip, his thoughts about his next adventure, his feelings about New York. He discoursed in the open-minded way with which he'd entertained Caroline and me in the cafés in Arles. But I was impatient to talk about Caroline.

At last he said, "I've been thinking how we create myths to console ourselves. Do you think of Caroline as a meteor who shone briefly in the sky before vanishing?"

"No, I don't. After she came out of the hospital the last time, she told me she was going to earn her college degree. She was on the verge of starting over."

The spontaneity and certainty of my reply gratified me. I continued, "I read afterwards that someone emerging from depression is at the greatest risk of suicide. They just don't have the energy when deepest into it." Then I told him about Caroline's discovering her grandfather after he shot himself.

Dave said, "They say suicide runs in families. I guess the first one makes it less unthinkable."

I went on. "And when she was a teenager, just four years later, her mother had her pose for leotard ads. On the way to the hospital that last night, Caroline berated her about it."

"The things parents make children do for their own vanity."

"Or they were simply proud of her," I said, lately feeling protective of the Sedlaks. "You probably noticed the bump above her nose. They airbrushed it out."

"I remember. Part of her intrigue—the defect in a lovely face. I guess it bothered her."

"She didn't act as though it did."

"But now you question everything."

"Everything, along with the abortion."

"Of course. You feel responsible for that."

"If I'd agreed to it, she would have had the child."

"Would she? That tirade she gave her parents about the leotard ads—it had to mean something, didn't it?"

"Apparently they were her last words," I agreed.

"Is it possible she thought her childhood had been such a disaster that she couldn't trust herself to be a parent in her own right?"

"She never said anything like that to me."

"Nor had she ever let loose a tirade like that before, had she?"

Dave was taking me where I needed to go. I'd hoped he would. I shook my head. "Not to my knowledge."

He said, "The girl who was forced to concentrate on making an external impression for those leotard ads responded by concealing her deepest feelings. When they finally burst out, they overwhelmed her."

"You're saying she had reasons to have the abortion that she kept to herself."

"And that if you'd said yes to having the child, she might have gone through with the abortion anyway, only with more peace of mind."

"Because?"

"This is pure speculation, you realize."

"Because?"

"Because," he sighed, "you would have said you loved her enough to accept whichever decision she made."

Here it was again, the inadequacy of my feelings for her. I cradled my glass, which still had a lot of beer in it, but felt no urgency to drink up. Hard as it was, our conversation was filling the hole that, at that time, normally required alcohol.

"I know you loved her," Dave said. "She knew it, too. If there was a problem, it would have been how it got expressed."

"You think I didn't show I loved her when we were together in Arles?"

"I sensed something weighing on you."

"I was in a bad job situation," I conceded.

"That will do it."

I thought some more before saying, "During that vacation, I felt like a square peg trying to fit into society's round hole. I assumed I'd put thoughts like that behind me in college, but I found myself asking all over again what someone who can't see is doing in a world ruled by vision."

It was a sentiment I never admitted, and I immediately regretted doing so. But Dave replied calmly. "Everyone's that square peg. You were just stuck knowing it from an early age. It seems Caroline was, too."

I nodded.

He said, "The thing about vacations is that new situations confront you with yourself—one reason I travel. It can be disquieting."

"You're a brave man, Dave."

He laughed pleasantly. "Something I observed was that Caroline never acted as though you had physical limitations. She adapted to your needs, but in the way we all adapt to our companions, one way or the other—the way you adapted to hers. You were happy together. It was nice to see, even after that bad day—what was it?—in the Camargue?"

"You noticed."

"Neither of you exactly hid it. But you got over it soon enough."

My turn to laugh. He'd called me on my determination to blame myself. Perhaps, as he was suggesting, I'd blown that Camargue day all out of proportion.

We turned to other things, from his physics to my environmental work, but it wasn't the same without Caroline. As I was to learn many times over during the years after her death, friendships have a time and place. Outside the bar, Dave and I shook hands, and then he, too, walked out of my life.

93

THE LATE EVENING I SPENT in Sheridan Square with Taylor, the student from Kansas, brought memories of Caroline flooding back and motivated me to set them down. Caroline's suicide had ended my creative writing aspirations. The only subject I'd wanted to write about was our relationship, but the idea had felt like exploitation. Yet, sparked by that evening's encounter, here I am, about to complete our story. Setting it down has been cathartic.

Taylor guessed I was lonely. In fact, for the past twenty years, six of them married, I've shared my life with Alison. When I said goodnight to Taylor and set off down the subway steps, I interrupted the stream of memories she'd unknowingly evoked to call Alison on my cell phone to say I was on my way. She assumed I'd had a long evening with my dinnertime friend. It was only when I got home that I told her about Taylor. I thought I detected a moment of concern, but she accepted my explanation, and a whole new conversation came out of it.

A lot of good has happened in the intervening years: meeting Alison, earning recognition at the office, new friendships. Alcohol moderation undoubtedly kept me alive.

I did resolve at least one uncomfortable question that arose during my relationship with Caroline, thanks to the example of a blind law school classmate who has raised a sighted daughter, much of the time as a single father. She's in college now. Their relationship has a nice balance of affection and autonomy. Blindness doesn't preclude parenthood. I might have become a father but for my fear of passing along a defective gene, but in the end, the simple fact is that I didn't want to.

With all that, Taylor's observation still hit home: Part of me is lonely. Not the pre-Caroline loneliness, when I'd yet to have a true relationship, but the kind that loss of a loved one leaves behind. The death of my mother, many years later, created a new loneliness, as I know my father's will when his time comes. We're all shaped by our closest relationships. Before Caroline, I was one person; after, someone greatly changed. When I think about her, I feel her absence. That feeling is a form of loneliness.

I'd learned from my years at the Alliance how inner torments play out at the expense of others. I believe Caroline assumed that lashing out over long-held grievances wouldn't really hurt anyone except herself. The most tragic part of all might have been this lack of self-esteem.

For a long time, I agonized over her "I want to go somewhere." There was no getting around my failure to comprehend when I might have saved her. But in time I understood she had said a loving farewell.

The words of the dead are crumbs for the hungry.

Looking back, Father Edward's mass was the turning point. It gave substance to my grief. I couldn't accept that Caroline had walked this earth for nearly thirty years only to decompose into indistinguishable particles. By treating death as a mystery, the funeral mass allowed for the possibility that she isn't forever lost. Possibility has settled into something akin to belief, though one I keep to myself, safe from argument.

A few years ago, I returned to Arles with Alison. We went for other reasons, but once there I became curious to retrace parts of my first trip. It didn't upset her. We don't pretend away past loves, some of whom have stayed in our lives and are now friends to us both. The arena and theater gripped my imagination all over again. There'd been at least one improvement: Lunchtime no longer reeked of sulfur. However, I couldn't remember the name of the hotel where Caroline and I had stayed, and between us, Alison and I couldn't find anything resembling it in our current hotel list or map. The map also didn't show any fields in the vicinity of the town center. Alison did see a mall on the map that I didn't recall being mentioned during my first trip. Whether it was the mall or some other development, time had tramped over the field where Caroline and I had admired the wild herbs.

Sitting there with Caroline, I'd caressed a stalk of rosemary, then a leaf of thyme, and relished their scents. I'd taken pleasure in living things not for the security they might give me, not for pet-like affection, not for my career, but for themselves. I like to think that was the moment she chose to become pregnant.

I envision her in that field, wherever it may be in a universe of reconstituted landscapes and revived ruins. It's the place she reached after trudging all the way to the end of those shadowed, ever-turning passageways where I'd long wished to pursue her and where she now rests. Or rather, where she and the part of me that is entwined with her have come to rest.

ACKNOWLEDGMENTS

Independence is never pure. Often without thinking about it, we all count on road builders, food suppliers, security guards, back office staff, and many, many others we may never meet. What distinguishes disability is that it can prevent people from doing on their own certain activities that others take for granted. This knowledge makes me aware of my indebtedness to a cast of, literally, thousands. Ever since losing my sight as a teenager, I have relied on people to read to me. The need is much reduced today, thanks to voice synthesized computers and other technology, but readers still have a place in my life. I am indebted to you all.

That said, the following people made very specific contributions to this book and its publication:

Charis Conn, the editor who worked closely with me on this project. Charis died on March 21, 2017. I'm sorry she isn't here for this recognition.

My friend Bascove, illustrator of many admired book covers, who graciously agreed to create the art and design for the novel's cover.

John Lescault, an audiobook narrator I admire for his fidelity to text, who did me the honor of agreeing to narrate the novel's audio version.

Laura, my wife, who read and improved early and late drafts of the novel and who gave me unstinting support throughout the long and solitary process.

ABOUT THE AUTHOR

Adrian Spratt practiced law for twenty years, mainly in consumer protection, before returning to his first love, fiction writing. He graduated from Amherst College and earned his law degree from Harvard. Retinal detachment led to his loss of vision when he was thirteen. Today, he lives in Brooklyn with his wife, the artist and photographer Laura Rosen. His website, where he maintains a blog and showcases selected stories, essays and memoir excerpts, is www.adrianspratt.com.

Made in the USA
Coppell, TX
20 February 2022

73872354R00198